Praise for the Missing Pieces

"The Lavene duet can always be counted on for an enjoyable whodunit." — *Midwest Book Review*

"[A] terrific mystery series." — MyShelf.com

DAE'S CHRISTMAS PAST

"Paranormal amateur sleuth fans will enjoy observing Dae use cognitive and ESP mental processes to uncover a murderer...Readers will enjoy." ~ Midwest Book Review

A FINDER'S FEE

"The Lavenes once again take readers into a setting with a remarkable past, filled with legends and history...The characters are vivid and fascinating." ~ Lesa's Book Critiques

A HAUNTING DREAM

"I felt like I couldn't read fast enough on this one..<g>but then I love all their missing pieces mysteries - can't wait till the next one. ~ Bookaholic

continued .

A SPIRITED GIFT

"This is the third book in the A Missing Pieces series. It's always enjoyable to visit Duck, NC and Mayor Dae and the interesting residents and this was no exception." ~ Fred Yoder

A TOUCH OF GOLD

"With a quaint coastal setting, a great cast and refreshing dialogue, this was an enjoyable and pleasant read and I look forward to reading the next book in this delightfully charming series." ~ Dru Ann Love

A TIMELY VISION

"Filled with likable (if eccentric) characters and boasts a vividly realized small-town setting. The combination of small-town ambience, a psychic main character, and plenty of antiques should give the authors plenty to work with in subsequent adventures." ~ Judy Coon for Booklist

. .

Dae's Christmas Past

By

Joyce and Jim Lavene

Dae's Christmas Past

By

Joyce and Jim Lavene

Chapter One

The Currituck Sound had a smooth, glossy surface leading to the horizon as I walked down the boardwalk. All the shops were closed, but there was one woman standing at the rail in front of my shop, Missing Pieces. She wore a dark purple suit with an amazing hat that matched it.

She turned to me as I came closer. "Hello, Dae. I've been waiting for you."

I thought she was wearing a marmalade-colored scarf around her neck, but it slowly moved as she turned. A large cat blinked at me with lazy green eyes, balancing on her shoulders.

"Do I know you?" I thought she looked vaguely familiar. Maybe a former customer.

"Yes. We met a few years back. I see the shop still bears my name." She glanced at the shop next door—my friend Shayla's place—Mrs. Roberts Spiritual Reader.

"I remember you now! You're Mary Catherine Roberts, the pet psychic. You opened the shop right after the boardwalk was finished and then moved to Wilmington. Have you moved back to Duck?"

"Not exactly. My cat, Baylor, and I will be here for a while. Something large and quite possibly dangerous is about to happen in Duck. Maybe you've heard something about it from the horses? Goodness knows news travels fast."

At large fish jumped out of the calm water and flew through the air toward her until it finally dove back down inches from the boardwalk.

She laughed. "You see? Everyone knows. I'll wager your little cat, Treasure, has been talking about it too. But don't worry. We'll handle it. I think you have some prehistoric horse figures we need to examine. I hope you have some tea too. I could really use a cup."

This promised to be an interesting conversation. I opened the door to Missing Pieces. "I actually came here for a cup of tea myself. Won't you join me?"

"Isn't there something you should be doing with the election and everything? I heard you won the election for mayor of Duck. Congratulations."

"Thanks, and thank goodness it's over. I stopped here for a little peace and quiet. There are parties later, but right now I need to hide for a while."

"I can come back later." She paused at the threshold.

"No. That's fine. I have to hear how you know my cat's name is Treasure. I know you talk to animals, but Treasure isn't even with me today."

She smiled at me in a knowing way from under her large purple hat. She had a smooth, creamy complexion and an attractive face. Her blue eyes were deep, holding fathoms of secrets, like the ocean. She was probably in her fifties—a little plump—but very stylish.

I held the door to my shop as she walked in. I'd owned Missing Pieces Thrift Store for a few years. There was a little of everything here from antiques and collectibles to used items I thought someone might like. There were also the items that had been lost and were waiting for their owners to find them.

That's what I do. I find lost things. I started finding things that belonged to other people when I was just a child, taking the gift from my grandmother. Sometimes those things seem important—lost keys and missing wills—even a missing child. As long as I could remember, I'd found items people were looking for by holding their hands.

Lately, I'd also been able to find lost people by holding their possessions. It had led me into a lot more trouble.

"What a lovely shop." Mary Catherine roamed around through my lost and found. Baylor stayed completely still as she walked.

I closed the door even though there was a nice breeze coming in from the Currituck Sound. It would've been lovely for it to swirl through as we sat down for tea. But I wasn't prepared to deal with anyone's problems or congratulations at that moment. It had been a turbulent road to becoming mayor—my first real election—the first time someone had run against me.

I thought Mary Catherine might be exactly the diversion I needed to begin putting it behind me.

"Thank you." I walked over to the hot plate, teas, and cups that I always kept ready for customers and friends when they dropped in. "I have some orange spice, Earl Grey, and lemon balm, if you're in the mood for herbal. It's very fresh. A friend of mine grows it."

"I'll take the Earl Grey, thanks," she said. "It was a long drive up from Wilmington. I hardly slept last night thinking about today. I came as soon as I could arrange everything."

I filled the kettle and turned on the hotplate. "You work

for the radio station in Wilmington now. I've heard your show. It's very popular here. People call you when they have problems with their pets."

She smiled, small lines fanning out from her eyes. "That's right. I make a living helping people understand their pets. Many times people think they're doing what's right for their furry loved ones, but it's as far away from what they want or need as the moon."

"So you really talk to animals?" I took out a few shortbread cookies, hoping they weren't stale. "That's amazing. I'm sorry. I don't remember you doing that when you were here."

"I've always done it. I just didn't figure out that I could do it for a living until the last few years. It's opened up a whole new world for me. What I do is no more amazing than you being able to find things and people, Dae O'Donnell. I read about that little girl you found. You have a wonderful gift."

"Thank you. Is that how you knew my cat's name?"

"Of course! Baylor told me before we got here. I believe animals may all be telepathic with each other. It's also how I heard the horses calling for help."

"You mentioned the horses. You talk to animals that aren't pets too?"

"Oh yes. Direct communication goes around the language barrier, you know. I don't have to speak dog to understand what a dog has to say."

"And the wild horses have been calling you?"

"Yes—although there have been the odd dogs, cats, and even a few dolphins warning of the problem to come. Animals have a better grapevine than people."

I put tea in the cups and poured the boiling water in after when the kettle started whistling. "And what are they saying?"

"Oh, it's all about the ancient horses. It started when they began digging up the horse statues. It seems the statues are part of a cult the horses despise and fear. This is something old and primitive. There was an ancient, primal scream that came from all the horses as they protested the invasion. I heard it from horses as far away as Charleston. If other humans could have heard it, they would've known not to dig at the site. I was concerned at that point, but I didn't know what it was all about. Since then it's gotten louder and more animals along the coast are involved."

I put a few cookies on the saucers that held the tea cups. "Cream? Sugar?"

"Both, thanks." She added what she wanted and took a cup and saucer to my burgundy brocade sofa.

"That sounds terrible, but I don't know what we can do about it. The site is considered a heritage spot now by the state. They've brought in archaeologists from the University of North Carolina and a whole team of people. It was astonishing to find out that horses were here before the Spanish ships. The whole idea of our history is changing. My friend, Jake, owns the property where they're digging. It was an accident that he found them at all."

I took my saucer, cup, and cookies to sit beside Mary Catherine on the comfortable sofa. The sofa was too big for the shop, but it was worth working around. I'd spent the night here on it more than once. It was one of my favorite finds.

"Jake Burleson rescues wild horses," I explained. "He lives near Corolla, a few miles down Highway 12 from here." The two-lane highway divided the Outer Banks and split the Atlantic Ocean from the bays and sounds that were along the coast.

"I remember Corolla." She nodded. "That lovely old lighthouse is there."

"Yes."

"From what I understand of the problem, they should never have disturbed the horses' resting place." Mary Catherine sipped her tea. "Excellent tea! Thank you. Just what I needed."

I appreciated her praise of my tea-making skills. "Jake

was fascinated by the whole thing when he found the smaller horse statues. He couldn't leave it alone. It's amazing when you see what's down there. It's spooky too. It feels dark to me—wrong somehow. But I couldn't tell you how or why."

"Have you laid hands on any of the horse statues yet?"

"No. Jake was hoping I would. He'd like a better idea of what the horse statues were used for. The experts are saying the site is part of a cult where horses were worshipped. I haven't touched the statues without gloves. Maybe it sounds crazy, but I'm afraid to."

Fear was something I had learned since I started touching possessions instead of people. Even the simplest old coin could have a terrible, hidden history that could take me days to get out of my mind. I was happy that I hadn't learned that skill as a child.

"I don't think it sounds crazy at all. I think you're right to proceed with caution." Mary Catherine tasted one of the shortbread cookies.

"I wasn't like that at first." I put down my cup and saucer. "Experience has made me cautious. What do the horses and the other animals say about it?"

"They say bad things are going to happen. The site needs to be closed and blessed, perhaps by a shaman with an understanding of these things. The animals can't adequately describe their fears but that doesn't mean they aren't genuine."

"I can talk to Jake and see what they're doing out there. You can come out with me and take a look around."

"That sounds like a plan." She put her cup and saucer on the sink. "Thank you for inviting me along."

I received two texts on my phone. Gramps was looking for me. So was my boyfriend, Kevin. I wasn't really ready to go back out into the world, but I knew if I didn't, the world would come and beat on my door.

"There are some parties the rest of today to celebrate the election. I hope you'll join us. Do you have a place to stay while you're here?"

She shook her head as she straightened her cat around her neck. "No. I came spur of the moment. I'll have to find a place. Maybe you have some ideas?"

"We have plenty of room at our house. I'd love it if you stayed with us."

"Us?" Her pretty face got pink. "That's your grandfather—Horace O'Donnell, right? I remember him!"

It sounded as though she *fondly* remembered him. Had I missed something when she was here last time? "Yes. We have an extra room. Gramps loves company."

"Thank you, Dae." She hugged me. "As for the parties, I'd love to go with you. It will give me a chance to mingle and get to know people. Will your friend Jake Burleson be there? Is he a friend-friend or a boyfriend?"

"He's a friend-friend." Her question made me smile. "I have a boyfriend—Kevin Brickman—although that's a silly word for our relationship. I don't know if Jake will be there or not. He's not from Duck, but he might come just because the party is for me. I haven't seen him for a while with all the events leading up to the election."

"I see. I'd still like to go out to the site even if he's at the party. I just thought it might be nice to meet him first."

"We'll have to see if he's willing to put on a clean pair of jeans and drive down here. Jake's not a party-goer by nature." I picked up my handbag. "I have to go home, take a shower, and change clothes. We'll head to the Blue Whale Inn after that for the first party. That's Kevin's place. I'm sure you'd like a chance to catch your breath too."

"That sounds great. Thanks so much. I could freshen up a little, change clothes. Do you need to talk to Horace first?"

"Nah. He'll love it. My house is only a short walk from here."

"I remember." She sighed. "People here walk everywhere unless they drive one of those little cars."

"Golf carts." I thought I might as well teach her the local jargon. "Gramps recently purchased a deluxe model. If he's home, we'll ride over to the Blue Whale with him. If not, I'll call Kevin. I'm not walking to the post-election parties in my good shoes."

She put her hand to her heart. "That's a relief! I love Baylor." She stroked the large cat draped around her neck. "But he's no lightweight."

"Did you bring luggage?" I hadn't noticed anything with her when I'd seen her on the boardwalk.

"I have one suitcase. I always travel light. I think we can clear the air on all these bad vibes in a few days."

"Did you drive to Duck?" I switched off the lights and closed up Missing Pieces. "I didn't think to ask."

"I don't like to drive." A breeze caught her large purple hat and almost took it off her head. Baylor yawned but otherwise didn't move as she grabbed at the hat. "I don't even own a car. But a friend was headed this way so I hitched a ride with him. I thought I'd be able to find someplace to stay for a few days. Now I don't have to. Thank you for your hospitality."

She'd left her suitcase beside my shop on the boardwalk. I'd been so busy thinking about the election that I hadn't even seen it. I offered to carry it and was surprised how heavy it was. She was obviously good at packing.

We walked past Curves and Curls Beauty Spa on our way to the parking area. My good friend, Trudy Devereaux, owned that shop. Our town hall was still located with the Duck Shoppes on the Boardwalk, but it would be moving soon. Construction crews were hard at work on the new stand-alone building that would house town offices. It was almost complete.

Our first municipal building was going to be next to Duck Park. We'd used some of the land, donated to the town years before, to put it there. Our town manager, Chris Slayton, had set up some great plans for our growth in the next few years. The new town hall was only the beginning.

As we passed the present town hall our clerk, Nancy Boidyn, walked out of the office, cigarette already in hand. She glanced at it guiltily. "Hi, Dae. I know how this looks.

I've been trying to stop smoking, but there's always something going on with my girls. I love them, but they drive me crazy!"

She was talking about her two teenage daughters. They were frequently in some sort of trouble.

I put my hand on hers. "You don't have to explain to me. I know it's hard to stop doing anything you're used to doing." I turned to my companion. "Nancy, this is Mary Catherine Roberts. Mary Catherine, this is Nancy Boidyn, our town clerk."

The two women shook hands. Nancy's blue eyes widened under her short, reddish-brown hair. "The pet psychic? I listen to your radio show all the time. Can you *really* talk to animals?"

"Yes. I can talk to animals. Thanks for listening to my show. I remember seeing you here, the last time I was in Duck, Nancy. You were running the whole town then! I'm glad you got some help."

"Thanks. Yeah. The 'good' old days!" Nancy's delicate features softened. "That last show where that man who called in had accidentally hit his dog with his car—that was heartrending. The dog wanted to forgive him, but the man couldn't forgive himself. I cried the whole time I was listening."

"It's true what people say. Dogs are very forgiving of our flaws," Mary Catherine said. "I'm happy I could reunite them. So many times pet owners are ready to find other homes for their animals and there's no reason. They just need to understand them."

"I have a terrier I wish you'd come talk to," Nancy invited. "He's so stubborn. How long are you going to be in Duck?"

Mary Catherine glanced at me. "I'm not sure yet. But if I have an opportunity, I would love to talk to your terrier."

"I need to go home and get ready for the parties tonight," I told Nancy. "Mary Catherine needs to freshen up a little too. She just got here from Wilmington."

Nancy grinned. "Yep! We have a victory to celebrate. Congratulations, Madame Mayor. You're in for another four years."

We hugged. "Thanks. It only happened because of my friends, and my wonderful campaign managers. You did a great job for me."

Nancy nudged Mary Catherine with her elbow and winked. "It didn't hurt that the other candidate was disqualified for a while because the police thought he might be a killer."

Mary Catherine laughed. "That's the best way to take care of it."

"I'd like to think I would've won even if that hadn't happened." Would my election always be clouded by the murder investigation into my opponent, Mad Dog Wilson?

"Of *course* you would have!" Nancy playfully slapped at me. "I have the car here today. I'd be glad to offer you ladies a ride to Dae's house."

"That would be awesome," I told her. "Thanks."

We went down the boardwalk stairs to the parking lot and got in Nancy's older Chevy. My house was only a few minutes away on Duck Road. At this time of year, early November, it wouldn't take long to get there. During the summer—when our population rose from five hundred and eighty-six to more than twenty-five-thousand—that drive could take half an hour.

Nancy chattered about her terrier and his bad habits all the way to the house. Mary Catherine sat in the front seat and pleasantly answered questions and discussed the dog.

I assumed being a pet psychic was a lot like being a doctor—everyone wanted to talk about their problems. The same thing happened to me when people from town had problems they wanted addressed. Sometimes it was about sidewalks. Sometimes it was about sewer issues. Mostly I referred them to our town manager, but I always checked back with him afterward to see if anything had been done.

Sometimes people wanted me to find things for them.

Everyone knew about my gift. My mother and grandfather had always seen it as a kind of responsibility to the people of Duck, not unlike being mayor.

"Looks like you've got company, Dae." Nancy's smile was suggestive. "I think that old pickup belongs to Jake Burleson, doesn't it? Maybe he's come to help you celebrate."

Chapter Two

Nancy had a 'thing' for Jake. I'd told her repeatedly that it was fine with me if she dated him—she was worried I had romantic leanings toward him. She'd been a single mother for many years and the cowboy from Corolla had taken her fancy. I wished they would get together. Jake was a good man and Nancy was a wonderful woman. Nothing would make me happier.

I would have known that rusted-out pickup anywhere without Nancy's alert. Riding in it was just slightly better than riding down Duck Road on a horse. You could see the road going by through holes in the floorboard. The whole vehicle seemed to be held together with wishful thinking and duct tape.

Jake usually brought the pickup when he was taking me somewhere. I didn't mind riding a horse in a nice, sunny meadow, but I didn't like being out on the street with one. He frequently came to visit and had eaten dinner many times at our house.

He rode horses most places. The wild horses were his true love, his passion. He didn't care about anything else. He worked with injured animals until they were well enough to be back with the herd. I respected that about him.

The horses were part of the Outer Banks, but their space was becoming more and more limited by civilization each year. Jake, and Wild Horse Conservancy director Tom Watts, worked tirelessly to help them.

Mary Catherine and I got out of the car. Nancy got out too—on the pretext of taking the suitcase inside—I knew she really wanted to talk to Jake. So far he'd shown no sign of being interested in her at all.

"I'm glad he's here," Mary Catherine murmured to me as we walked toward the house. "I'm not as good at reading people as I am animals. I'm curious to meet this man who thought nothing of upsetting a fine balance."

I started to remind her that Jake had no idea what he was doing when he'd found the horse statues on his property. He'd thought they were remarkable, something worth saving, like the living horses. He never intended things to get so far out of control. The state had come in when they'd heard about the find and it had quickly escalated from there. The excavation had changed his life and work. That was never what he'd meant to happen.

Jake walked out of the house with Gramps. His gaze was locked on me. The expression on his face was grim. Gone was the teasing, flirty man who'd tried so hard to charm me into believing that there could be something between us. I hardly recognized this stranger.

There were terrible, dark circles under his sunken eyes.

His handsome face was drawn, thinner than the last time I'd seen him. His clothes were dirty and wrinkled as though he'd been wearing them for a few days. It was the only time I'd seen him without his Stetson.

I glanced away from his gaze. It was too painful to see him this way. What was wrong?

There were introductions all around—except for Mary Catherine and Gramps. It seemed they had known each other very well when she'd lived here before, even though it was only a brief time. He would still have been the sheriff of Dare County when she'd set up her shop on the boardwalk. I had just left college after my mother's death.

He greeted her with a warm hug. I wondered how his thinning white hair and full white beard compared to the last time she'd seen him. The white accented his ruddy complexion and blue eyes. I thought it made him look distinguished. His face was still strong and rugged from spending so much time at sea on his charter fishing boat.

"Welcome back, MC. I hope you've spent enough time in Wilmington to know what you've been missing not being here in Duck."

Mary Catherine was equally excited to see Gramps. "Horace, you old salty dog. You were about to retire from the sheriff's office when I was here last. Did you finally give it up?"

"I did indeed. Come on inside and let me warm you up with some coffee. I have a nice apple strudel that just came out of the oven. I'll get your bag. How long are you staying?"

They walked inside together, heads bent close. Nancy, Jake, and I stayed outside in the driveway. The breeze played with the last leaves that were left on the trees around us and pushed at the squeaky weather vane on top of the old house that had been built by an ancestor of mine.

My grandfather and my mother had both been raised here. So was I. Now I lived here Gramps who'd been my inspiration to open Missing Pieces—he'd told me I was bringing home too much junk and that I needed to find somewhere else to put it.

It was the best move I'd ever made.

None of the three of us that remained in the drive had anything to say. For once Nancy was even quiet instead of chatty. She gazed at Jake in quiet adoration.

"I have to talk to you, Dae." He brought a brown cloth bag from behind his back.

It was the bag he'd used to put a few of the ancient horse statues into the last time I'd been out at his property with him. He'd wanted me to use my gift to understand more about the background of the horse cult they'd been excavating. Jake hadn't grown up here, but he'd heard rumors about my gift of sight.

I'd been too involved in other things to look at them properly—at least that was my cover story. The real truth was that I was scared of them, as I'd told Mary Catherine though I hated to admit it. I'd only examined them with gloves protecting my hands because I could feel their dark power.

The whole idea of the horse cult was frightening to me. Archaeologists were saying the statues were at least a thousand years old. I'd touched dozens of antique items— either purposely or by accident—that didn't go back that far. Not all of those were pleasant experiences. Most still brought nightmares.

It had been easy to put Jake's request on the back burner since I was busy and hadn't wanted to do it. I knew wasn't being fair to him. I just didn't know what to say.

"We're on my way to my post-election parties, Jake." I summoned up a bright smile. "I'll have to wait to examine the horses until later. Come with us."

His usually warm gaze was cold and hard on me. "I need you to do it *now*. You've put it off too long. Tom Watts wants to help Martin Sheffield and the others continue this madness. I thought he was my friend. You've said *you're* my friend. Now's the time to prove it."

Tom and Jake had been good friends for many years. I

hated the idea that this excavation had come between them.

Martin Sheffield was the lead archaeologist on the horse project. I'd only met him a time or two, but I knew that Jake's feelings about him ran deep. Dr. Sheffield had offered Jake a substantial sum of money to sell his property outright so that the excavation could take over everything. Jake had flatly refused. The tension between the two men had continued to grow.

It was one of those awkward times when someone was intent on having me touch or find something or someone for them that went against my better judgment. Sometimes I had to say no for my own good. Very few people understood that. They hadn't seen the terrible things I had.

Nancy glanced between us with worried eyes. "I think I should go home and get ready for the parties, Dae. I'll see you later. Bye, Jake."

He didn't reply.

"Thanks for the lift, Nancy," I said. "I'll see you later."

I wasn't afraid of Jake, but I was very uncomfortable with him at that moment. I was sorry to see her go. She'd supplied a buffer between us. Now I was out there alone with him. He was making me nervous.

"Let's go inside and talk," I suggested. "Wouldn't you like a piece of Gramps's strudel?"

"You said you'd help, Dae. What are you afraid of? I'll be here with you, I swear. I just need to know the truth. I don't know if I can stop Sheffield and Tom without an ace in my pocket. You're the only card I have up my sleeve. He doesn't know about you. You have to help me before it's too late."

"Jake, you're letting this take over your life. You wanted to dig up these things from the horse cult. Why are you backing out now?" I knew the answer. I was just making conversation, hoping to see some little spark of the man I knew in his dead face. "When did you sleep last? You look like you're falling apart."

"I'm not afraid of the horse cult. That was a long time

ago. I'm afraid of these buzzards circling around wanting my land. If I can't stop them, I can't take care of the *living* horses that need my help. I can't lose my property over this."

"How will anything I find by touching the horse statues make any difference? I don't think Martin Sheffield is going to care what I think about the horse cult. Maybe you need someone else to come in—another archaeologist or historian. You know a scientist isn't going to recognize my gift as anything important."

He grip bit into my arms, and his eyes bored into mine. "Please, Dae. You can do *this*. Don't be afraid. I'll protect you."

The bag with the horses dangled on his wrist close to mine. I could feel the vibes, as Mary Catherine had called it, even through the cloth. The cloth protected me, like gloves, kept me from being drawn into the past and whatever secrets were buried with the horse cult statues.

I pulled away from him. "I can't do it, Jake." I said the words in a firm tone so that he'd know this was it. I'd been too wishy-washy about his request. I had to disappoint him, make sure he knew I wasn't going to touch any of the horse statues that he'd dug out of the sand. "I'm scared. I don't think it's a good idea for me to do this. Please try to understand."

I could feel his anger as strongly as I felt the darkness surrounding the stone horses in the brown bag. He grabbed me again, his hands tightening again on my arms. He pulled me closer until there was barely an inch between us. His need to see this done battered at me like gale-force winds.

"Hey, everything okay out here?" Gramps pushed open the back door. "Dae, you don't have all the time in the world to get ready, you know. You'd best come inside. You can see Jake at the party."

I wasn't sure if Jake was going to let me go. His gaze burned into mine and his hands continued to clench on my arms.

Then suddenly he let go and stepped to the side. He

glanced at the bag he held. "All right. I guess you have to do what's right for you. I have to do what's *necessary* for me. I'll see you later."

I was happy to see him climb in the old truck and back down the drive. I sighed, rubbed my arms, and walked toward the house where Gramps was still waiting with a concerned look on his face.

"What was that all about?" he asked. "If you're having trouble deciding between Jake and Kevin, you'd better say something *now*. That looked pretty intense to me."

"That's not what he wanted." I explained about the horse statues.

He'd known about the problem for a while. Like Kevin, he understood what could happen if the pull of something I held with my bare hands was too much for me. He'd lived with my grandmother having the same abilities.

"He's gonna have to get over it." He shrugged, already dressed in his khaki cargo shorts and a yellow button-down shirt with colorful fish on it—his idea of party clothes. "You need to keep saying no, Dae. And mean it. I've heard the way you say no sometimes, and it sounds more like maybe. Do you want me to talk to him for you? I can handle this once and for all."

I felt like I was a teenager again. "No, thanks. I can handle it. I'm going to get ready for the party." I changed the subject. "So you and Mary Catherine, huh? Or should I say MC?"

"Get in there and get ready and stay out of my personal life," he said. "Just because we live together doesn't mean you get to poke around in my stuff and tell me what to do."

"That's funny. Wasn't that what *you* were just doing with me, Jake, and Kevin?"

"I can do that. I'm older and wiser. The sooner you acknowledge that, the better off you'll be. I recall explaining how this works years ago. It hasn't changed. No matter how old you get, I'll still be older."

I laughed out loud at his statement, given in his

professional law enforcement voice that I remembered so well. "You're addressing the newly-elected mayor of Duck North Carolina," I reminded him. "That gives me a certain amount of wisdom and foresight that someone my age wouldn't necessarily have."

"Whatever. Don't forget to feed your cat before you go accept your accolades, Madam Mayor. If I decide to come home early, I don't want to hear him crying all over the place and looking pitiful."

Mary Catherine was staying in the spare bedroom. I ran lightly up the stairs with my cat following me. I'd named him Treasure because he'd come to me like so many other important gifts I'd found. Now he was so much a part of my life, I couldn't imagine how it would be without him.

I wouldn't say I could talk to animals—not like Mary Catherine—but Treasure and I communicated. I sat on the bed, and he jumped up beside me. I could tell that he wasn't happy that I was going out again.

"I'm sorry." I rubbed his white tummy. "People expect me to celebrate winning the election. I'll be back later. I'll feed you before I go."

He meowed and jumped on the floor before pacing back and forth with his black tail swishing.

"I know you don't like having Mary Catherine's cat here. It won't be for long. You'll just have to get along with him. I think he mostly goes out everywhere with her. I know. You'd like to do that too. But you're not the scarf type that I can drape over my shoulders."

I smiled and stroked his shiny black fur. "I have to take a shower and get dressed. Life will be back to normal tomorrow. Maybe you can come with me to Missing Pieces. You like that."

He was still complaining when I went into the bathroom. I ignored him, getting into the shower and rubbing some flower-scented shampoo into my short brown hair. The hot summer sun had bleached it out more than normal this year since I'd been outside so much. My tan was darker than usual too. Kevin had reminded me several times about using sunblock.

The hot water felt so good. I closed my eyes and let it pour down on me.

I felt guilty about not helping Jake when I could see he was in such bad shape. He needed someone. I just wasn't sure I was that person. I didn't know how to overcome my fear of the artifacts. Mary Catherine said she thought it was healthy. I felt cowardly about it.

Convincing myself to get out of the shower—I couldn't hide here either—I swiped my hand across the steamy bathroom mirror. I practiced my big mayor's smile that had become second nature to me. The smile looked as it always did, but didn't reach my troubled blue eyes.

What if Mary Catherine was right and bad things were about to happen to us? Storms and floods we'd weathered—what about a horse cult? I didn't really even understand yet how something like that could be a threat.

I'd made it through a pirate's ghost, and a dead man trying to help me find his daughter. I'd been hoping for a slowdown in that kind of thing. I needed a nice, long vacation where only good things happened. It could be me and Kevin on a nice, calm beach together. No ghosts. No secrets. And definitely no possibly evil horse cults.

I opened the closet door and went to find the outfit I'd set aside for my possible re-election party. It was breezy, blue and purple, mid-length. I had beautiful, though uncomfortable, shoes that went with it. They matched so perfectly I couldn't leave them at the shop.

My spirits began to pick up once I was dressed. I remembered all the exciting plans I had if I was elected mayor for another term. I was proud of my town and wanted to be part of its future.

Because it was the first time I'd worn the dress, I could also see that it was made in Duck at Sunflower Fancy. I could see my friend, Darcy, in her little sewing room in the back of the shop. She was a wonderful seamstress and I enjoyed wearing her clothes. They felt happy. It was much better than sensing a dress had been made in some far-off country by people who were miserable at their jobs.

The shoes were a different matter. As soon as my feet were in them, I could feel the large factory in China where they were made. At least, I reminded myself, no one had died while they were wearing them before me. I'd once put on a dress that a woman had drowned herself in. Not a pleasant experience.

There wasn't much to do with my hair. I combed the flyaway brown wisps—it dried straight, like always. I put on some eye makeup and lipstick, and studied myself in the mirror again.

Treasure yowled.

"I know I look stupid smiling at myself. I can't explain it. Mayors have to do it. Be glad you're a cat!"

He slunk away. He really didn't like that idea at all. I didn't blame him.

I met Mary Catherine in the hall as I left my room. Treasure walked out before me. Baylor was on the floor at her side. He watched my cat intently but didn't run after him. Treasure hid behind a chair, frightened.

"You look fabulous," Mary Catherine complimented with a wide smile of her own. "The people of Duck are lucky to have such a beautiful and clever mayor."

"Thanks. I take it you like purple." I noticed that she'd changed clothes but was still wearing purple, in a different shade, with a wide-brimmed hat that matched.

"I adore it." She started down the stairs. Baylor shadowed her every move. "I think it's good for a woman to know what works for her, don't you?"

Gramps was waiting at the bottom of the stairs. "Maybe for the woman, but not for the men around her." He took her hand as she came closer to him. "You look like a queen, MC. I'd be honored to escort you to the parties."

"What about Dae?" she asked.

"She has Kevin. We'll pick him up after the first party at

the Blue Whale Inn. You're gonna love that place."

"Then I would be honored for you to be my escort, Horace." She laid her hand on his arm as she reached the bottom of the stairs. She looked down at Baylor who butted his big head against her leg. "Not tonight. Wait here like a good boy. I'll be back."

Baylor jumped on Gramps's recliner and made himself at home. Treasure watched him from a crouched position on the floor. I could tell he wasn't sure yet what to make of the large tabby.

We were ready and out the door very quickly. Gramps started the golf cart, and we ambled down Duck Road. The golf cart was very slow compared to a car but it was great for getting around town. In the summer when traffic was at a standstill, walking and riding in a golf cart were the only ways to get through. During the rest of the year, it still saved on gas and was easy to maneuver.

"I've never seen a golf cart with sides." Mary Catherine touched the clear plastic panels Gramps had installed for rain.

I was riding on the seat behind them, watching the road slip by behind us. Listening to their conversation without being involved was nice. I could save my energy for the parties to come when all my friends and the people of Duck who had voted from me would have plenty of questions.

The sky was a delicate shade of pink across the Currituck Sound. We turned left and headed toward the other side of the island which faced the Atlantic Ocean. People were walking toward the Blue Whale for the party, waving and smiling as we went by. Others were in golf carts too. One or two cars passed us, but there weren't many.

The Blue Whale Inn was right in front of us as we dead-ended at the beach. Kevin had restored the old three-story hotel after retiring from the FBI. I'd helped paint the crazy shade of blue that closely matched the original color and made the inn easy to find. There was a circle drive with a stone fountain, in the grassy middle, that featured a pretty mermaid and a hitching post. Usually there were plenty of places to park—but not this evening.

"Looks like the whole town is here." Gramps pulled the golf cart into a spot by the old hitching post. There was a hand-painted sign that said the spot was reserved for Mayor Dae O'Donnell and family. It was a nice touch that warmed my heart.

I got out of the golf cart and started up the stairs to the wide verandah where dozens of wood rocking chairs usually waited for Kevin's guests. This evening they were filled with my friends and neighbors who rocked and waved to me as they gossiped. Most of them had a drink in one hand and a cupcake or some other confection in the other.

It's time, I told myself. *The spotlight is on you.* I put my big mayor's smile on my face and joined the party.

Because the night was so fine, the double doors at the back of the inn were thrown open to the breezes and a glimpse of the surf. People began congratulating me as I walked in.

Trudy, my best friend since elementary school, hugged me as she grabbed Tim Mabry's hand. The three of us had grown up together. He'd thought he was in love with me for the longest time, but then he and Trudy had found one another. I was so happy for them. There was already talk of marriage in the months ahead.

"There you are!" Cailey Fargo, Chief of the Duck Volunteer Fire Department, saw me. "Congratulations! I knew you'd do it, Dae!" Cailey had also been my fifth grade teacher and one of my campaign managers for the election.

"Congratulations, Dae." Carter Hatley owned Game World, a popular skeet ball and video game arcade on Duck Road. I'd gone to school with his daughter. We'd spent long afternoons there after school, learning to master every game.

There were also people who were relatively new to Duck. Luke Helms was a retired attorney and volunteer firefighter who had recently become the new DA for Dare County. We'd dated once but it hadn't amounted to anything. We just weren't right for each another.

Cody and Reece Baucum had only been in Duck a few years. They'd opened their restaurant on the boardwalk, Wild Stallions. Both brothers congratulated me. Cody's wife, Sally, had their new baby in her arms. This was my town. My home. My people. But there was only one face I searched for in the crowd. Kevin Brickman had changed my life. I finally saw him putting out trays of snacks and topping off glasses. He'd been with the FBI for twelve years before deciding to retire and start a small business. He told me that he had researched dozens of small, coastal towns. Duck had been on the top of his list. I was thankful for that.

"Madam Mayor." He kissed me and took my hand. "I'm glad you could make it."

Kevin was a little over six feet, strong and lean. He'd been wearing his dark brown hair slightly longer in recent months, and it had taken on highlights from the sun. His eyes were more gray than blue, reminding me of the ocean only a few hundred yards away. His handsome face had relaxed since he'd moved to Duck. I could see the changes in him— he was less impatient and tense, a little more friendly and approachable.

He'd seen and done terrible things working for the government. I hoped one day not to see those shadows from his former life lingering in his face.

"I wouldn't have missed it. Everything looks great. Thanks for hosting this."

He put his arms around me, tucking me close against him. "It was the only way I could be sure to see you tonight. There must be six other parties with people who all want to talk to you."

"And that's why you planned yours as the earliest, right?"

"That's right. You know I'm strategic. I'm not a seat-of-the-pants kind of guy." He touched my face with a gentle hand. "You look wonderful for someone who almost died before the election. Every time I think of you out there, fighting for your life, it makes me shudder. I should have been there with you."

"You can't follow me around all the time waiting for me to get into trouble," I reminded him with a grin. "You'd have to be at my side twenty-four-seven."

Gramps laughed from behind me. "That's for sure. I've tried to keep this girl out of trouble her whole life. It's coming to a time when I don't know how much more I can do."

"Maybe I can help with that." Kevin got down on one knee.

I hadn't even noticed how the crowd had cleared a space around us. This was Duck— everyone knew this was going to happen. Everyone but *me*. How'd they manage to keep it from me?

Trudy was already crying, trying to keep her makeup from running. Shayla Lily, who ran the psychic reader shop that Mary Catherine had started, was also crying. Betty Vasquez from the Boutique and Floral shop was sobbing into a pretty lace handkerchief.

"Dae O'Donnell," Kevin said to me. "I'm not good at speeches. But I love you, and I'd like you to be my wife."

Chapter Three

I felt like someone had hit me with a sledgehammer. I truly hadn't seen this coming.

How had I missed it? There should have been signs from Gramps or Shayla. I should have heard whispers and seen the sly looks. Nancy was terrible at keeping secrets but she'd managed to keep this one.

Kevin was silently waiting for my answer. The crowd had grown completely quiet so everyone could hear.

My first reaction was to try to talk him out of it. It sounds crazy, I suppose, but I thought he was probably just feeling guilty, like he said, about not being able to protect me. That wasn't a good reason to marry someone.

On the other hand, I loved Kevin and I believed that he loved me. That was the *best* reason to get married. I'd just never seriously considered it.

I glanced at Trudy standing beside Tim. She frowned at me and tapped on her watch. I was taking too long. I realized then that I was going to have to say yes—then Kevin and I could talk it over. It would be mean to leave him hanging with no answer or to say I wasn't sure in front of this crowd.

"I love you too, Kevin Brickman. And if you want to marry me, let's do it." There was probably a more elegant answer, but that was all my shocked mind could come up with.

It was enough.

The crowd around us let out a long, worried sigh and then started yelling congratulations. Champagne bottles popped. The party that was supposed to be for me winning the election became the party where I got engaged.

Kevin slid a beautiful ring on my finger with a knowing smile on his face.

It took me by surprise since he knew what I went through when I touched something new. He hadn't prepared me at all. I closed my eyes as hundreds of impressions raced through me.

"You *made* this?" I asked after seeing the images of him creating the white gold ring with the moonstone in it. "How? When?"

He shrugged. "I took some classes and met a man who helped me. I knew better than to give you an antique or something made in questionable circumstances. This way I know what you're sensing from it."

"You remembered that I love moonstones." I threw my arms around him. "Maybe we really *should* get married."

He pulled back a little to study my face. "Was there any doubt?"

The attention had wandered away from us and toward the food and champagne. A small, local band was playing in the corner. People had started dancing.

I was safe now expressing my views without making him look stupid. "Well, I'm not really sure—and I know this is a bad time to say it—I don't want you to marry me because of what happened with Chief Peabody. Even if we are married, you can't protect me all the time."

Kevin kissed me gently on the lips. "I'm not just asking because of what happened with Peabody or anyone else. I thought about it for a while and then it took me months to make this ring. I want to be with you. Don't ever doubt it. I love you."

"Okay." I started crying even though I'd promised myself I wouldn't if I ever heard the question. "Thank you for the beautiful ring. I love it. And you."

"Punch?" he asked. "Or champagne?"

"Punch," I said. "Are those little dumplings over there on that tray? If so, I'd like a few dozen of those too."

He kissed the ring on my hand. "I'll be right back."

Phil DeAngelo and his sister, Jamie, hugged me and wished us well while I waited for Kevin. Jamie had married Chris Slayton, the town manager, last year. It had been a lovely wedding.

August Grandin, who owned the Duck General Store, grudgingly said he was happy for me, and hoped I'd work to keep sales tax low. Cole Black and his wife, Molly, from the Curbside Bar and Grill, said they hoped the new plans Chris Slayton had for Duck would increase tourism.

A few people from Duck weren't necessarily happy about me becoming mayor again. Martha Segall had voted for Mad Dog Wilson. She made no bones about it when she wished me well with my engagement. "And I hope you'll do a better job as mayor this time around. You're still a little too young and wet behind the ears to hold such an important position. But I'll be there to let you know how you're doing."

By that I knew she meant she'd be complaining the whole time about everything, as she always had. No surprises there.

I was surprised to actually see Mad Dog at the party, laughing and drinking punch with his wife, Laura. He didn't speak to me, but he nodded in my direction.

By running for mayor, he'd given up his seat on the Duck Town Council. His seat was one of two that would have to be filled by an appointment from the town council. He'd be free to run for it again in the next election.

"Dae!" LaDonna Nelson had been the owner of the second seat that was empty. Her mother, Beverly Michaels, was there with her and LaDonna's brother, our police chief, Ronnie Michaels.

"I'm so happy you're going to be mayor again." LaDonna hugged me. "Just remember to make wise choices for those two empty seats."

"One of them could still have you in it after the next election," I told her. "I can't imagine a town council without you. You've been there since we incorporated. Are you sure you won't reconsider?"

"No. I don't think I can handle the stress anymore," she told me. "It's time for some changes. Maybe you could convince Kevin to take one of the seats. I'd love to see him on the council."

"Maybe." I glanced up to see Kevin making his way through the crowd toward me. "We'll see."

Tom Watts and Dr. Sheffield were at the party to congratulate me on my election win. I thought about what Jake had said about Tom agreeing with Sheffield that the excavation should continue.

I wished I knew something to say that would end the whole debate between Jake and Tom. They were too important to the welfare of the wild horses to let the horse cult, or Dr. Sheffield, come between.

"Congrats, Mayor Dae." Duran Hawkins's smile was sweet as were his velvet brown eyes. He was Dr. Sheffield's young, personal assistant. He placed his limp, cool hand on mine. "You should come out to the site again. We've dug out the whole big horse now. It's amazing!"

I thanked him for the invitation and then thought of a reason to walk away. I didn't like Duran, though I had no reason for it. He was just a young college student, excited about his first archeological dig. I felt guilty for not liking him, but it didn't make me any more comfortable in his presence. Each time I saw him, I vowed to like him and be more pleasant the next time. I didn't want him to tell everyone that I was nasty to him.

And once again, I'd failed.

We'd been at the Blue Whale for about two hours when Gramps reminded me that we needed to move on to the next party. It was being held at the volunteer fire department a few miles away.

I was in a better mood, stuffed full of Kevin's delicious dumplings, my head slightly spinning from too much champagne. It was a good way to approach the rest of the evening.

"I'm sure Kevin will want to drive his golf cart," I told Gramps. "We'll meet you and Mary Catherine there."

"Okay, honey." He smiled and kissed my forehead. "You were surprised by his proposal, weren't you?"

"Probably more surprised than I've ever been. How did you keep it from me?"

"It wasn't easy. People kept asking about it. I just knew someone was going to give it away."

"They didn't. It's kind of weird, you know?"

He laughed. "Did you think you were going to live with me forever? You know sometimes having a granddaughter in the house cramps my style. With you over here at the Blue Whale, I can get some action going." He glanced significantly at MC and waggled his eyebrows.

"I don't even want to know what you mean by that!" But I laughed. I hadn't thought about not living in our old house. All the ramifications of marrying Kevin hadn't sunk in yet. Not that I would mind living at the Blue Whale with Kevin— I just hadn't thought about it yet. I felt sure it would all catch up with me later.

Gramps and Mary Catherine went out to the golf cart. Kevin was helping his part-time staff clean up before he left. He'd be there until he felt comfortable that the people who worked for him could finish. I offered to help, but he said I couldn't clean up after my own party.

I wasn't in any hurry to leave. The parties would go on most of the night. After being turned down to help put things away, I went out on the verandah to look at the stars and take a deep breath. Everything was happening very quickly.

I pulled on the light sweater I'd brought with me and sat in one of the rockers. One of Kevin's many cats walked by on the railing after a sharp look in my direction. A small, brown bat flew out from under the eaves, and I knew what the cat was really looking at.

Everything was going uphill from here, I told myself. The problems of the past few weeks before the election were gone. Kevin wanted to marry me. I was mayor again for another four years. It was an awesome responsibility but one I took on gladly.

I could hear the ocean hitting the shore behind the inn. I thought about walking back there but wanted to be ready when Kevin was finished. There were still five more parties with food, drinks, and congratulations to get through. I didn't want people who had put their trust in me standing around wondering where I was.

There was a scratching noise from the side of the verandah. It came from the same direction where the cat had headed. Thinking it might be in trouble, possibly no match for the brown bat, I went down the stairs and searched for it.

There were several bright floodlights that Kevin used when guests were staying at the inn. He'd turned those lights off after the party. Instead the old fashioned lanterns were on, softly illuminating the evening. They fit the early 1900 timeframe when the Blue Whale had been built. I admired their charm, but they weren't much help for looking for a cat.

"Here kitty-kitty." I scraped my hands on the dark bushes. My sweater got caught on a branch, and I carefully disentangled it. "I'm sorry I don't remember your name, kitty, but if you're in trouble, I'll be glad to help."

There were no more scratching noises in the bush. No doubt the cat had run away, laughing at the stupid human who was getting caught in the branches. I turned to go back on the verandah and a dark shape rose up before me.

"I'm sorry, Dae."

It was Jake. I couldn't see his face but I knew his voice. I started to accept his apology for what had happened at my house earlier. Maybe we'd even have time to talk before Kevin came out.

But before I could speak, he thrust one of the stone horse statues into my hand. There was an instant when I was cognizant of the statue's weight and the coldness of the stone. I didn't have time to think how he'd betrayed my trust. Images of the statue's terrible past overwhelmed me, and I sank to the damp ground, unconscious.

Chapter Four

The hot night was made hotter and brighter by a hundred torches. The smell of the tar they had been dipped in hung over the area like the heavy smoke from the large bonfire. Dozens of men were dressed in animal skins. They chanted loudly, monotonously. The large figure of a horse, at least twenty feet tall, presided over the event. Dozens of living horses raised a protest with snorting and stamping feet.

Something was coming out of the fire. The men held the stone horse statues in the air, cheering when they saw the beasts rising from the flames. Their enemies would soon be vanquished.

One man stood to the side, alone. He was covered in blood, and held a large animal bone in one hand. He stared through the flames and the smoke, his eyes narrowing. He reached out, trying to grab what he saw—
I woke up, back inside the Blue Whale. The windows were dark and a fire burned in the hearth. In the quiet, I could hear the logs crackling and shifting as they burned.

Something is coming out of the fire.

I jumped from the chaise in the lobby area. My hands were shaking and cold. Even though I hadn't seen what was coming from the fire, my insides were knotted in fear. I knew what it was. It had no name. But I could feel its wrath and devouring hunger.

"Dae!" Kevin put down a tray of tea he'd brought into the room. "Sit down. You look terrible. How do you feel?"

"Thanks." My voice trembled, and I fell back against the chaise. "That's what a girl always wants to hear from her new fiancé."

"Are you hurt? Did you hit your head?" He stared deeply into my eyes. "The cowboy said you'd passed out after he handed you one of his stupid horses. I wanted to hit him in the head with it."

"No more than I deserved." Jake walked out of the shadows, his hands in the pockets of his dirty, wrinkled jeans. "I'm so sorry, Dae. I didn't understand. Are you all right?"

I didn't know how to answer. I couldn't find the words to express how hurtful his actions had been. Handing me a piece of ancient history with no preparation, no safeguards, was as though he'd thrust *me* into that fire. I couldn't believe he'd do something like that. He was my friend.

"I think you should leave." Kevin's voice had a dangerous edge to it. "You've seen that she's alive. That's all you're going to get."

"Wait." Jake took another step toward me. "I need to know. What did you see? What was the statue's history?"

"That's it." Kevin grabbed him and twisted one of his

arms behind his back as he shoved him toward the door. "Get out of here before I kick your—"

"I just want to know the truth." Jake was pleading with him. "Please, Kevin. I didn't mean to hurt her. Dae!"

I didn't raise a finger to help him as Kevin threw him out of the inn and closed the door behind him.

"Sorry. I told him he could stay until you woke up. He's your *friend,* after all."

"That's okay." I smiled at him despite the pain in my head and the terrible sense of what had happened at the excavation site in nearby Corolla so many centuries ago. "I don't know what he was thinking. He's obsessed with finding out about the horse cult so he can shut down the dig. I understand. I really do. Just that—"

He handed me a cup of hot tea. "I know. If it's any consolation, he at least brought you inside. I don't think he realized what he was doing, but I'm not making excuses for him either."

I sipped the strong Earl Grey, not in a forgiving mood. "It's no consolation at all. He's supposed to be my friend. Why would he force me to do something I'd told him I couldn't do?"

"He doesn't know any better." He put his arm around me and held me close. "Can you talk about it?"

Kevin knew how to handle these events. He'd worked with a psychic partner in the FBI for ten years. No doubt he'd seen and heard much worse than anything I could ever tell him. He didn't like to discuss it, but his knowledge and experience was a great comfort as I discovered more about my gift.

"The horses—I saw everything." I shuddered, my hands still freezing despite being wrapped around a hot cup of tea. "There were horses, real ones, and the big statue I saw out at Jake's place. The whole thing was at least twenty feet tall. The men were dressed in animal skins. They were chanting and calling something from the fire."

He frowned. "*From* the fire?"

"They were like horses, but not horses. I think they were demons. They were red and black with yellow eyes. The men were calling on them to murder people in another village. I could feel how much the demons loved it. They couldn't wait to get to the kill. The men thought they were using the demons. It was the other way around."

"This sounds like a long time before the Spanish or English got here. Did they come in boats?"

"No." The image was clear in my mind. "There was still a narrow strip of land connecting the Outer Banks to the mainland."

Kevin whistled softly. "So we're talking a thousand years ago?"

"Yes. There was blood everywhere. I couldn't tell if it was real or part of the vision. And there was a man. I-I think he saw me. He reached out and then I was gone." I shuddered, thinking about it again. It would be a while before I forgot that vision.

Someone knocked at the front door. My real life came rushing back to me. How long had I been out? We needed to go on to the next party.

Gramps and Mary Catherine were at the door.

"Are you okay, honey?" Gramps hurried into the room to sit beside me.

"I'm fine." I tried to smile and hoped he'd believe it. He knew almost as much as Kevin in how to deal with the problem after living with two women who had similar gifts for so many years.

He hugged me. "What was Jake thinking doing something like that? I knew something was wrong with him when I saw him earlier. He's losing it. You can't see him anymore, Dae."

It was so reminiscent of my childhood that I laughed. "You know I'm too old for you to decide who I can and can't see, right?"

"You're not that old. You'll never be that old." He kissed my forehead. "What a night. What does a man have to do to get a drink around here?"

"Come into my bar," Kevin joked. "I think I can help with that. I could use one too. Mary Catherine?"

"No thanks," she said.

"What about the next party?" I asked. "We're going to be late."

Gramps patted my hand as he got up to follow Kevin. "I'm sorry, honey. You missed it all. I told everyone you had too much to drink and passed out. They understood."

"What?"

He laughed. "I just told them you weren't feeling well. Everyone knows you've been through a lot the last few weeks. They understood. You just get some rest and then we'll go home."

When they were in the old bar, Mary Catherine sat close to me. "What happened, Dae?"

I told her everything I'd seen and understood from the vision.

"No wonder the animals are so upset." She shook her head. "Excavating this site is going to bring out these demon horses. Now I understand."

"I don't know." I searched my memory. "I think so. It seems impossible. At some point, everything was destroyed or buried to prevent it from happening again. I can only guess that the energy surrounding the site is still enough to bring them back."

"That doesn't sound good. What can we do to stop it?"

I thought about the man who'd reached out to me. He was involved in what had happened all those centuries ago, but I wasn't sure how. "I think there's a ritual of some kind that has to be performed. It's not enough just to dig them up again. We might be safe as long as no one performs the ritual. If they do—"

"Put it behind you," Mary Catherine said. "It won't help to dwell on it. You know the truth now. We just have to figure out what to do."

"We have to stop the excavation." That part was very

clear to me. "I don't know how we'll do it. If it was happening in Duck, we could just change the zoning or rescind their permit. With it being in Corolla, I'm not sure."

"I don't think you should worry about it tonight," she said. "You need to clear your mind."

I took a deep breath. "I guess the animals didn't understand what was wrong, but they knew it was something bad."

"Are you channeling animals now?" Kevin asked as he and Gramps returned to the lobby.

"No. That's my thing." Mary Catherine smiled. "I talk to animals. That's why I'm here. All the wild horses are concerned. I'm sure it's a race memory. They've carried the terrible secret of the horse cult, fearful that it could happen again."

Kevin sat down. "That's right. You're the pet psychic."

"Yes. But I find that wild animals are just as chatty. Am I stretching your comfort zone?"

"No. The government has been working on developing talent in all the various psychic abilities for the last fifty years. They might have agents now who can talk to animals."

"That sounds exciting." Mary Catherine considered the idea. "I'll bet it pays better too."

"Probably," he agreed. "But you might not like the work as well."

Gramps finished his whiskey and thanked Kevin for helping me. "I think we should go home now. Let's get away from what happened and start fresh tomorrow."

Kevin hugged me as I got to my feet. "You don't have to go," he whispered in my ear. "You could stay here with me tonight."

Part of me wanted to stay with him, but the biggest part wanted to sleep in my own bed with familiar things around me. "Thanks, but I can't. Not tonight anyway."

"That's okay." He kissed me. "I'll see you tomorrow on your first official day as mayor."

"Not to mention the future Mrs. Kevin Brickman."

Gramps grinned. "I'll wait for you outside." Mary Catherine took his arm, and they went out to the golf cart.

"I won't officially be mayor until the swearing in ceremony on Thursday before the council meeting." I kissed Kevin. "You haven't seen my special mayor's coat that was handmade in Duck."

"I have," he corrected. "You were wearing it the first time I saw you at the Fourth of July parade. I've been trying to forget it ever since."

"Yeah. Me too. You don't know how tempted I've been to accidentally lose it and have to find something else to wear for formal occasions."

"It doesn't matter about the coat. It's what's inside that counts. I think I fell in love with you when I saw you that day." He kissed the ring on my finger. "I'm so glad you said yes tonight."

"Because you would've felt like an idiot on your knees if I would've said no in front of the whole town?"

"That would've been bad," he said. "I should've thought about that before I did it. But I could've lived with it. I hope never to live without you in my life again."

"Me too." I kissed him again as Gramps was honking the small, annoying horn on the golf cart. "I better go before someone shoots him."

I went outside, looking away from the bushes where Jake had confronted me with the horse statue. I still felt the terror and evil from the vision. Evil wasn't a word I used often, but it was apt in this situation. I had no idea how to stop the state archeologists from continuing work on the project.

I knew I could count on Jake for help, but Tom and Dr. Sheffield wouldn't be as easily moved. I had no legal sway in Corolla and it was doubtful the town council would back me since everyone saw this as a goldmine for the community.

Jake had been so overwhelmed by the need to know what was buried behind his barn. I understood it was that passion that had led him to force me to hold one of the statues.

That didn't mean I could forgive him—at least not for a while. It was going to be hard to talk to him and see him right away. But I was going to have to grit my teeth and work with him before something came out of the ground and we couldn't put it back.

Chapter Five

The drive home in the golf cart was cold, but what I needed to snap myself out of what was left from touching the stone horse.

I stared out at the Currituck Sound as we passed the boardwalk. Mary Catherine and Gramps were chatting in the front seat. I was glad that the two of them seemed to have such a wonderful rapport. If I was going to leave my family's old house and move in with Kevin someday as his wife, it would be good to know that Gramps had someone too.

I realized that it might not be Mary Catherine. She hadn't said anything about staying in Duck beyond this crisis.

She would probably go back to her life in Wilmington. There were no good-sized radio stations that could hire her to do her pet psychic radio show here. I was pretty sure Gramps would never leave his family home.

It was a quick trip since the roads were empty between the Blue Whale and our house. The air was sharp and crisp. It was nice to get inside where it was warm and cozy. I excused myself to give Mary Catherine and Gramps some privacy. The house wasn't very big. I knew what it was like to be there with someone you wanted to speak with alone.

"Goodnight, honey," Gramps said. "Get a good night's sleep. I'm sure things will look better in the morning."

"Goodnight, Dae," Mary Catherine called. "Your grandfather has promised me blueberry pancakes in the morning. We'll see if he can fulfill that vow."

I looked at the two of them standing close together, gazing into each other's eyes.

I could imagine having her in our lives. Gramps had been alone too long. "I could go for some blueberry pancakes too. Don't let him wiggle out of that promise!"

I went up to my room, thinking about what this house had been like when I was a child. My grandmother had died before I was born. My mother and I lived here with Gramps. He was the sheriff when I was young. He had been strict with me—probably with good reason since I liked to goof around a lot.

I had never known my father—at least not until the last few years. Gramps and my mother had decided it was better to tell me that he was dead instead of telling me that he was a criminal. He'd come back to Duck long enough for me to get to know him before he left again. He'd been in and out of jail most of his life. He hadn't changed, still looking for that big score that was going to make his life perfect. Instead it had almost killed him, and he'd had to run away.

I was sorry for him that he'd had to miss spending time with my mother and me. He hadn't even known she was dead until I told him. He'd claimed to love her, but that didn't seem like love to me. Gramps was hard on him too, I'd found out later. He thought my father wasn't good enough for his daughter.

It was complicated, I guess.

My mother had died while I was in college. She'd left me feeling guilty about the last time we'd seen each other. We'd argued about something stupid before she'd gone home to Duck that day. She'd lost control of her car and it had gone off the bridge from the mainland. Her body had never been recovered. I still had dreams about her sitting in the car beneath the water.

No one ever knows if they will have a chance to make it right with someone they care for.

I'd seen ghosts, and even helped a family pirate ancestor prove he wasn't guilty of the crime he'd been hanged for. But not my mother's ghost. The one spirit I really wanted to summon seemed to be content where she was. Sometimes I blamed that on the family 'gift' skipping a generation. Grandma Eleanore had the gift of sight, but not my mother. Instead, it had come to me.

These weren't the best thoughts to think as I lay in bed staring at the ceiling. I was supposed to focus on good things to get away from what I'd seen in the vision. That wasn't working. I stroked Treasure's soft fur. He always slept with me. But knowing he was there didn't make me feel any better. There was still that pent-up emotion and fear lingering inside me. I couldn't sleep.

I put on my robe and slippers and walked up the narrow stairs that led to the roof and the widow's walk. I'd spent hours here as a child, trying to figure things out and enjoying the view. The ornate wrought-iron rail was frosty as I put my hand on it.

From here I could see the beams from the working lighthouses across the Outer Banks. Their large, bright lights swept across the water as a reminder to sailors that the shoals around the islands were dangerous. Called the Graveyard of the Atlantic for more than four hundred years, the waters still took their toll. Most of the larger vessels had electronic devices now that kept them safe, but smaller vessels still sometimes ended up beneath the surface of the deadly water.

Treasure came soundlessly up the stairs after me. He looked up and meowed, and I lifted him in my arms. We stared out at the Currituck Sound, smooth and clear, and the edge of the Atlantic. The rooftops around us covered the sleeping houses in Duck and farther along the coast.

Women had once watched for their loved one's return from these high walks. Day after day, a wife, sister, or mother would wait for the tall masts that would signal the safe and successful voyage of a ship.

Sometimes their husbands, brothers, sons, and fathers would be gone for months, even years, as they traded goods with other states and countries. Many times they never returned, which was how the high rooftop got its name. I'd read countless ghost stories of widow's walks when I was a child. Some female ghost was still looking for her missing lover.

I'd always thought how unfair it was that men weren't up here pining for their women. There had been a few female pirates and ship captains, but not enough to tell stories of. It hadn't sounded appealing to me—being gone for years from the people you loved. I was glad that didn't happen anymore.

Something icy and white hit the top of Treasure's head. He hissed at it before batting at the next one with his paws. *Snow!* I let him down so he could run back to the stairs. I couldn't believe it was snowing.

Snow was an infrequent guest in Duck. The white stuff didn't last long, but it was always welcome and exciting. Everyone stopped what they were doing to marvel at it. The snowflakes started coming down faster and harder, covering the widow's walk and the rooftops below me.

I ran down the stairs after Treasure, who had curled up on the bed again to go back to sleep. "Don't you want to go outside and see the snow? Who knows when we'll have it again?"

He made it clear to me that he wasn't interested in anything cold or wet. I threw an old shawl over my robe and went downstairs to the living room. I didn't bother putting on real shoes, afraid the snow would stop before I could get outside. I ran out in my slippers and reveled in the sparkly white stuff that covered everything in the yard.

I tried to scrape enough snow from the golf cart to make a snowball—there wasn't enough. I whirled around in it and caught snowflakes on my tongue. I grinned as my hair and shawl were covered in it. The snow catching in trees and bushes revealed hidden depths. It was thrilling, and exactly what my wounded heart needed to feel light again.

Skidding across the drive, I headed to Duck Road, glancing up and down. No cars had been through to mar the clean, white surface. But there was something large and dark in the middle of the road. Maybe it was a rug or something that had fallen off the back of a truck. Snowflakes were rapidly gathering on it.

I hoped no one had carelessly injured or killed a dog and left it there as I walked toward it. I walked down to the spot, slipping and sliding on the road, not knowing what I would find. When I reached the dark form I considered that it was too big to be a rug. Probably not a dog either.

It was then that I realized it was a man.

He was wearing dark dress pants and a dark suit coat. He was lying on his chest, his head turned to the right so I could see his face in the dim streetlight's glow. *Tom Watts.*

Maybe he had passed out after drinking too much. Kevin's party wasn't the only one where people had been drinking. I needed to touch him, try to wake him. I didn't dare do it without protection after going through the vision earlier.

I slipped my hand inside my shawl and bent close to him.

"Tom?" I pushed at him. He didn't move. "It's me, Dae O'Donnell. You have to get up. I don't think I can move you by myself. Even in Duck, it's dangerous to be in the middle of the road."

A bad feeling was slowly overwhelming me. I beat it off with a reminder that things weren't always the way they appeared. I had to move him before a vehicle came down Duck Road and hit him. "Tom—can you hear me? We have to get you out of the road."

I thought his eyes were closed until I put my covered hand on his face and realized that they were wide open, staring into the snow-filled darkness. He was dead. The words whispered through the silent night.

"Tom." I pushed away the tears that slid down my cheek as I knelt in the street beside him. "What happened? Why are you out here?"

I wanted to insist that he get up. He couldn't be dead. He was a good man and a good friend to the wild horses. His work was so important. Who would step in to take his place? This couldn't be happening.

Being the granddaughter of a retired sheriff, I noticed things about the scene that other people with grandfathers who were dentists and accountants wouldn't have noticed. There was no blood. Blood would have been visible even in the dim light. His jacket was torn on the right side. One of his hands was stretched out. The other was tucked under him. He had an ugly mark on the side of his head. It was a deep gash, but it had some kind of shape.

I stood to go inside and get Gramps. He'd make the appropriate calls and verify what I already knew. There was a rush of icy air that swirled the newly fallen snow on the street. I heard the thunder of horse's hooves and smelled the scent of them coming toward me.

Then I was engulfed in what felt like a stampede as hundreds of horses seemed to rush down Duck Road. I cringed and tried to protect myself from them as they raced by me. Their loud snorts and screams echoed through the night. I was afraid I would be crushed by their frantic pace.

But when I looked up, there were no horses. It was some kind of strange mirage, maybe part of the vision still lingering inside of me. And yet there were hoof prints up and down the street, marking the clean snow and covering Tom's body, as though horses had run across him.

Spooked, I ran into the house and woke Gramps. I was surprised to find him sleeping in his bedroom. I hadn't seen him use it in ten years. Usually he slept on the recliner in the living room, across from the TV. Who knew he'd make appropriate changes for our guest?

"What do you mean there's a man in the road?" He stuffed his legs into worn pants and shoved his sockless feet into boots. "Why were *you* in the road, Dae?"

"It's snowing." I fought to find an explanation. "I went out to see the snow."

He eyed me critically. "You're a little old to run out in the middle of the night to look at the snow."

"Maybe. But you're missing the point."

He put on his fishing hat and jacket. "Which is the man in the road. I get it. Do you know who it is?"

"It's Tom Watts. I think he's dead. We have to move him so no one hits him. I couldn't do it by myself."

"Well, of course not," he complained. "Let's go."

He brought a flashlight, and I retraced my steps into the street. There were still no tire tracks, only hoof prints, visible in the snow. The hoof prints extended into the yard, almost up to the porch, and around the side.

"What the hell? There were *horses* out here?"

"I don't think they were real horses." I told him what had happened.

"Whatever they were, they left physical evidence. Go back and get your phone. Take some pictures before this snow is gone. We won't be able to see the hoof prints after that. You'll need to take some pictures of Tom too—just in case we need them."

I ran inside to do as he said, leaving him to check Tom. I came back out with my phone. Gramps was setting up old wood sawhorses as roadblocks. I knew then that I was right about Tom.

Swallowing hard, I took dozens of pictures of Tom lying still and lifeless on the road. I took even more pictures of hoof prints. The hoof prints not only extended up into our driveway but into our neighbor's drive and yard too. I'd never seen anything like it. The wild horses had never come this far into town.

Gramps lit flares that sparkled red in the darkness to alert anyone coming this way. Both sides of Duck Road were blocked from traffic. "You were right," he said. "Tom's dead. Looks like he took a bad blow to the head."

"I noticed that."

"He's covered in hoof prints too. I think one of those may have been what caused the fatal blow to his head. Did you get pictures of it, Dae?"

"Yes. But I don't see how it's possible. I was standing in the middle of the road when the horses stampeded by. There weren't any *real* horses."

"Maybe not that time." He took out his cell phone. "But that man is dead and the horses that don't exist left their calling card."

"Maybe it's the demon horses I saw in the vision."

"Shh. I don't want to think about it. Let me get with Ronnie and Tuck. We can talk about it like normal people."

It kind of hurt my feelings when he said that. I understood what he meant—it was one thing for me to hold his hand and tell him where he'd dropped his wallet. It was another to tell him that demon horses from the excavation in Corolla were running up and down Duck Road, possibly killing Tom.

"I'm sorry, honey." He squeezed my hand. "I shouldn't have said that. You know I didn't mean it that way. I'd just like this to be something the police can take care of without your help. You've been through enough recently."

"That's okay. I understand."

Gramps went to find a tarp he could use to cover Tom. I went inside to get dressed and found Mary Catherine. She was waiting by the door with Baylor.

"What's going on?" she asked.

"I found a dead man on the road."

"I assume that's not a normal thing."

"No. I have to get dressed. We're about to have a house full of law enforcement. I'd rather not be here talking to them in my robe."

"Dae?" She stopped me. "Does this have anything to do with the horses? Baylor and I felt something . . . unusual. I can't describe it, but the local animals were terrified. I think you'll find many of them have run off. They don't want to be here."

In a hushed tone, I told her what I'd experienced. "I don't know what to make of it. It felt like there were horses, but none were there—at least none that I could see."

She put her hand on my arm. "I think you *do* know. Don't be afraid to be certain of your gift. I know sometimes other people don't understand, but it's important for you to take hold of it. Make it your own."

"Thanks." I heard the distant sound of a siren coming our way. "I have to get dressed."

"I'm going to hide upstairs. There aren't many animals I dislike, but sheriffs, police chiefs, and officers make me nervous. Excuse me."

I watched her go into my mother's old room before I disappeared into mine. I quickly pulled on jeans and a red Duck Jazz Festival sweatshirt. I ran a comb through my hair and shoved my feet into boots.

It had been a strange and terrible night. I wanted to be prepared in case anything else came my way.

Chapter Six

Treasure didn't move from the bed as I dressed. He didn't even lift his head to see what I was doing. I closed the bedroom door and went downstairs, taking out the large coffee urn that we always kept around for these times.

I could remember dozens of these nights as a child, and as an adult. Sheriff Tuck Riley sitting around the old wood table in the kitchen drinking coffee and eating any pastry we had on hand. Duck Police Chief Ronnie Michaels would be there too, shaking a donut at Sheriff Riley and reminding him whose jurisdiction they were working in.

That was going to be a problem in this case. The crime

happened in Duck, although Tom Watts lived in Corolla. That was another town and another county. I knew Sheriff Riley would jump on the chance to take the case. Our police chief would have to participate. But it seemed fair for the new Corolla police chief to take part in it too.

I cut up what was left of the strudel Gramps had made yesterday and put it on small plates so it would go further. There were some day-old cookies from the grocery store that I put on a plate. No one would care that they were stale. While they discussed a case, they'd eat anything and drink gallons of coffee.

Several other sirens got closer. I was glad Gramps had blocked off Duck Road to protect the crime scene.

Tuck Riley got there first. He had to come all the way from Manteo and should've been the last person there. He tipped his flat-brimmed hat to me as he came in the kitchen. His brown uniform was clean and pressed as always, but there was something slightly askew about his overall appearance. I couldn't put my finger on it. Maybe it was the button in the wrong hole or the collar not quite pressed down flat.

"I guess this is good morning, huh?" He poured himself a cup of coffee.

"For us," I replied. "How did you get here so fast?"

"I was out and about when I got the call." He cleared his throat and glanced away, pretending to take a sudden interest in the pastry. "Is this strudel homemade?"

Sheriff Riley never asked questions like that. It was easy to tell he was up to something. But what?

I continued my assessment of his appearance. His dark brown hair wasn't perfectly combed and in place like always. His brown eyes flitted restlessly instead of his usual inquisitive stare.

"Yeah, I made the strudel yesterday." Gramps came out of his room and down the stairs. He'd changed clothes into dry cargo pants and a blue flannel shirt. "Sorry to drag you out so early. You made good time getting here. You must've flown."

Sheriff Riley's face turned red. I couldn't believe it. He was embarrassed about something!

"Good coffee, Dae," he finally gruffly muttered. "Now, what the hell happened out there on the road?"

Gramps filled him in as he poured a cup of coffee and winked at me to say thanks for making it. "I don't know where Chief Michaels is. It seems like he should've been here first. I did what I could to preserve the crime scene and protect Tom Watt from getting hit by a car."

"Don't you mean another car?" Sheriff Riley asked. "Looks like one of your partygoers from the mayor's celebration last night had too much to drink and mowed him down. Hit and run. You have another theory?"

"Nope. Not right now. You can't even see the crime scene clearly yet. Let's wait until it gets light."

"What about that gash on his head?" I asked.

"I suppose you found him." Sheriff Riley showed his even white teeth in a sardonic smile. "Leave it to Dae. What were you doing out on the street at that time of night?"

"I went out to look at the snow."

"Of course you did." He nodded and shrugged at Gramps. "What else?"

There was a knock at the door. I went to answer, hoping it was Chief Michaels. They'd probably only want me to write a statement about what happened. They could share it.

But it was the new Corolla police chief, Heidi Palo. I'd only met her once before. There was a meeting of several mayors from local towns in Corolla a few months back. She'd been the deputy police chief then. With the arrest of her boss on murder charges, she'd stepped in to take his job.

"Hello." She coughed and tugged at her gray uniform. "Is this where everyone is meeting to discuss what happened to Tom Watts?"

"Yes. Come in."

"Heidi! Let me get you some coffee," Gramps said. "This is my granddaughter, the mayor of Duck, Dae

O'Donnell. I suppose you know Sheriff Riley. We're waiting on the EMS people and Chief Michaels. Come on in and warm up."

Heidi Palo was at least six-feet tall, very blond, with startling blue eyes and high cheek bones. She was about my age, mid-thirties, and handsome, not pretty. "Hello, Mr. O'Donnell. You used to be the county sheriff. It's nice to see you again."

I shook her hand and gave her my big mayor's smile. "It's a bad night to be out. I'm glad to finally meet you."

She took my hand. "It's nice to meet you too, ma'am. I've seen you around, just haven't had the opportunity to introduce myself. I'm sorry it has to be during this circumstance."

"Please call me Dae. We aren't too formal around here."

"Thank you. I hope you'll call me Heidi."

As I grabbed a mug of coffee that Gramps had poured, I caught a sneaky, sidelong glance between her and Tuck Riley. His face turned red again, and he quickly looked away.

So that's how it is.

"You must've been monitoring your police scanner, Chief Palo," Sheriff Riley said. "Otherwise you wouldn't have known about this since it's not in your county, right?"

She nodded quickly. "Uh-that's right, sir. I picked up the message on the scanner. I came right down when I heard one of my people was involved."

Gramps scratched his head. "I don't remember saying who was involved when I called it in."

Chief Palo faltered—her expression stricken.

"Oh, it must have been my call that you picked up on." I stood close to her. "I called the Corolla police. I thought they should be involved."

Sheriff Riley brought his hand down hard on the wood table, one of his funny habits. "I understand this happened right outside your door, Mayor, but you had no right to call in someone outside this jurisdiction."

"Sorry." I shrugged.

"Thank you, Dae." Chief Palo gave Sheriff Riley an angry glance. "I appreciate you thinking about me."

I almost laughed out loud. Sheriff Riley had been alone for a while after his wife had divorced him. Heidi Palo was much younger, but I could see where the two of them could be good together. They just needed to acknowledge their relationship before everyone else noticed it. Either way it would be fodder for the small town grapevine that ran up and down the highway.

"Whatever." Sheriff Riley took a big swig of coffee. "Where's Ronnie? How long does it take to get here from his house? He must be driving a golf cart."

Chief Michaels came in with a blast of cold air still filled with snowflakes. "Sorry I'm late. It's been the weirdest night."

"Weirder than having a dead man in the middle of Duck Road?" Sheriff Riley asked with his usual sarcastic tone.

"As a matter of fact—" Chief Michaels took off his heavy coat. He was shorter than Tuck Riley and older, in his sixties. He and Gramps had been deputy sheriffs together.

Ronnie Michaels reminded me of a drill sergeant with his curt tone and immaculate uniform. His patent leather shoes were always shiny. "We've been run ragged by phone calls about horses running through the streets and trampling people's yards. Ever hear of such a thing?"

Gramps glanced at me. He buried his words in a stale cookie.

But it had to be said. They were going to see the hoof prints anyway. "When I was on the street, I heard horses run by me. It was more like a stampede, with hundreds of horses."

Sheriff Riley whistled. "Close call. You might've been killed. I never heard of so many wild horses being down in this area. Are you sure you didn't have a little too much to drink, Dae? I heard you only made it to one post-election party because you were ill. Was it something else?"

"I know you don't like it when I tell you these things,

but there were no *real* horses. I could smell them and hear them. But there was nothing there."

"That doesn't explain the hoof prints all over the road and on top of our victim." Gramps passed my phone around with the pictures I'd taken. "You were right to call it a weird night, Chief."

Chief Michaels looked at the photos. "Every call we went out on was the same. Tim, Scott, and I went out to dozens of houses tonight. Lots of hoof prints, but no one actually saw any horses. Everyone *heard* them, though, and they did plenty of damage. Fences were trampled, lawn furniture destroyed, even a broken window."

Sheriff Riley laughed. "Are we talking ghost horses now? Because if so, I'm going home. I've never seen or heard a horse that wasn't really there. And I don't want to."

"But what if Mr. Watts was killed by these horses?" Chief Palo handed the phone back to me after examining the pictures. "It seems too coincidental to overlook that he was killed during this stampede."

"Maybe someone is training killer horses." Sheriff Riley hooted. "That's even funnier than ghost horses."

"Well then you'll love this," I added. "The horses came *after* I found the body. Tom was already dead when the horses, or whatever it was, ran by me."

"Now that makes sense," Sheriff Riley said. "Someone hit this man with a car and let loose a few wild horses to cover it up. Sound like anyone we know? Maybe someone with a grudge against Tom?"

Chief Michaels nodded. "We all know Jake Burleson fits the bill, Tuck. He was here in Duck tonight skulking around the Blue Whale during the post-election party. I saw him myself."

"There have been some confrontations between them," Chief Palo confirmed. "I've had officers out at the ranch almost every day. Mr. Burleson wants to keep his land for the wild horses. Tom agrees with the state that it should be taken for the excavation. It's been ugly out there."

"I don't think you understand what I'm saying." I looked at their mostly closed faces. "There were no *real* horses on the road."

"Thanks, Dae," Chief Michaels said. "Why don't you write down exactly what happened, and what you did? We're gonna go down and have a look at the crime scene. Keep the coffee coming."

I didn't attempt to convince them after that. This wasn't the first time they'd wanted to overlook my gift and things I'd seen. I hoped this would be different and I wouldn't have to prove it to them. I also hoped—despite my hard feelings toward him—that Jake wasn't responsible for what had happened to Tom. They had been such good friends for so many years.

Chief Palo hadn't gone out with the men. "Thank you for sharing your experience, Dae. And congratulations on your re-election. I was wondering if you wouldn't mind actually walking me through what you saw tonight. I've found in the past that people remember better if they're where it happened."

"Sure. Let me get my coat, Heidi. You might find that things are a little different here. Sometimes, I can see things when I touch people or their belongings. That might sound strange, but I've been doing it my whole life. And I've been helping the police since I was a teenager."

She had a beautiful smile that altered the sternness of her face. "I moved from Minnesota to take this position. We have psychics there too. I've never worked with one, but that doesn't mean I don't believe it's possible."

"A word of advice." I zipped my coat. "The towns around here are very small and people love to gossip. If you're going to try to keep your relationship with Tuck Riley a secret, you'll have to try harder."

"Oh no!" She frowned. "What did I say that gave it away?"

"It wasn't just you," I told her as I pushed open the front door. "Tuck wasn't on his best game either. I've never seen his hair a mess. I don't think I've ever seen him blush either."

"He's not going to like it."

"I won't tell anyone, but these things have a way of getting out. The two of you should come clean and face the inquisition. It will be over quickly, I promise."

"Thank you, Dae. I'll talk to Tuck and see what he thinks."

I didn't tell her that Tuck Riley could be a stubborn mule when he chose. She'd find that out by herself. We walked down to the road where the EMS was waiting to collect Tom. They couldn't move him until the medical examiner said it was okay. That could take a while since he was coming from Manteo.

Heidi and I walked the street together with me explaining exactly what I'd done and seen. The snow was already melting. I bent down to have a look where I'd photographed one of the hoof prints.

"Dae." She pointed to a spot on the road that she'd cleaned with a gloved hand. "This hoof print looks burned into the pavement. How is that possible?"

Chapter Seven

I called Gramps over to have a look at what we found. Each place we wiped free of snow where a hoof print had been, there was now a print etched in the road.

"That's crazy," he said. "What could've caused such a thing?"

I knew what it was, but I didn't say—not in front of Heidi. I told him later when everyone was gone and the medical examiner had finally arrived to take Tom's body.

"It was the demon horses," I told him as he was getting ready to go to the Duck police station. "That's why I couldn't see them."

"Dae, maybe you shouldn't take that vision so literally. It could just be the way the horses hooves hit the blacktop. I don't know. One thing I do know—the ME said horses didn't kill Tom. He said the object that hit him in the head caused his death and that object didn't have the weight and power that would come from a horse. It wasn't a horse's hoof, although he seems to think the wound is shaped like one."

"Exactly! The demon horses have no weight. Gramps, you know I'm right. No one ever wants to admit it, but how many times have my visions been right?"

"You have to let the process work. We have to understand what it isn't to know what it is sometimes. You know I've always supported your gift. Your grandmother's ghost would haunt me if I didn't, bless her soul. But you can't expect most rational people to understand what you can do. Let's just let the ME go through the evidence. We'll know soon enough what happened."

He kissed the top of my head and left. I assumed he'd said something to Mary Catherine before then. Missing Pieces was supposed to be open again today, but I waited for her to come downstairs before I left.

She was dressed in emerald green, Baylor draped around her neck and shoulders. Her hat was a matching wool cap that was very attractive.

"Good morning . . . again. How did everything turn out when the police showed up?"

"I wish it had been better. I told Gramps my theory of what happened after I found Tom. He didn't want to hear it."

"Not surprising. Your grandfather is a good man, but he doesn't have a psychic gift. Someone like that can understand and commiserate. He'll never really know—not like we do. I'm afraid your new fiancé will be the same way. That's why I go so long between husbands. It's not like I wouldn't like to find husband number six. I'm just not always sure it's worth the hassle."

I sighed, knowing she was probably right. "But I don't want to be alone my whole life either. At least Kevin and

Gramps have some idea what's going on."

She nodded and stroked Baylor.

"Come on. Let's go get some coffee and a bagel." I called Treasure and put him in my tote bag. "Then I have to go to Missing Pieces. I have a UPS delivery and a pickup. I need to be there for a while anyway. My sales are always off in November. It's hard to make summer money last the rest of the year."

"Sounds exciting!"

The snow was completely gone by the time we went outside. The frosty branches and white rooftops were just a memory. But the hoof prints etched into the road were still there. I showed them to Mary Catherine and took a few pictures.

"I never knew horses' hooves could do that," she said.

"You're right. They appear to be burned right into the pavement. How odd. I'll listen for any horse chatter around the island. I'm sure the horses are frightened and confused too. This is probably what they've been worried about."

Walking down Duck Road with Mary Catherine was a strange experience. Two sea gulls flew down and walked with us for a while, squawking the whole time. She talked to them like she was talking to two old friends. They answered back, and she frowned.

As we reached the edge of the Duck Shoppes' parking lot, a rat came right up to her and rested its head on her shoe. She smiled and even scratched its ear. The rat ran away into the tangled brush.

"What was that about?" I asked.

"Oh, the rat was nothing. He just wanted to say hello. But the seagulls were interesting. They've already heard the story of the invisible horses. They aren't frightened by them—they're creatures of the air and not subject to the same fears as we who live on the earth. But they were very interested and shared your view about the supernatural aspect of what happened to your friend."

"Wow. That's amazing. Do they always just run up and

talk to you?"

"Oh no. Many times I have to go looking for animals I need to talk to. They aren't always as forthcoming as seagulls."

We walked into the crowded coffeehouse and bookstore in the Duck Shoppes' parking lot. The people waiting in line and seated at tables were as chatty as the seagulls, but more afraid.

"I want to know what someone is going to do about those horses knocking down my fence," Martha Segall said in a loud voice. "And here's the mayor. What are you going to do about this, Dae?"

It would have to be Martha's fence.

Everyone turned to stare. I plastered my big mayor's smile on my face and addressed the situation. "Chief Michaels and Sheriff Riley are looking into the events of last night. Try not to worry. I'm sure there's a rational explanation for everything."

"What about the dead man they said was found on Duck Road?" Barney Thompson asked. He owned the Sand Dollar jewelry store.

"The police are looking into that too," I promised. "I'll have the town clerk send out emails to everyone on her list when we have any updates."

"What if we don't have a computer?" Agnes Caudle ran the Beach Bakery. "I don't have a computer."

"In that case, someone from public works will call you." Chris Slayton was standing behind me. "Jamie has a sign-up sheet at the counter. If you aren't on the email list, leave your name and phone number."

There was a lot of grumbling and complaining. People were nervous and afraid after the unsettling night. I knew exactly how they felt and could only imagine what the council meeting would be like tomorrow. I hoped things would quickly settle down.

Mary Catherine and I finally reached the counter. I ordered two coffees and two bagels with cream cheese. We took them to the shop so I could open for the day. It was better to leave before there were any other complaints too. People weren't as likely to come into Missing Pieces to ask questions.

Maybe that was cruel, but I was short on answers that anyone would want to hear besides being scared that my vision could be true and demon horses were visiting Duck.

There weren't many people in the parking lot or on the boardwalk. It was early, though. People might come later in the day. Hurricane season was over, but many shops were closing down for the winter. Everyone knew about the seasonal issue and stayed away.

Chris had a brilliant plan for bringing people to Duck and other parts of the Outer Banks for the holiday season. The Tourism Association had not only picked up on the idea but also made Chris head of the event. It was called OBX Christmas. Every town was supposed to light up and dress up for the holiday between Thanksgiving and the first of the year. We'd never done it before, always seeing November as the end of the season.

Chris already had the backing of the Duck Business Association and the Chamber of Commerce. Most of the shop owners were members of one of the organizations so they already knew the plans. We'd been asked to come up with discounted merchandise for the promotion too.

I got the door open to the shop just in time for the UPS man to arrive. My usual driver was on vacation, but Josephine was helpful and picked up my packages in no time. She was immediately followed by my first customers of the day. Jessie Morton, and her husband Chase Manhattan, were visiting from Myrtle Beach.

"What did you have in mind?" I asked the attractive couple.

"I'm always looking for antique craft items for Renaissance Faire Village," she told me. "Chase is just along for the ride."

"Unless you have any swords or interesting horses," he

called back from the side of the shop where he was already perusing my merchandise. He was a large man with big shoulders and a long brown hair tied back on his neck.

Jessie was average in appearance except for her height. She was tall, like Heidi Palo.

Mary Catherine and I exchanged curious glances when Chase mentioned horses. She continued to eat her bagel and drink her coffee.

"What kind of interesting horses?" I wondered if he was really a reporter and had already heard about what had happened last night.

"He collects horse figures," Jessie explained. "He's a knight at the Ren Faire and trains jousters and knights. He's also a member of the Templar Knights. He isn't too fussy about his horses. You have the wild horses here, right?"

"What about this sword?" Chase took one of the more valuable pieces off the rack. "What's its history?"

"You've got a good eye," I complimented, glad that we'd gotten away from the subject of horses. I was also happy that he didn't immediately ask how much. That was one of my rules for selling some of my more valuable possessions. "That sword belonged to the first mayor of Charleston, South Carolina. They said he was originally a pirate that couldn't be defeated by the English so they bought him off with a land grant and position."

He examined the sword closely. "I like the hilt, but it doesn't look English. French, maybe."

"You're right about that." My little heart thrilled when an educated collector came to Missing Pieces. "The sword was given to him by his French wife. She'd sailed with him when he was a pirate. They settled down, married, and had ten children. I came upon this sword at an estate sale in Charleston. The last member of their family had died. All their possessions had been kept so well. This sword was the best of the lot."

Chase smiled at Jessie.

She rolled her eyes. "Really? You have a lot of swords."

"And you have a lot of other things. Besides we have more room now. There can be more swords *and* horses."

"Whatever." She turned her back to examine an old spinning wheel.

"I'll take it." Chase put the sword and his VISA card on the glass counter.

"I'm very happy it's going to live with someone like you who'll appreciate it." I wrapped the sword in protective paper and processed the transaction.

I tried to help Jessie find something too, but she couldn't settle on anything. Happily, the purchase of the sword was enough to keep Missing Pieces open for a few months. I didn't sell many items this valuable, but when I did it was a big help, stretching my money to make ends meet.

"Was all that true about the sword?" Mary Catherine asked after Jessie and Chase were gone. "Did you hold it?"

"I knew almost everything about it before I held it. There was a bloody history with it from the mayor's pirate past, but I saw it as a love story too. Those two people were very happy together. I hope it brings the same luck to Jessie and Chase. Imagine living at a Renaissance Festival."

"I've been there, but only for a short time," Mary Catherine said. "I had a wonderful weekend with a man who was king of the village. I think his name was Harold. It was a while back."

It didn't take long for the concerned citizens of Duck to realize that I was at Missing Pieces. People stopped in to gossip and express their concerns about a man being killed in the middle of town. There were hundreds of rumors floating through Duck about what had happened the night before.

I was sad that most of them hadn't known Tom since he had lived in Corolla. They knew his work though, and were sorry that he'd been killed. Many wondered, as I had, who would take his place as director of the Wild Horse Conservancy.

The natural answer seemed to be that Jake would be the one to do it. I hoped that would be the case, and that Chief

Michaels and Sheriff Riley didn't seriously consider him a suspect in Tom's death. But just because I wanted it to happen didn't make it so.

August Grandin from the Duck General Store came by before he opened to see if I had any other information about the event. "I'm really concerned that Tom Watts is dead. It seems to me that it has to be hit and run, probably by someone from Duck who left him there. I hope Chief Michaels is checking cars to find the culprit."

I assured him that everything was being done that could be done. I hoped I was right about that. It wasn't that I didn't have complete faith in our police department. It was more that the odd nature of the death made me wonder if anyone could actually figure it out without some psychic help.

Business was slow. More people came in more to discuss Tom's death than to shop. At lunch, I treated Mary Catherine out at Wild Stallions. Most of the time, I just ate a sandwich at Missing Pieces. But things were slow, I had a guest, and I'd made a large sale. I decided we should go out. I left a sign on the shop door pointing anyone looking for me in the direction of the restaurant.

"What a wonderful place to work," Mary Catherine said as we stepped out on the sunny boardwalk. "I remember thinking that when I bought this shop." She smiled as we passed Mrs. Roberts Spiritual Advisor.

"Were you actually advising people with tea leaves and tarot back then?"

"When you're in my line of work, you do what you have to do survive. I'm a little more solid now—more than anything thanks to a generous bequest from my third late husband. I'm not so worried about the future anymore."

Shayla hailed us as we passed what had become her shop that she rented from Mary Catherine. "I need to talk to you, Dae. Where are you off to?"

"Lunch," I told her. "Why don't you join us?"

"I don't want to take up your time." She glanced significantly at Mary Catherine.

"Don't be silly." Mary Catherine smiled. "I'd love to get to know you."

Shayla seemed fine after that. She accompanied us to Wild Stallions, wearing her usual chic black pants and sweater. It didn't matter what she wore, she always had style and panache. Her black hair was drawn away from her face in braids that she'd looped around her head. She had brown eyes and finely drawn brows in her cocoa-colored face.

Mary Catherine and Shayla were chatting about the business of being psychic as I told Cody Baucum that there would be three of us for lunch.

"Make that four," Kevin said from behind me.

"Good party last night." Cody shook his hand as he grabbed four menus. "I couldn't believe someone died after it. Any update on that yet, Dae?"

"I haven't heard anything since early this morning," I told him. "You know these things take time."

"I know." Cody led us to a table that overlooked the Currituck Sound. "You know, I'm thinking about throwing my hat in the ring for one of those two council seats. You all are deciding on that tomorrow night, right?"

"Yes. We'll be filling the seats, at least temporarily," I told him. "There won't be an election for two years. Whoever we choose to fill those seats will be there until then."

Cody summoned a waitress. "I think I'd be good as a council member, don't you? We need business owners represented on the council. I also think we need some *younger* blood." He said it like it was a dirty word, sneaking glances behind him to see if anyone was listening.

I didn't want to get involved in talking about the council's decision. I thought Cody would be fine, but it wasn't only my vote. I knew there were other people interested in the seats too.

"We'll have to see what happens," I told him with a smile. "You might be the only one interested in a seat. When I ran for mayor the first time, no one ran against me."

"And they probably won't ever run against you again,

right Kevin?" Cody slapped Kevin on the back. "I mean, you slaughtered Mad Dog in the vote."

I thanked Cody for his kind words and he left to welcome other diners waiting at the door. The waitress, Cole Black's daughter, Amy, took our drink orders and left to get them. She was in her second year of college and was having a disagreement with her parents. She was refusing to work at The Curbside until it was over.

"Is that the way your day has been going?" Kevin asked me.

"No. I almost forgot about the council meeting tomorrow night after finding Tom Watts dead on Duck Road and having ghost horses run through me."

"I thought it must be something like that since I've heard about Tom from ten other people, and nothing from you."

"Sorry. There was a lot going on. Are they calling them ghost horses?"

"Yes. That's all anyone wants to talk about. I think the horses ran through everyone's yards last night. They were at the Blue Whale too. I found hoof prints everywhere, but no damage done."

"It was quite a night," Mary Catherine declared. "I felt the horses. They had no substance. I couldn't communicate with them."

"I heard you could do that," Shayla said. "I've listened to one or two of your radio shows. Nice shtick."

"I've heard animal voices since I was a child," Mary Catherine said. "I wouldn't have chosen it as a gift."

"So what did you actually see when you found Tom?" Kevin changed the subject.

Amy came back with our drinks and took our food orders. I explained everything to Kevin from finding Tom to the hoof prints embedded in Duck Road. I passed around my cell phone with the pictures.

"Wow!" Shayla's dark eyes were huge. "What is the world could cause something like that? Normal horses don't leave marks in pavement. How could ghost horses leave marks?"

"They aren't technically ghosts," I explained. "They're more like demon horses that were summoned by the early tribal people.

"You are getting weirder and weirder," Shayla said. "No wonder your aura is so far off this morning. Your chakras are probably all messed up again."

Tim and Trudy stopped by our table. The only aspect of his appearance that gave away his all-nighter was his pale blond hair. It was usually combed up into a tall flat top. Today it was just flat.

"Afternoon," he said with a nod, his hands resting on his duty belt.

"Why don't you two join us?" Kevin suggested. "We have plenty of room."

We made space for them at the table. Trudy tucked her arm through Tim's, still nervous about their relationship, especially around Shayla. She saw Shayla as a rival, though Shayla had never even liked Tim.

"Anything new on the investigation?" I asked Tim when they were seated.

He nodded. "Chief Palo from Corolla called to tell us that Tom's truck is still at his trailer. Chief Michaels thinks someone just dropped him off on Duck Road after he was killed. It doesn't look good for your friend, Jake Burleson, Dae. He's everyone's favorite suspect right now—if we can ever find him."

Chapter Eight

Kevin frowned at me. "You didn't tell me that part."

"Sorry. I just didn't get to that part yet." I turned back to Tim. "What do you mean? Why can't you find Jake?"

"I don't know. Chief Palo has been out there. He wasn't home. We have an APB out on his truck and him," Tim said. "It won't be long."

"Jake doesn't get around much," I added. "I can't believe that he killed Tom. He just isn't that kind of man."

"Really?" Kevin stared at me. "You still feel that way—even after last night?"

"What about last night?" Trudy asked.

She was hoping she could turn the conversation away from boring police matters, but she also didn't like talking about supernatural things.

"Jake gave Dae one of his stupid horse statues to hold, even though she told him she didn't want to know anything about it. She passed out on the ground." Kevin sipped his water and didn't seem to care that he'd started a ball rolling that couldn't be stopped.

"Is that what happened?" Trudy's gaze was disbelieving. She'd known about my gift as long as I had. "I knew everyone said you were sick when you missed the other election parties. I didn't know that's what they meant."

"He just didn't understand." I contradicted Kevin. "I told him no, but I haven't completely explained to him why I have to be careful."

Tim's eyes narrowed. "You shouldn't have to explain. When a woman says no, it's no. Sounds like we have something else we should discuss with Jake when we find him."

"I don't think handing me an ancient horse against my will is a crime exactly." I didn't like where this was going, and I wasn't happy with my new fiancé sending it there.

"I understand what he's saying." Trudy, not surprisingly, took Tim's side. "It's kind of like mind rape."

"I'm not sure I'd go quite that far," Mary Catherine said.

"No. I think Tim is right for once," Shayla agreed. "Dae said no. Jake should've respected that. I might be able to whip up a little spell to help find him."

"I'm sure the police will be able to find him," Tim said. "We do a good job around here. We have the sheriff helping too. We don't need any hocus-pocus."

"Just offering." Shayla shrugged.

Amy brought our food out with Cody's help. I was glad to see it. Everyone needed something else to occupy their minds.

The food brought a fresh change of subject to the Christmas festivities that were coming up. Everyone was excited about the concept. It was one of Chris's better ideas, and that was saying a lot since he came up with great ones every day.

"August Grandin is putting up Christmas ducks." Trudy laughed. "They are the sweetest things. They have little red bows around their necks. He's going to float them on the sound the last day of the event. Isn't that a cute idea?"

We all agreed that it was.

"What are you going to do, Dae?" Shayla asked.

"I don't know yet. There's been so much going on, I haven't had a chance to think about it. But I've got some old decorations in the closet. I'll probably put those up."

"The Duck Shoppes leasing company is putting up a big, lighted tree on the boardwalk." Trudy clapped her hands. "I've got dozens of snowflake lights to put up, and I'm holding a contest each day to win a free service. You know—like manicures, waxing—that kind of thing."

"Maybe I should offer free palm reading," Shayla said. "I've got some red and green skull lights to put up."

"Skulls?" Trudy couldn't believe it. "Oh, wait. Is that like from *Nightmare Before Christmas*?"

Shayla had no idea what Trudy was talking about. Cody joined us for a moment. He and his brother had plans for their Christmas events and decorations too. He was also hosting a children's parade around the boardwalk leading to a visit from Santa at town hall.

They were all wonderful ideas. I didn't quite feel in the Christmas spirit yet but I hoped it would come to me soon. When the lights and decorations started going up and late fall visitors started stopping by, I'd feel much better. I was just in a funk of sorts. I never stayed down for long.

My phone rang. It was Nancy at town hall. She needed me to come down right away. She didn't elaborate, but I knew she wouldn't call unless it was important. I told her I'd be right there.

"Do you want me to go with you?" Kevin asked when I said I had to go.

"I'll be fine. I'm not even leaving the boardwalk. You stay and finish lunch. I'll be right back."

Everyone else continued eating and talking. Kevin grabbed my hand as I turned to go. "I'm sorry if you're upset about what I said."

"It's the truth, I suppose. But now it's going to be everywhere." I squeezed his hand. "Don't worry about it. The story will pass in a few days."

I walked out of Wild Stallions. The Currituck Sound was beautifully blue with white puffy clouds above it. The clouds urged me to sit and daydream for a while. While I wanted nothing more at that moment, I had to go to town hall.

There was a spot where the boardwalk turns to the left from Missing Pieces. Duck town hall was tucked into a shadowed corner there where rain didn't fall and the sun had a hard time reaching into the shade. The boardwalk stayed damp all year and moss grew at the sides where the wood slats met the buildings.

As I walked into the area, I was aware of someone being there, watching me. I looked across and saw the man who'd been in my vision of the horse cult in the past. He was short, a little hunched, and dressed in animal skins. His hair was long and ragged, as though it was normally cut with a knife. He had a full beard and no shoes.

My heart skipped a beat. How he could be there? The other men in the vision were from a far distant past that no one alive could remember today. And yet there he stood, glaring at me from the dark corner.

"Who are you?" I asked in a trembling voice. I cleared my throat and blinked a few times. "Why are you here?"

I'd spoken to assure myself that this wasn't real. This man was still from my vision of the past. He wasn't really standing here on the boardwalk with me. That wasn't possible.

His words in reply were gibberish to me. It wasn't any language that I'd ever heard. He pointed and waved the big bone he held. I still couldn't understand him.

He lunged at me with the bone, and I took a step back. Far from proving that he wasn't real, I'd proven that a nightmare could follow me back from the places that I went. The idea was terrifying.

"I can't understand you. I'm sorry. I don't know what you're saying." I held my hand cupped by my ear hoping he'd understand."

His hand lifted to point at the parts of Duck that we could see through the open entrance to the boardwalk. His words were unintelligible, but his meaning seemed clear to me when he pounded the bone.

I shivered. "Something else bad is going to happen, isn't it? Something worse than Tom's death."

His dark gaze roamed the sunny water on the other side of the boardwalk behind me. He searched for some way to communicate with me as he ran back and forth to the rail and pounded the bone on the wood.

"I don't know what you mean." I thought about the horses I'd heard but couldn't see. "Are you talking about the demon horses?"

The door to town hall opened behind me. "There you are, Dae," Chris Slayton said. "Thank goodness."

I glanced back, and the other man was gone. I walked to the edge of the damp wood. The shadows were empty. "Did you see him?" I asked Chris.

"See who?" His head shifted back and forth outside the doorway. "Were you talking to someone? I'm sorry. I thought you were just pumping up before you came inside. I didn't see anyone out here with you."

"That's okay." I put my hand on the door as he started to shut it again. "Whoever he was, I guess he left."

Chris stared at me for a long moment. "Are you okay, Dae?"

I couldn't quite summon my bright mayor's smile, but I did the best I could. "I'm okay. What's going on?"

Dozens of Duck residents had come to town hall and were refusing to leave until someone explained to them why there were wild horses running up and down Duck Road in the middle of the night.

"I started having them come back here in the meeting room until Chris showed up," Nancy whispered an explanation. "More came in with Chris. They wanted to talk to Chief Michaels, but the chief is out with the sheriff looking for Jake Burleson. I'm hoping maybe between you and Chris you can handle the situation before I have to shut down the office."

Nancy was out of sorts, unusual for her. Usually she handled every crisis calmly. She was still wearing her pink bunny slippers that she always wore at work but her hair was frazzled and her mouth had become a thin line.

"We can handle it from here, Nancy," Chris said. "The people like the mayor. They trust her more than anyone. I'm sure they'll believe what she tells them."

I stared at him. "And what's that going to be? I can't explain what happened last night. The horses ran right past me—maybe even through me—I'm not sure. They left hoof prints burned into the street. How do I explain that?"

Chris pushed me into the meeting room with a gentle but firm hand. "I don't know. But I'll be there with you. There are a lot of frightened people, Dae. They need someone to tell them it's going to be all right, even if that someone isn't really sure it will be."

About fifty people, the maximum amount of chairs we normally have in the meeting room, were full of scared, questioning Duck citizens. They were noisy, shouting back and forth at each other, until they saw me and Chris. Then silence hit them, and they stared at us with watchful eyes.

I forced another smile and avoided the podium at the front of the room. We pushed our chairs together to form a semi-circle. Chris grabbed a chair and sat close by.

"Hello, everyone. I know you all want a chance to speak. Let's take it one at a time, no shouting, and we'll try to work through everyone's problems." I tried to appear confident and helpful even though I was as nervous and worried as they were.

One man stuck up his hand. I nodded and acknowledged Andy Martin from the Ice Cream and Slushy shop.

"Mayor, I don't know what's going on, but those horses crushed a bunch of my wife's azaleas and broke some pots. Why are they coming up this far?"

Everyone around Andy nodded. They wanted to ask the same question.

"I can't really explain why this happened, Andy. Sheriff Riley and Chief Michaels are looking into it."

"Did the horses kill that man from Corolla I heard about?" Mark Sampson from the Rib Shack asked.

"I don't think so. The last I heard, Chief Michaels thought Tom was a victim of hit and run." It was close to the truth.

There was a great deal of whispering and shock that anyone in our small community could be responsible for something so terrible.

"But if it was horses," Mark continued. "They'd need to be put down or something, right? They must be rabid if they're going around attacking people."

"Horses didn't attack Mr. Watts," Chris said. "He was killed, but not by horses."

"That doesn't answer the question of why those wild horses were up here in Duck," Agnes Caudle charged. "They never come up this far. I guess there should've been a horse round-up this summer to get some of them off the island. They're probably looking for food."

"Looking for food is one thing," Carter Hatley said. "Did you get see the streets and the ground around your houses? I understand that the ground is wet from the snow, but I have hoof prints burned into the concrete on my driveway. I saw some hoof prints burned into the streets on the way here this morning. What kind of horse is responsible for that?"

"It's coming from Corolla," Vergie Smith, our Duck postmistress, said. "We all know it's from all that digging and those crazy statues down there. I heard the police say

Jake Burleson killed Tom. I'm telling you, it's all coming from that historic excavation on Jake's property. Somebody needs to shut that thing down before we all go to hell in a hand-basket."

I could see heads nodding and people agreeing that Vergie was right. Residents of the Outer Banks who'd grown up here tended to be a superstitious lot. They still believed that the ghost of Rafe Masterson came back once in a while to stir up trouble. He was a pirate that had pillaged and plundered along the coast of the Carolinas hundreds of years before.

"I don't think the excavation is causing these problems." Chris' answer was rational.

"Something is going on that we don't understand," I told them. "But we're going to figure it out. Now I want each of you to take a piece of paper from that table over there and write down what happened to you last night. I know some of you called the police, and that's fine. But let's see if we can discover some kind of pattern that could help explain this."

People went to get pieces of paper or took them out of their pockets and bags. It was action toward solving their fears. In my experience, that was what everyone wanted, to feel that there was something they could *do*.

"How is this going to help?" Chris whispered.

"I don't know yet. Let's see."

As the residents scribbled on their pieces of paper, the door to the meeting room burst open and Jake came into the room.

"I'm here to set the record straight," he said. "Evil has come to our home. The end of the world is at hand."

Chapter Nine

"There's an evil coming out of the ground in Corolla at my rescue ranch. We have to stop it!"

Chris and I shared horrified glances at Jake's words.

"I'm sure Jake doesn't mean evil like we're thinking about something from the movies," Chris joked. "Right, Jake?"

Jake looked as wild as the horses he tended, maybe more so. His gait was unsteady, and his hands shook. There was a crazy, restless gleam in his eyes that I'd never seen before. He was like a man possessed or stone cold drunk.

"No, Chris. I'm talking about pure evil like we normally

see in the movies or hear about in church. I can't explain why those stone horses are evil, but I know they are. The excavation is driving our native horses crazy. They don't want us digging around out there. I think what we're seeing here in Duck is what we've been seeing in Corolla since the excavation began. The horses are running wild. They're trying to tell us to stay away from that site. Tell them, Dae. You saw it."

Jake's words weren't helping the situation. Everyone knew him and understood that he had knowledge about the horses that the rest of us didn't. If he said the excavation was evil and causing the wild horses to attack Duck, everyone would believe him. We had to find some way to stem his rhetoric.

"Why don't you come with me so we can record this?" Chris suggested in a friendly voice. "I've got the recording equipment in my office."

"All right." Jake pushed his lank hair back from his face. "If you think we should record this, I'm game."

Chris nodded to me as he led Jake out of the meeting room. "Call the police," he whispered.

Nancy was standing at the door. She heard him and nodded.

I was glad that she was willing to call Chief Michaels. I wasn't sure if I could. Whatever he'd done, Jake was my friend. I wanted him to have a chance to explain himself.

"I'm sorry about that," I said to my friends and neighbors. "Whatever is going on in Corolla is affecting Jake too. I hope he didn't scare you."

"You mean the horses aren't evil?" Carter asked.

"Of course they're not evil," Vergie answered. "It's something else."

I was glad she spoke up and added, "I know all of us have been out with the horses on the beach and seen the colts after they've been born. How could those horses be evil? That doesn't make any sense."

"Not those horses, Dae," Carter said. "It's the horses

they're digging up that are evil. We have to stop that excavation. I'm going to the state capital in Raleigh with a petition to make them stop. Who's with me?"

All of the shop managers and owners who'd signed up for the Christmas in OBX event backed away from that proposal. They were too busy to make the trip to Raleigh and talk with legislators. But a group of ten people, mostly retired folks, agreed to help get a petition together and go with Carter to Raleigh.

"Aren't the legislators out for the holidays?" Anne Maxwell asked.

"Yes." Carter rolled his eyes. "I guess we'll have to get the petition together and take it up there after the holidays. We can probably get a larger group to go with us once the shops are closed for the winter too."

Mark Sampson shook my hand. "Thanks, Dae. I'm glad you're going to be mayor again."

"Yeah, me too," Vergie said. "I don't like to think what's gonna happen to this town once Dae is gone."

"I'm not planning to go anywhere," I told them. "And I'll be glad to sign that petition when you're ready. I don't know if the excavation is evil or not, but it seems to be affecting people badly."

"Never a good idea to dig up the past." Andy shuddered. "Let that stuff stay buried."

"I don't agree with that," Mark argued as they walked out the door together. He was a member of the museum board and obviously wouldn't want history to be left buried in the sand—unless it was evil.

Within a few minutes, the meeting room was empty again. I sat in a chair with a sigh of relief. At least that problem was solved for the moment. If the horses continued to cause damage, people would be back again. Maybe it was cowardly, but I hoped Chief Michaels would be here next time.

I said goodbye to Nancy. She'd called the police to report that Jake had been there. "But Chris said he left before

I called," she said. "That poor man needs help, Dae."

"I know." I hurried back to Wild Stallions—after a last long look at the shadowed area where the man from my vision had accosted me. No one was there. I wasn't sure if he was real or I'd imagined him. Maybe I was still affected by the vision. How could I be sure?

Mary Catherine and Kevin were on the boardwalk watching the antics of a gull as it spun and dived toward Mary Catherine. Several silver fish also jumped out of the water as I approached.

"Can you believe it?" Kevin laughed. "A crow started pecking on the window by our table in the restaurant. All she had to do was tell him to go away, and he disappeared."

"Sometimes it's okay to chat," she said with a smile. "Sometimes they have to wait."

As she spoke, a crow flew down from the roof of the Duck Shoppes and landed on the edge of her handbag. It squawked and cried until she paid attention to it.

"What is it saying?" I asked as the crow fluttered its wings.

"He's complaining about the horses. He didn't like the noise and he says it's an omen." She stared at me. "He tells me you had a visitor with an omen too, Dae."

I didn't know what to say. Her gifts were incredible. I shouldn't have been surprised that the bird saw what had happened outside town hall. I was glad anyone else had seen him, even if it was only a crow. I told Mary Catherine and Kevin about the man who'd warned me about the horses.

"Maybe he was warning me about the horses anyway. I'm not sure. He was scary, just like the men I'd seen in the vision I got from the stone horse. He spoke some odd language I couldn't understand. He kept waving around a large bone. I don't want to know where it came from."

"Oh my dear." Mary Catherine took my arm. "That must've been very frightening for you."

"I don't know if it was any worse than the group of people waiting inside town hall. Everyone is upset about the horses. To make it worse, Jake was there too. He was half out of his mind and told everyone that the excavation in Corolla was evil and had to stop. Nancy called the police. What a mess."

"What's going on out there?" Kevin asked. "I wonder if the police have looked around the site on Jake's property."

"The new Corolla police chief, Heidi Palo, said she's over there all the time breaking up fights. Funny that Chief Michaels and Sheriff Riley are out looking for Jake and he was right here." I squinted at the far horizon. "I guess everyone is done eating."

Mary Catherine pulled out a box. "I had them put yours in a to-go box. I didn't want you to be hungry."

"Thank you." I took my little box of tomatoes, shrimp, and rice. "If nothing else, I'll eat it for dinner."

"What are you, and the rest of the town, going to do about this thing with the horses?" Kevin asked. "I'm sure this won't be the only visit to your office about it."

I figured it was the perfect opportunity to ask him about being on the town council. "You could help us make that decision." I dangled the opportunity before him.

"How? Are you going to do some kind of poll?"

"No. We need two people to be on the town council until LaDonna and Mad Dog's terms expire and we hold a new election. Interested?"

"I don't think so," he bluntly answered. "I've got a lot on my plate right now with the Blue Whale. I'll leave the politics to the politicians."

"Then you can't complain about what happens." I warned him using the same words Gramps had said to me about being mayor.

He put his arms around me. "I think one politician in the family is enough."

Mary Catherine giggled. "In the family, eh? Are you expecting the wedding to be anytime soon?"

My face got hot. I wasn't used to the idea of being engaged yet. It was still a lot to take in. "I-I don't know," I stammered.

"No rush," Kevin said. "We'll figure out a date later."

I was glad to hear him say it, and hurriedly changed the subject. "I hope the horses don't come back so we won't need to have another impromptu meeting about them. I expect to hear something from Chief Michaels later about how Tom actually died."

Kevin nodded. "The longer Jake is on the run, the worse it will be for him. I don't like him, but I thought he had more sense."

I knew he was right. I wished Jake would turn himself in and get it over with. He'd been acting so crazy at town hall. I was worried about what would happen if the police didn't find him soon. He could hurt himself or someone else.

Kevin had to go back to the Blue Whale to set up an author's tea. The author was from out of town, staying there overnight. Jamie from the bookstore was handling book sales. It was a good mutual effort that I loved to see happen between businesses in Duck. I fostered it wherever I could, though this time it had nothing to do with me.

Mary Catherine and I went back to Missing Pieces for the afternoon. Customers were in and out. They mostly looked around, ignored me, and left. Some days were like that.

"I remember being in this same position after I opened the shop next door—sitting and waiting for customers. I'm not a very patient person. Radio has been better for me. I still couldn't sit around waiting for a sale like you do, Dae."

I was standing behind my glass case that held some of the more valuable items I had for sale. Some of these things could only be given or sold to certain people. The bigger items were in the back closet. I didn't show those even though some of them were very valuable. I had no intention of selling them. There was no amount of money I would take for them.

My laptop pinged and I checked my email. Dillon Guthrie had sent me a message from the old site of

Jamestown in the Caribbean where he was still busy looking for antiquities. He planned to be there for a while and asked if I'd changed my mind about joining him.

While being there for the salvage operation would have been fascinating, I told him again that I couldn't leave Duck. My life and my commitments were here. He'd never understand my feelings because he moved from place-to-place on a whim. There was no romantic interest between us, at least not on my part. He just wanted someone to share his passion for ancient artifacts. I could do that, but it had to be from here.

I'd already told him that ATF agents were looking for him. He wouldn't come back until that was over. I didn't know why they wanted him, and I didn't want to know. Agents Brad Jablanski and Allen Moore stopped by regularly for a while after Dillon had left. As time had passed, I saw them less frequently.

It had been a bad situation for me. With being mayor and the daughter of the former Dare County sheriff—not to mention that my boyfriend was ex-FBI—anything that didn't smell right was impossible. I'd always kept my dealings legal. I didn't plan to change that regardless of some of the amazing merchandise that could be had.

One of my rules for finding things for people had always been that it had to belong to that person, and it had to be legal. I had bent that rule for some people that I knew very well, but I wouldn't change it for most.

I sent my email to Dillon. He wouldn't be surprised when I turned him down again. I didn't regret it. I loved my life.

"Oh my goodness!" Mary Catherine said from the burgundy brocade sofa. "What's going on?"

Hundreds of moths had somehow come inside and lighted on her. She was covered in the brown, white, and orange creatures. They made a fluttering blanket across her.

"Quiet, Baylor," she hushed her cat. "It's not funny, and you can't eat them."

Treasure meowed when he looked at her. Baylor hissed at him. Maybe if he couldn't eat the moths, neither could my cat.

"Are the moths trying to tell you something?" I watched in astonishment. "I hope they aren't here to eat my winter coats."

The shop door opened and a breeze blew in, displacing the moths for an instant, but they came right back to Mary Catherine.

"What in the world is going on?" Shayla came in, closing the door behind her. "Is she talking to the moths now? Did Kevin tell you about the crow incident at Wild Stallions? I think she really can talk to animals. Maybe moths too."

"They tickle a little." Mary Catherine laughed. "If they have something to say, I wish they'd say it. I feel bad moving and disrupting them, but I have an itch on my shoulder."

Shayla took in a big gulp of air, and her eyes widened. "Wait. I know this one. Moths sometimes are the harbingers of spirits. People used to believe that a spirit could catch a ride with a moth and visit their loved ones."

"I don't know anyone who's died recently," Mary Catherine said.

"Maybe it's something to do with the horses," I suggested. "You didn't know him, but Tom died right outside the house last night."

"Don't ask me." Shayla shrugged. "I'm just repeating a story I heard as a child. Maybe you just need an exterminator, Dae."

"Let me take a picture of you." I used my phone to snap a photo of the moths. "I don't know what to say. Are they talking to you?"

"I'm not sure. I'm listening, but I don't hear anything." Mary Catherine closed her eyes.

Shayla shook her head and looked away from Mary Catherine. "I wanted to do this Christmas thing with everyone, but I'm going to have to head home for a few weeks. There's some trouble with my crazy family. Could you keep an eye on the shop for me? I don't expect you to read tea leaves or anything. Just don't let any horses trample through it."

I noticed that Shayla was wearing a long, black dress and carrying a large leather shoulder bag. "You're leaving right now?"

"One of my clients has a private plane and offered to take me to New Orleans if I could be ready right away." She shrugged. "That's a lot of money to save on a ticket."

I hugged her. "Okay. Well, let me know how it goes. Be careful."

"You be careful, honey. You've got the crazy ghost horses running around Duck. Next time you hear them, get out of the way."

"I will. Have a good trip."

"Sure. And Merry Christmas." She smiled, and was gone.

I had an odd feeling that she wouldn't be back. I couldn't describe it, but it felt very real. I hoped I was wrong, and if not, that it was something wonderful that kept her in New Orleans. I'd miss her.

Mary Catherine opened her eyes. "I'm just not getting anything. The insect mind can be very difficult to understand. They have such a different perspective on life."

The door to the shop flew open again and the moths fluttered out of the shop.

This time it was Nancy. "Dae, you won't believe what just happened."

"Try me." Nothing she said would surprise me.

"Chris went up on the water tower to hang a Duck Christmas banner. I don't know exactly what happened, but he called to tell me that he's hanging from a rope and needs help."

Chapter Ten

The three of us walked out on the boardwalk and gazed toward the big blue water tower. There was Chris, hanging upside down, with a rope attached to one ankle. The Duck Christmas banner was draped around him.

"I called the fire department," Nancy said. "I hope they have a ladder that goes up that high."

It struck me that the best thing to do would be to pull him up to the steel ladder that went around the water tower. "Let's get over there in case they need our help."

The water tower was close by and we were prepared to walk, but Mad Dog Wilson was in the parking lot with his deluxe golf cart that seated six people. He was on his way to the scene, so we hitched a ride with him.

I hoped the bad blood between us that had happened during the election was over. I wanted it to be in the past, and I hoped he did too. He'd been friends with Gramps since I was a child. He was also one of the founders of Duck's incorporation.

"Whose bright idea was it to have the town manager hang a sign on the water tower by himself?" Mad Dog glared at me as if he already knew the answer.

"Not mine," I told him. "We never hang a banner up there. He didn't even tell me about it."

"He wanted to surprise everyone for the Christmas event," Nancy said. "He didn't even pull the public works guys to help him."

Mad Dog huffed at me, all six-foot-four, three hundred pounds of him, grimacing in disapproval. "That's even worse. People who work for Duck shouldn't be making those kinds of decisions. That should be up to the mayor and the town council."

He was probably planning to get his old seat on the council back. I hoped the council would agree that Mad Dog shouldn't make decisions for the town anymore. We needed fresh blood, as Cody Baucum had said.

I didn't bother commenting on his words. He didn't say anything else to me either, and pushed the limit on how fast the golf cart would go. We arrived at the water tower a few minutes later.

Cailey Fargo, the fire chief, was already on hand. Her volunteers were in turnout gear around her. I waved to Gramps, Kevin, and Luke Helms who were in their boots and helmets.

I didn't see Tim or Scott, our police officers, or Chief Michaels. The public works guys—Roy, Shelton, and Harry—were up at the top of the water tower, waving down to everyone as though they were trying to get our attention. Chris was still dangling by one leg. I hoped he was all right. I couldn't tell from the ground if he was conscious.

"Is he okay?" Jamie finally got there from the bookstore. She shaded her eyes to look up at her husband. "What was he doing up there?"

"He didn't tell you either?" I asked her.

"No. I would've remembered if he was planning to jump off the water tower."

"He was trying to hang the banner." Nancy pointed to the swath of white material that was covering most of him. "It was something special. He even paid to have it made."

Jamie shook her head. "Well it's *very* special. Has anyone talked to him?"

"He called me," Nancy said. "He couldn't find the fire department's number on his cell phone."

By this time Cailey, Luke, and Kevin were climbing up the narrow blue ladder that led to the top of the water tower. Everyone else was on the ground, watching to see what happened. More people crowded in at the base of the tower, some with binoculars and cameras. The event was causing a big disturbance right in the heart of Duck.

I was watching Chris when I saw the man in the animal skins who'd tried to speak me at town hall. He was standing on the ground, near one of the metal legs that supported the tower. He was staring right at me. I wondered if he had anything to do with what had happened to Chris.

"Someone has to direct this traffic." Gramps put on his reflective, orange vest. "I guess that's gonna be me."

He stomped off toward the street, muttering about Chief Michaels not leaving one of the Duck officers for emergencies while he was chasing Jake. I had a sudden premonition about what would happen next, but I wasn't fast enough to stop it.

An older Cadillac came steaming down Duck Road. I saw it coming and yelled out a warning to Gramps, but he was so busy directing traffic coming from the opposite direction and he didn't hear me.

The driver of the Cadillac never stopped or swerved. He

hit one of the onlooker's cars that were parked on the narrow road. The car spun sideways and hit Gramps. The Cadillac finally stopped after hitting another car and a golf cart.

"Oh my God!" Nancy yelled.

Chris's precarious position on the water tower was forgotten as everyone ran into the street to see what they could do to help.

I reached Gramps first. He was conscious, but his leg was broken. I called an ambulance that would take a while to reach us. I had to get him out of the street.

"Cody? Can you help me move Gramps?" I asked him.

He yelled for his brother. "Reece? Come help us."

Reece had been mesmerized by the drama on the water tower. He ran across the street and helped us move Gramps to his golf cart. "Let's elevate that leg," he said. "It doesn't look too bad."

"Thanks." Gramps's voice was shaky. "What's next?"

"Don't ask." I glanced back, but man in animal skins was gone. "Are you okay?"

"I've had a broken leg before, Dae. Don't baby me. At least the bone isn't sticking out of my leg like last time."

I had to agree with that. "Stay put. Don't make things worse."

Mary Catherine and Barney Thompson from the Sand Dollar jewelry store were checking on the driver in the Cadillac.

"I think he had a heart attack," Barney said. "We need help."

I got Reece and Cody to help us move the man out of the car. We laid him on a blanket that had been in Gramps's golf cart.

"We have to get these cars off the road before it happens again," I decided. "Does anyone have the number for Dalton's Towing? It's in Southern Shores, but I think that's the closest service to us."

"I have it," Phil De Angelo from the coffeehouse said. "He just picked up a car for me last week. Want me to give him a call?"

"Sure. Thanks." It was good to delegate, I reminded myself. I'd learned that at my training seminar on being a mayor when I first took office. "In the meantime, we need someone on each side of this directing traffic away."

Cody and Reece volunteered. "Where should we send them, Dae?" Cody asked. "It's a two-lane road."

"Back where they came from," I said. "Better angry drivers than injured ones."

As we were trying to get everything in order on the ground, the team on top of the water tower was beginning to pull Chris up. It wasn't easy. Chris kept bumping up against the metal with every tug on the rope.

"Good thing he's got a hard head. I hope he's going to be okay." Jamie's hands were pressed tightly together. "He's always got to go that extra mile to impress everyone."

"He does a great job." I hugged her. "He'll be fine. Just try not to hit him with something when they get him down."

She laughed, but wiped a worried tear from her eye. I walked back to the golf cart. Mary Catherine was sitting with Gramps.

"Everything okay here for now?" I asked.

"If you call having a broken leg and feeling like an idiot okay, things are peachy," he grumbled.

"It could've been much worse," Mary Catherine reminded him. As she spoke, two small terns landed on the golf cart roof.

"They follow you everywhere, don't they?" I asked.

"Yes. I'm always easy to spot in a crowd. I'm the one with birds or fish jumping at me."

Gramps laughed. "I remember you used to be good to take along on a fishing trip."

"Until I figured out that you were using me as bait to bring the big fish in closer," she scolded. "I was angry at you for a while after that."

"I saw the man in the animal skins again." I explained to Gramps what had happened earlier at town hall. "I hope he's not responsible for this."

"How could he be?" Mary Catherine asked. "You said he doesn't even speak our language."

"Next time, hold him for Chief Michaels," Gramps said. "Maybe he could get some information from him."

I agreed, but I knew I wouldn't do it. I tried to avoid situations like that with Chief Michaels. If he ever decided I was completely crazy, I couldn't help Duck anymore.

Sheriff Riley pulled up with a deputy's car behind him. He checked out the mess on Duck Road and put his men to work. It wasn't long before one lane of traffic was moving freely to allow cars through the intersection.

No one left the area. More visitors and residents came to see what all the fuss was about. Sheriff Riley's deputies wouldn't allow them to park on the side of the road so they drove to the Duck Shoppes' parking lot and walked down.

They were making progress with Chris too. He was very close to the walkway around the top of the water tower. When Kevin and Luke reached down to help him over the rail, there was a loud cheer from everyone above and below. Chris waved and blew Jamie a kiss. The firefighters and public works guys helped him hang the Duck Christmas banner before they left. There was applause from everyone.

Dalton pulled up and began moving cars out of the way with his tow truck. The ambulance arrived and took the Cadillac driver to the hospital. Gramps refused to wait for an ambulance and instead asked me to take him to the emergency room at Kill Devil Hills.

Mary Catherine offered to stay and keep Missing Pieces open for me. Kevin came down from the water tower and said he'd drive me and Gramps to the hospital.

Gramps complained that he wanted to take our old car to the clinic. But it hadn't been started in months, so I told him we were riding with Kevin. He didn't like riding in Kevin's pickup, but it would have to do.

After getting him settled in, I went through the driver's side and sat in the middle on the bench seat. I could tell

Gramps was in pain, despite his stoic manner. He never complained no matter how badly he was hurt. It made it difficult to decide exactly how bad it was. I always just assumed it was worse than he let on, and went from there.

"What happened in the street?" Kevin asked as we started toward Kill Devil Hills.

I explained the accident, and that I'd seen the man in the animal skins again. "He said there would be trouble."

Kevin shrugged as he kept his eyes on the road. "I could make prophecies like that too. Like weather predictions—if you say it's going to rain enough times—it's bound to rain. Are you sure he's real?"

"I'm not sure, except that Mary Catherine's crow saw him too. Maybe it's possible that he's still part of the vision from the stone horse. I wish it would go away."

"Maybe it's your subconscious warning you that bad things are going to happen," Gramps suggested.

"I don't think it needs to do that," I retorted. "It pretty clear."

"I talked with the sheriff," Kevin said. "No sign of Jake yet. I told him he was at town hall earlier. Chief Palo brought together a group of citizens in Corolla to look for him. She also temporarily closed the excavation site."

"I wonder why she did that." Gramps shook his head. "I don't see how that will make the situation any better."

"Me either," I agreed. "But maybe she's afraid people will come looking for the ghost horses."

Kevin shook his head. "That doesn't seem very likely."

"Then you don't understand people," I told him. "They do crazy things when they get scared."

"That's true," he agreed.

We were barely out of Duck when I saw someone stumbling down the road. Even though I couldn't make out his face, I knew who it was. "Stop, Kevin! There's Jake."

Chapter Eleven

Jake was in worse shape than Gramps. His clothes were all but ripped from him. He had large deep scratches all over his arms and legs as though he'd been beaten with something.

I pushed his blond hair back from his face. His cowboy hat and boots were gone. "Jake, it's me—Dae. Everyone's been looking for you. What happened?"

His eyes cleared for a moment and his dirty hand touched my face. "Dae? I'm so sorry. It didn't help at all. I was too late. It's all over."

Then he started talking out of his head again. The

primary thrust of his words involved the demon horses. He even spoke of seeing men wearing animal skins dancing around a fire. He'd seen what I'd seen in my vision. I didn't know how, but that must have been why he'd come to town hall earlier.

"I think we should call Chief Michaels and the sheriff," Kevin said.

"He's hurt," I told him. "He needs medical attention first and then we can call everyone."

"They can see to his problems." Kevin got to his feet. "I'm done with him. I can't believe you're not."

I didn't get up from the place I'd been kneeling beside Jake. "He needs help, not the police. What happened to me wasn't illegal."

"It should be, and killing Tom was," he reminded me. "Come on, Dae. I'm not saying we should leave him on the road—although I think that's what he deserves. We'll wait until someone else gets here."

"We don't know that he killed Tom, and we're headed to the clinic anyway. Let's just put him the back of the truck and bring him with us. We don't know how long it will take for someone else to get out here."

He sighed, and opened the tailgate. "Okay. But we call the police on the way to the clinic, right?"

I smiled and hugged him. "Right. Thanks."

Jake wasn't a big man but he was heavy. His arms and legs flailed around—it was all we could do to get him into the pickup. Kevin offered to knock him out so he'd keep still. I wouldn't let him do it.

I decided to ride in the back with him. Kevin didn't like it, but he got in the truck, pulled out his phone, and started driving.

The hodgepodge of words coming from Jake meant nothing. I tried to bring him around but he was delirious and probably running a fever. I hoped his wounds weren't infected.

Something had been wrong with him at the Blue Whale,

and again at town hall. That wasn't the Jake I knew. Maybe he'd been poisoned or drugged. A doctor would be able to tell with a blood test. I hoped he'd be all right. He was only trying to protect his land. He'd never wanted the publicity for having found the horse cult statues.

I was sorry he'd found anything out there at all, though I was as interested at first as he was. Not everything that was lost needed to be found.

Chief Michaels, with Duck officers behind him, arrived at the hospital a few minutes after we did. They walked up quickly as we were trying to get Gramps out at the patient drop-off.

"Where'd you find Burleson?" Chief Michaels abruptly asked us.

"He was out on the road," I told him. "He's sick. He needs a doctor."

"We'll get him a doctor after he answers a few questions."

"He's not even coherent," I argued. "And a doctor might be able to tell you what's wrong with him. He's not a suspect yet in Tom's murder, only a person of interest. Let him see the doctor and then question him. You don't want him to come back later and say you questioned him under duress, right?"

Chief Michaels glared at me. "All right. But one of us stays with him at all times. Now, if you're done protecting this man you hardly know, let's get Horace out of the truck and inside. Okay?"

I was glad when Gramps was on a stretcher and in the emergency room. They took him immediately for an x-ray, which gave me a chance to check on Jake.

He was being examined in a small room that was heavily guarded by the three Duck police officers. It seemed like overkill to me, but they'd agreed to let him see the doctor first so I wasn't complaining.

"Have they said what's wrong with him yet?" I asked.

Chief Michaels was seated in a green plastic chair at the

door. "Not yet. It will probably be a while. Did he say anything to you about what happened to Tom?"

"If he did, I couldn't understand him. Nothing he said made any sense."

His gaze was angry and suspicious. "You know that as the mayor of Duck you're obligated to tell us anything that could help solve the murder case."

"I know the medical examiner isn't even finished with the autopsy so we don't really know for sure what happened to Tom. I'd tell you if Jake said anything important, although it would be hearsay so it wouldn't do you any good anyway."

He shook out his newspaper with a pained expression on his face. "Save me from the public trying to tell me how to do my job!"

It was perfect timing for Kevin to return with a cardboard holder filled with cups of coffee.

"Chief, I think you take yours black." He gave the first cup to Chief Michaels. "I'm only guessing about yours, Tim and Scott—I brought it with cream and sugar. Dae, plenty of milk and sugar. Anybody have any information yet?"

We thanked Kevin for the coffees and told him there was nothing yet. The door opened behind Chief Michaels and the doctor tried to get out of the exam room.

"What's the verdict?" Chief Michaels got to his feet and moved the chair.

"I'm not completely sure," the doctor said. "I think he might be high on something. He needs some stitches and has a broken wrist. We'll have to keep him at least overnight to try to figure out what he's taken."

"He doesn't do drugs," I told him. "If he has drugs in his system, someone else gave them to him."

"You don't know that, Mayor," Chief Michaels contradicted. He turned back to the emergency room doctor. "Any chance you could be finished with him sooner? He may be a suspect in a murder case."

The doctor adjusted his glasses. "It could kill him if we don't monitor his condition overnight."

Chief Michaels grunted, and gave me an evil look. "That's what I get for listening to people who aren't in law enforcement. Officer Mabry, you stay here with the prisoner. Let me know if there's any change."

Chief Palo joined us, removing her hat from her sleek blond hair. "Thanks for the call, Chief Michaels. We'll take over now."

"I don't think you will," Chief Michaels told her. "It was just a courtesy call. He may be your citizen but he's my murder suspect."

"Please don't fight over my patient in the hall outside his room," the doctor said. "I have more jurisdiction here than either of you."

"I'll leave an officer," Chief Palo said.

"So will I," Chief Michaels responded. "We'll call when we have something."

"No need." She smiled. "My man will be here too."

Since I wasn't going to hear anything else about Jake right away, and I didn't want to hear them arguing about him, I left to wait near the x-ray room where they'd taken Gramps.

Kevin went with me. "You were right to have Jake treated first, Dae." He settled in a chair beside me. "Sometimes I forget that I'm not in the FBI anymore."

"I suppose it's easy to fall back into that routine." I sipped my coffee. "I think anyone, not involved with law enforcement, would opt for medical treatment first. They can always talk to him later. If he was drugged or poisoned, he'll make a lot more sense when it's out of his system."

He put his hand on mine. "You think that's what made him give you the statue, don't you?"

"It wasn't like him," I told him. "He's not that kind of person."

"Everyone knows he's in love with you." Kevin glanced at me. "How do you feel about him?"

"Do you even have to ask?" I showed him the beautiful engagement ring on my finger. "You must know me well enough by now to know that I wouldn't sneak around even if

I wasn't completely in love with you. I'm too serious to have any fun—that's what Shayla always says."

I told him about Shayla leaving and my feeling that she might never come back. "I've been having a lot of strong impressions during the last few days. Maybe it's the horses."

"Or maybe it's being around another psychic, even if she only talks to animals." He grinned. "You manage to get involved with some odd characters. It must be your other 'gift'."

"That's exactly what I first thought about you. Since you worked with a psychic in the FBI, I thought that's why you were attracted to me."

"Are you saying I'm odd?"

I shrugged. "You must be since I get involved with odd characters."

They brought Gramps back from x-ray. It was a different doctor, thank goodness. The break was simple and would be easy to repair. Gramps was impatient and ready to leave. Kevin and I sat with him while he waited for his cast.

"What about Jake?" Gramps asked. "How's he doing?"

"They're keeping him overnight for observation," I told him. "Chiefs Michaels and Palo aren't happy about it."

"Not surprising. No one likes to wait for answers." Gramps looked around the tiny cubicle. "I'm dry as a frog on a sunny day. Could you get me something to drink?"

"Let me." Kevin put his hand on my shoulder as I started to get up. "I'm sure he'd rather you be here than me."

"Thanks, Kevin," Gramps said. "If you see any beer, be sure to get it."

"I'll do my best."

I hugged Gramps. "What a mess. I'm glad Chris was safe, but it sure took a lot to do it."

"The banner looks good."

"Yeah. I hope it was worth it."

He laughed. "It probably will be unless Jamie kills him when she gets him home."

Kevin brought a glass of water. "You'll just have to

pretend it's beer, Horace. They're probably going to give you something for pain. You shouldn't have alcohol too."

"You mean you saw beer out there and passed it by?" Gramps chuckled. "You're not the man I thought you were."

"I'm sure that's true." Kevin sat beside me and squeezed my hand. "They definitely decided to leave Jake here overnight. He'll have plenty of armed guards so he should be safe."

"I hope whatever someone did to him will wear off," I said. "Maybe we'll have a chance to figure out what really happened to Tom while Jake is getting better."

Kevin shook his head as he looked at Gramps. "Your granddaughter has an amazing ability to forgive."

"Yes she does. She gets it from her mother and grandmother. She sure doesn't get it from me. If I'd seen Jake give her that stupid horse, I might've shot him."

"You would not," I argued as the attendants returned to have Gramps's leg put in the cast.

"We'll never know," he said. "You better be here when I get back."

When he was gone, I left Kevin to go to the ladies room. What a day! I'd be glad to go home when this was over. I called Missing Pieces, and Mary Catherine said everything was fine. There were no sales but some customers had wandered through the store.

"Gramps should be done here soon. I appreciate you doing this. I'll have Kevin pick you up and bring you to the house."

"Don't worry about me," she said. "Just take care of you and Horace."

I put away my phone and walked out of the ladies room. There was a small courtyard in the back of the building. I could see plants and shrubs surrounding some benches and a pretty fountain.

I also saw the man in the animal skins again.

Should I go out and talk to him? It seemed stupid if he wasn't really there. I couldn't understand him either way.

What was the point?

But I pushed open the door to the courtyard and looked around. He was waiting for me. "If you were trying to tell me that bad things were going to happen, you were right."

He answered, waving the bone around again and jumping up and down. My visitor—whether real or imaginary—looked nervous. He kept pacing the marble stones with his bare feet.

"Do you know anything about what happened to Jake?"

He nodded as though he understood me, but didn't still didn't say anything that made sense.

I took a step back as he came closer. He stared directly into my eyes. His eyes were bloodshot and yellow around a pale brown iris. I didn't have a chance to get farther away from him before his hand came down on my head. The world spun dizzily, and finally turned black.

Chapter Twelve

I awakened with a start, gasping as though I'd been holding my breath. I was worried that he was going to hand me an artifact, and grateful when he didn't, but curious about what had happened to me.

This didn't seem like a normal vision. This felt real, as though it was happening to me at that moment. But I wasn't in the garden at the hospital any more. I didn't know where I was or why I was there. I wasn't observing as usual. I was part of whatever this was.

I was sitting on a patch of rough, damp soil. It was a dark place, only lit by a few torches that sputtered, leaving shadows on the walls behind them. It appeared to be a cave.

Where were Kevin and Gramps? Were they looking for me?

The tall horse statue I'd only seen complete in my vision was right in front of me. Jake had shown me part of the head when he'd first started digging. The rest of the body had been buried in sand and dirt. It had been excavated by the archaeologists in the past few months. Why was it underground again?

Its craftsmanship was remarkable. It was a beautiful piece of work, with such detail in the dull, brown stone. How long had it taken someone to make it? This was a part of American artistry that would be a shame to lose.

And yet I'd seen it in my vision by a fire where terrible evil was being planned. The horse statue wasn't really part of that, I reminded myself. It was the human interface that was the problem.

I got up and walked around it, careful not to touch it. Touching it might only make matters worse.

There were meticulous carvings on the legs and face. The eyes appeared almost real, gleaming in the light from the torches. Whoever had carved this had been a master.

I saw the man in the animal skins. He was huddled in a rough corner, the bone at his side. "I wish I could understand you."

He touched his head. "You understand now."

His words had been spoken in whatever language I'd heard before, but now I could understand them. "Because you touched me? Is that why I can understand you now?"

"You. Me. The same." He wrapped his hands together.

The same? "You mean we both have a psychic gift. Is that right?"

"Yes."

I glanced around the cave. "Why did you bring me here?"

"I die here."

"You die here now?"

There were no records of people living here a thousand years ago. There was no way of knowing who they were or what had happened to them. Perhaps there had been an earthquake that had sealed the horse in the sand. Or the sea could have risen on the island and then gone back again.

One thing I noticed—there was no way out. The walls were irregular, but no doors or any other openings existed. I was afraid to run my hand along the edges for fear of what I might find, but I grabbed a torch and searched carefully. If there was an exit, I didn't see it.

"Now." He nodded. "I was first. I die to keep the demons away."

"You were the first to bring the demons through the fire?" I sat close to him for the comfort of being with another human even though we were so different. "You were punished for it?"

"Yes." His lined face was worn and sad. "Too much killing. Not let demons out again."

He'd been locked inside the tomb they'd made for the horse so the demons couldn't be called again. I got it.

And I was terrified.

Panic built inside me. It was hard to breathe. The air was stale, like a basement that had been closed off for too long. The damp and mildew were beginning to bother me.

I tried to think of it rationally. I was really lying on the flagstones or grass in the courtyard at the hospital. That strange little man had touched me and brought me here but it was only in my mind. I wasn't really here at all. There was no reason to panic. I'd wake up soon or Kevin would notice I'd been gone too long and come find me.

"What is your name?" I asked the man across from me. "I'm Dae O'Donnell. You could be an ancestor of mine."

"Osisko." He patted his thin chest and then drew a horse figure in the sand. "Horse man."

"The horse was your totem." I tried not to notice that the torches were flickering as the oxygen was used up. "That's why you were able to call them. That's why you have to die."

He nodded. "Dae stop evil."

"I hope so."

The underground area was sealed. No air. No fire. The flames grew dimmer and began to die out. My heart fluttered with them. How many times had I asked myself what would happen if I died in a vision? If Osisko died, would I die too because he'd brought me there?

I forced myself to be calm. Any minute now, I wouldn't be here. I'd be back at the hospital waiting for Gramps. This would all be something I could tell him and Kevin. There was really no reason to be scared. I wasn't really here.

The last torch sputtered and died. The black was so absolute that I couldn't even see Osisko right in front of me. I literally couldn't see my hand in front of my face. There was nothing but endless darkness.

My breath came harder. I squeezed my eyes shut and hoped someone would wake me. I didn't belong here. I was supposed to be in the light many years from now. It was getting harder and harder to breathe. The air whistled in and out of my lungs. I felt lightheaded and sick to my stomach. *Come on, Kevin!*

I finally lay down in the sand. I couldn't sit up anymore. I gasped for air. The world was beginning to fade away. I didn't want to let go of my life.

It was ridiculous to even think that since I wasn't really here.

I had to leave. Now.

My eyes closed and I said a small prayer that I wasn't really alone in this terrible place. Then I fell asleep, or lost consciousness. I don't know which.

That seemed to be it for Dae O'Donnell.

Then I slowly realized that there was bright light on the other side of my eyelids. I opened my eyes and looked around. I wasn't in the dark hole with the giant horse statue and Osisko anymore. I was on a sunny beach with the one man I never expected to see again.

"And what are ye doin' here?" a familiar voice asked.

"Am I dead?" I asked my nefarious ancestor, Rafe Masterson.

He laughed as he threw some sticks on a fire. He was the same as I recalled his ghost that had visited me when he needed help clearing his name. It was then that I'd learned that the Scourge of Duck was in my family tree.

"I hardly think so. As to why ye're here, that might be any man's guess. I assure you, madam, that I am very much alive, and so are you."

I scrambled to my feet. "You're not alive. You're a ghost. That has to mean that I'm dead too. But why am I dead here?"

"Ye're beginning to sound a bit mad. What makes ye think that I'm dead?"

"Because I'm your great-great-grandniece, Dae O' Donnell. We can't be alive at the same time. You were dead a long time before I was born, remember? You wanted me to clear your name because you were hanged for being a pirate, but you hadn't done anything illegal."

He stood up straight, towering over me, his hands on his hips. His flinty eyes stared into mine. "I think ye'd best be leavin'. This here beach might not be big enough for the two of us. Off you go. I don't like killing women as a rule, even the mad ones."

"I can't leave. Where would I go? I don't belong here. I'm from the future. It's not like I can stay in this time." I considered what I was saying. "Unless this is heaven—or the other place. Either way, I'm not going anywhere until I figure it out. Where are we supposed to be?"

"It's not where we're supposed to be, lass. It's where we are. This is the edge of the Carolinas that falls into the sea. There's nowhere to go from here—especially if ye're like me and ye have a price on yer head."

I studied him closely. I'd been wrong at my first glance at him. This was a younger version of my ancestor than the ghost that had visited me. He was probably still in his pirate days. He looked lean and mean, doubtless waiting for his crew to come and get him after he'd finished burying his treasure.

"I can see I made a mistake." I made a little curtsey to him. "You aren't the man I thought you were. Good day to you, sir."

"Ye wait up there. Ye seemed so certain of who I was just a moment ago. I believe ye know who I am now. I can't let ye leave after all. A man like me can't be too careful." His cutlass slid out of the scabbard hanging from his belt.

I glanced at the rock formation behind him. It was the rocky outcropping that was shaped like a duck. I was right about why he was here. This was the tiny island off the coast of Duck where he'd buried his treasure. Of course he didn't want me to leave with that information.

"I thought you didn't kill women," I said as I backed away from him.

"I said I didn't like it. It leaves a foul taste in me mouth. But that don't mean I won't do it if I need to. I'm sorry, Mistress O'Donnell, but I can assure ye that a long drink of rum will get rid of that foul taste."

He kept advancing on me with his cutlass raised high. *Good grief!* I'd been sure that I'd died in that cave with the horse, and now I was facing a brutal death at the hands of my own ancestor.

"If you kill me now, there won't be anyone to set things right for you after you die," I warned.

He threw back his head and laughed. "I don't plan to worry about it. Once I'm dead and buried, that's it for Rafe Masterson. I'll take my chances with Davy Jones."

I had backed into another rock that was behind me. He wasn't going to let me skirt around it and run away. I was trapped again, only this time I didn't have faith in the idea that I was actually at the clinic and would come to my senses at any moment.

That is what you get for using your gift. If you'd left it alone, you wouldn't be about to die at the end of a sword.

I didn't have as much as a stick to fight back with. So I

closed my eyes and hoped something better was on the other side. There was a loud thud that was followed by a painful groan. I opened my eyes, squinting in case the sword was still coming at me.

But now there was a woman staring down at Rafe who was lying on the beach with his eyes closed. She was dressed as a pirate in dark short britches and a tattered blue shirt. She wore a scarf over her hair with a worn hat on top of it.

She turned to face me and smiled. "Hello, Dae. I would have known you anywhere. You look just like your mother."

"Grandma Eleanore?" I could hardly form words. "I seriously must be dead."

"No. Not yet." Her blue eyes were smiling at me as she gave me a big hug. "I had a feeling we'd run into each other at some point. I can't tell you how good it is to see you. I'm sorry I couldn't make it until you were born. I knew you would have the gift too. There were so many things I wanted to teach you."

"But how can I be alive and you're here?"

"It's difficult to explain." Rafe groaned and moved his head. "My knocking him out with a rock is only going to last so long. He's got a hard head. Let's get out of here and find someplace we can talk."

I took her hand, and there was an instant when nothing was there. It was a blank screen—that's the best way I can describe it. One moment we were standing on the sunny beach, and the next we were in a pleasant room, sitting at a table with a steaming tea pot and two cups in front of us.

I blinked several times. How was this happening to me? Was I travelling through time? I'd seen plenty of things in the past. Had my gift brought me to this place where anything was possible?

"There. That's much better, don't you think?" Grandma Eleanor was exactly as I'd seen her in many pictures. But those photos hadn't shown me the vitality in her face or the curiosity in her eyes. She had a bit of impishness about her mouth that I'd never noticed in a photo.

"I really don't know. What's going on?"

She poured us each a cup of Earl Grey tea. I recognized the aroma at once. The cups were matching rose Victorian china, set on matching saucers. "Our paths have intersected for a moment, Dae. Just as yours had with Rafe. It won't last long. I wish it could so we would be able to get to know each other. When you use your gift, you move through time to see where an object or a person has been. I'm here using my gift from a point before you were born."

Only one word could do this justice—"Wow."

Grandma Eleanor laughed. "Yes. I'm so sorry I wasn't there to guide the development of your gift. Your mother, bless her heart, didn't share it. She tried to understand, but it's not the same. She must be very proud of you, Dae. You're a beautiful young woman."

I sipped the tea. Was it real? I wasn't sure, but I needed something to keep from bursting into tears. "She's been dead a long time."

The blue eyes like mine welled with tears. "She was so young. What happened?"

I explained the situation. There wasn't much to say. Each word was more painful than the last. "Every year I have a séance and try to call her back. I just want one last chance to make things right between us. Is that crazy?"

"Not crazy, sweetheart. But if she had something to say, she would have said it."

"I've heard that."

"Tell me what you do. Do you have a young man in your life? How is your grandfather?"

I told her everything I could think of from Gramps and his fishing business to Missing Pieces and Kevin. She nodded and sipped her tea. She reminded me so much of my mother.

"I'll bet Missing Pieces was Horace's idea, wasn't it? He was always the practical one. It sounds like you have a wonderful life, Dae. I'm glad you're thinking about getting married, and hopefully having children one day."

"Thank you. Kevin is a great person. But what about learning to control these visions? You obviously have a way to do it that I don't. What should I do?"

"You have to take control of each vision. Before you touch someone or something, get your mind prepared. As soon as you find yourself wherever the vision takes you, make it yours. You have to dominate it. Be the vision, if you will. I know that sounds very Zen, but it's the truth. My vision had brought me to that island where I found you and Rafe—I've run into him before. But I could make this reality from it when I knew we needed to get away."

"It would be great not to always fall down and pass out." I grinned at her. "I'll get it. Thank you."

"Just remember that you can't go into the future, but you can go anywhere in the past. If you find yourself in a bad situation, like the horse in the cave that you described, just close your eyes and concentrate on where you want to be. You can do it, Dae. It's part of your heritage, like the rest of your gift."

She glanced over her shoulder. "I'm afraid I have to leave. I need to get back. I'm sure we'll meet again. I love you, sweetheart. Give my love to your grandfather, and your beau. If Kevin's as sharp as you say, he'll understand this right away."

I hated for her to leave me. There were so many things I wanted to ask. "Is there something I can say to Gramps to make him understand? Something only the two of you would know?"

"There is." She whispered a secret message. "Now I have to go! I love you, Dae."

Grandma Eleanor disappeared. The table and pleasant room went with her. I was left standing on a beach. It wasn't the island where Rafe was. Just a beach that I couldn't identify.

The way she'd described going back to where I wanted to be reminded me of Dorothy and her ruby slippers in the *Wizard of Oz*. I wished there were magic shoes that did the job, and that I was wearing them.

But there were no magic shoes. I closed my eyes and imagined the courtyard in the hospital where I'd last been. I took a deep breath, and saw the space clearly, with me in it. Kevin was there too, with a nurse that I'd seen at the front desk.

When I opened my eyes, I was there. It was exactly as I'd seen it. Kevin was sitting on the ground next to me, my head on his lap. The nurse was worriedly checking my pulse and urging him to get me inside.

"I'm fine," I quickly told her as I came back to myself.

She jumped. "Are you prone to seizures or forms of epilepsy?"

"No. Not at all. It's difficult to explain."

"That's what I was telling her." Kevin got to his feet and helped me up. "Are you okay?"

"I'm fine. It was the man in the animal skins again. His name is Osisko. He put his hand on my head."

"So you were assaulted?" the nurse demanded.

"No. I'm sorry. Is my grandfather back from having the cast put on his leg?"

"I think you should have a complete workup with an MRI." She gathered her medical bag. "People just don't go around passing out for no reason."

"Thank you for your concern." I shook her hand. "I'm really thirsty. Can we find something to drink?"

Chapter Thirteen

As I sipped my can of Coke, I told Kevin about the horse in the cave, Osisko, and the meeting with my relatives.

"That's incredible. Your grandmother is right about the control. I hope you were able to understand what she was telling you."

"It's how I got back here. I think I can make it work for me in the future. Just think of it—my grandmother was dead before I was born, but because she was in the past looking for something, we were able to connect."

"I can't imagine what that was like."

"It means that it's possible that I could go back and see

my mother. I don't know how to do that right now, but I think it will come to me."

"What about the horses? Any ideas on the cult background or who killed Tom?"

"Nothing right off hand. I know what the horse statue was used for, but I don't understand how it relates to what's happening today. Osisko thought his death would stop the demons from returning. I guess he was wrong."

A nurse glanced into the lunchroom. "Mr. O'Donnell is ready to go. You'll need to check him out at the front desk."

Gramps was woozy from the sedative they'd given him to set his leg and put on the cast. Kevin and I got him into the pickup, but he couldn't sit upright so I had to ride in the back again.

I didn't mind. It was chilly, but there was so much to think about. I'd never had a vision that had led to another vision—and actually meeting my grandmother . . . wait until I told Gramps. He'd be surprised.

The drive back was slow, but we finally made it to the house and tucked Gramps into his recliner. He woke up for a moment, long enough to thank me and Kevin and then went back to sleep.

I knew Kevin was busy with his guests and getting his Christmas decorations up, but I didn't want to leave Gramps alone. I asked him to pick up Gramps's prescription and Mary Catherine from Missing Pieces.

"Sure." He kissed me quickly and asked if I needed anything else. Then he was gone and I sat on the sofa, trying to absorb everything that I'd seen and heard.

I'd thought from the beginning that the horse cult was nothing to fool around with. It seemed that there was a good reason the stone horses were buried. The people who'd put them there never meant for them to be out in the light again.

The ancient horse demons that Osisko had first summoned flashed through my mind. Someone knew about them and was actively summoning them back into the world. It had to be one of the workers at the excavation. Anyone else would be too noticeable.

But had that person also killed Tom?

"Dae?" Gramps yawned and stretched a little before yelping in pain. "That's right. Broken leg. I thought when I gave up being sheriff I wouldn't have to worry about that kind of thing again."

I carefully hugged him. "You'll be up and taking charters again in no time. Want some coffee?"

"Yes, thanks. And if you could scrounge up something to eat, I'd be grateful. Wasn't Kevin with us? I thought I remembered seeing him."

"He went to get your prescription, and Mary Catherine. She stayed at Missing Pieces to keep it open for me."

"She's really something, isn't she?" He grinned. "I never really thought I'd see her again. I knew she'd kept the shop, but her goodbye was pretty final when she left. I've never met another woman I could compare to your grandmother besides MC."

I started the coffee and took out some eggs. He was going to need something in his stomach to take those pain killers. "Speaking of Grandma Eleanore, I finally got to meet her."

He did a comical double take. "What? Have I finally lost it—or have you?"

"Neither. I had a vision, and she was in it."

"That's not the same thing, Dae. You see all kinds of strange things in your visions."

"And Grandma Eleanore explained how to control them instead of letting them control me. We talked about you, and Mom, and Kevin. She told me to tell you that she loves you."

"It's not real, Dae. I know you understand that." He was beginning to look worried and uncomfortable.

"It's no less real than anything else I've seen. She gave me some helpful advice."

I scrambled the eggs, and poured some coffee in a cup. I could tell he didn't know what to think about me seeing my grandmother. Like she'd said, it was difficult for people without a gift to completely understand. I found an old TV tray, and put his eggs and coffee on it so he could eat in the recliner.

"I'm not saying you don't see real things when you have visions," he corrected. "All I'm saying is that you see what you want to see sometimes. I remember that with her."

"She said you'd say that. She gave me proof for you since you're so practical."

He smiled as he sipped his coffee. "She always said that. But it was your grandmother who got us through on a deputy sheriff's pay for many years."

"That's not my proof," I told him. "She told me about the sapphire brooch that belonged to your mother. You found it in a junk box and were going to throw it away. She stopped you by grabbing it so she could tell you where it came from."

"That's right." He nodded. "I remember."

"That was the night you proposed to her. You thought she fainted, and when she came to, she told you about the brooch."

"She told you that? I'm not sure if your mother even knew about it."

"She wanted you to believe that I'd seen her in my vision. Do you believe?"

He stared at me with tears in his eyes. "If I say no, will she come and haunt me every night?"

I got up and knelt beside his chair. "We can try. I love you, Gramps. I never realized from the pictures how much I look like Grandma Eleanore."

He smoothed back my hair with his rough hand. "I realize it every day. And I'm glad for it. You're a comfort to me just like she was."

Kevin and Mary Catherine got back. They'd brought take-out from the Curbside Bar and Grill. Cole and Molly had called Kevin and insisted that he should take food to us after Gramps's accident.

Gramps wasn't hungry, but the three of us were starving. We ate the fried chicken and potato salad while Mary

Catherine entertained us with stories about her day at Missing Pieces. She'd brought Treasure and Baylor back with her. They were eating too—from separate bowls of course.

"It was fascinating being there today," Mary Catherine said. "I can only imagine what it must be like to know the story of everything you have on your shelves."

"Except for the bad things," Kevin said. "Speaking of which, did your experiences today convince you that the man in the animal skins is real, Dae?"

"Yes. Osisko is real. I think he has a gift too, and that's why I keep seeing him here in the present. He's definitely not a ghost. I'm sure of that."

"I'd feel better if you weren't the only one seeing him." Kevin took a sip of his sweet tea.

"The crow saw him too," Mary Catherine remarked. "They are very truthful creatures."

Gramps held his head. "I don't know. Talking to crows might be crossing the line for me."

Mary Catherine laughed. "Well we're all back safely from our travels today anyway. Maybe tomorrow there will be some answers that everyone can understand."

Kevin kissed me goodbye before he left. "You know I only want to make sure that you're safe. It's not good for someone who has visions to imagine little green men."

"Not green—dark and covered with animal skins." I smiled even as he continued to scowl. "Don't worry. I'm sure we'll figure it out. With demon horses running around Duck, I don't think Osisko is so bad."

"Just be careful. I'm glad you met your grandmother. I know spirit guides can be helpful. I'm not so sure about the little man."

We walked to his truck through the chilly night air. "I'll see you tomorrow. You be careful too. I wouldn't want you to get run over by a herd of invisible horses."

Gramps and Mary Catherine went to bed early. I couldn't sleep, so I sat in my room and looked at town documents that Chris had posted on the town administration site for the meeting. It was all new ordinances that were going to be introduced tomorrow night and information about speakers that had requested time at the council meeting.

One of them was the corporation that wanted to put in a gambling ship that would use Duck as its home port. The town would have to pass several new ordinances to allow the ship to dock on the Atlantic side, close to the Blue Whale.

There was also an ordinance to allow the ship to have gambling even though they couldn't use it until they were twelve miles out. I still didn't understand why the town had to pass that ordinance since it was regulated by the state and the Coast Guard. But if Chris said it was something we needed to do, we needed to do it.

Shops in town had been very vocal about allowing the gambling ship to dock here. Everyone thought it would be good for business before and after tourists left the ship. Some people were still old fashioned about it, and felt like nothing good could come from gambling. They believed it would attract a bad element to Duck and wanted us to vote against it.

I stared at the ceiling for a few minutes, thinking about the upcoming controversy. I'd already received emails from the only two council members still on the board. Both of them wanted to hold the vote tomorrow night.

But I was against that idea. The gambling ship investors wanted us to give final approval for the project as quickly as possible. I thought we should appoint our two new members for the council and then hold a special meeting the week after so they had enough time to review the information. Five heads were better than three. It was easy to say yes to something, but difficult to get rid of it once it was in place.

I heard a sound outside on the road and immediately, my heart started pounding. Treasure meowed sleepily and put his head back down. The sound continued to grow, like thunder coming from a storm at sea. I ran up the stairs to the widow's walk, and looked down on the town.

From that vantage point everything looked calm and serene. But the sound grew louder, becoming a roar coming toward me from Corolla. I cowered behind the wrought iron railing, peeking between the scrollwork.

I still couldn't see anything on the road, and yet trees were swaying, wind chimes loudly ringing out. The wind grew stronger, pushing against the house. The noise became more distinguishable—the clatter of horses hooves on the pavement below me. As the sound grew closer and more abrasive, I could see bushes being trampled alongside the road. Snapping sounds—like pottery breaking and glass shattering—accompanied the turmoil. It was like a hurricane rushing by us, destroying everything as it went.

Was I the only one who could hear the snorts and other screams related to a large herd of horses?

And there was Osisko again, standing under a streetlight, watching as the ghost horses blew by him, a cloud of sand and dust flying in the air as they passed.

Even though I was behind the rail, the man on the ground looked right up at me, his eyes fixing on my face. I admit to being cowardly and sneaking down from the widow's walk. I didn't want to see him or talk to him that night. I was still recovering from our meeting in the cave.

I turned off the light and the laptop in my room, and held Treasure tight against me. He wasn't happy with the extra cuddling while he was trying to sleep, but he put up with it and finally settled down.

There was a knock on the bedroom door. I was terrified that Osisko had come into the house, but it was only Mary Catherine. "Are you awake, Dae? May I come in for a moment?"

I was glad to have her company. I didn't want to wake Gramps after the day he'd had. Mary Catherine sat on the bed beside me, holding Baylor.

"I know you heard that," she said. "Whatever it sounded like—it wasn't horses—at least not the living kind that I can connect with. I pushed out my awareness to try to communicate with them. I thought there might be something left of the animals they once were. But there was nothing, but blackness. Those things have *never* been real horses. I don't believe they come from a place animals could exist. They're only taking their shapes to terrify people as they always have."

My hands that were buried in Treasure's fur were shaking. "I saw Osisko down on the street again. I was too scared to face him."

"As well you should be. These are not forces to be trifled with. They are stronger and more deadly than the elements. You should stay away from that man, Dae. I don't like to think what could happen to you if he has a chance to touch you again."

"I don't know what to do. I can't think of any way to help Duck. I think the excavation is what's causing this, but I don't see what I can do to stop it."

"I think we should plan our trip to Corolla tomorrow, don't you? I'd like to spend some time with the wild horses. I think they might be able to help us better understand what's going on. I'm willing to bet that they relate to us more than they do to those things out there."

I nodded, hoping it would be light soon. "We could go over to the excavation site. I have a standing invitation from Dr. Sheffield to visit. I don't want to touch anything else out there, but there might be something to be gained by a visit."

So we agreed to try to go back to sleep and be ready tomorrow for our early morning trip. Corolla wasn't that far from Duck, but I needed to have Missing Pieces open and begin putting up Christmas decorations. I really wanted to check on Jake too. I hoped sure I could accomplish all that in one day.

I finally fell into a restless sleep that was haunted by Osisko and the tomb where he'd died. My dreams of him in a time long past were vivid and scary. I was up early, eager to get away from those nightmares, and the feeling that he was still out there waiting for me.

Chapter Fourteen

Gramps was up early too. I helped him out of bed and into the kitchen. He refused to sit around in the recliner all day. "I have a pinochle game. I can't miss that. I called Howard. He's willing to come get me. Don't fuss, Dae. I'll be fine."

I made a large stack of pancakes. They were ready to eat as Mary Catherine joined us. She was dressed in brown today with touches of orange that went well with Baylor draped around her neck.

"He's insisting on going with us today." She sat at the table. "He says he has some ideas about what's going on. I think he just wants to get out for a while. How can he possibly have any clue about the horse cult?"

Gramps chuckled. "I can't believe you're still letting that cat boss you around, MC. Come with me to the pinochle game. You'll have a lot more fun than hanging out with Dae trying to figure out the secrets of the universe."

"I'd like to, Horace. Maybe some other time." She laid her hand on his. "Something rare and unusual is happening here. I don't think the police will understand it. I'm glad I could be here to help Dae so she doesn't have to do it alone."

Gramps was blustery after that remark about the police not being able to handle the situation. As ex-law enforcement, he didn't believe there was anything that couldn't be handled by the police.

"I'm going to check in on Chris Slayton and make sure he's okay after his misadventure yesterday," I told him to break his tirade. "If he can't make it to the meeting tonight, I'm cancelling. We're already down two council members. I don't want to make any mistakes."

"The people from the gambling ship won't be happy about that," he said. "Are you planning to take a vote on that tonight?"

"I hope not. I'm going to try to get the two members on the council to hold off on that vote until we have our two new members seated." I shrugged as I served the pancakes. "I guess we'll see."

"You know how I feel about it." He stabbed some pancakes with his fork.

Boy, did I!

"We don't need something like that here. It will only cause trouble. That's why I had Tuck and Ronnie sign that document against it. I added my signature to support the rest of us old folks who like Duck just the way it is."

"I know, Gramps. And that's why we're having the public hearing tonight before the vote. That way everyone can express their opinion."

"Government in action." Mary Catherine took two small

pancakes from the plate. "I can't imagine dealing with all that bureaucracy. But you do it beautifully, Dae. The people of Duck are lucky to have you as mayor."

I rushed into a conversation about our plans to go to Corolla that morning before the shop opened. I knew Gramps would argue against the gambling ship for hours if we let him. I hoped he and his friends didn't plan a filibuster that evening.

He wasn't happy about Mary Catherine and me going to Corolla by ourselves. As if on cue, Kevin walked in the door. "I could smell pancakes all the way to the Blue Whale. I hope there's coffee too."

"You're just in time," Gramps said. "MC and Dae could really use a practical escort to take them to Corolla today. I'd go, but this stupid leg is going to keep me home."

"Sure." Kevin speared a few pancakes and put them on a plate. "I'd be happy to go."

"What about getting ready for the Christmas celebration?" I asked him as I handed him a cup of coffee.

"I can do that when we get back. I assume that's what you're going to do at Missing Pieces today too, right?"

"Yes," I admitted. "But I'm going to see Chris first."

"I'll get the truck," he promised. "You want to see how Jake is doing too?"

"If there's time," I was surprised that he was offering to go see Jake. "Mary Catherine wants to talk to the horses too. Then we're going over to the excavation."

Kevin and Gramps exchanged a worried look.

"I'm not going to touch anything," I assured them. "I'll take gloves with me."

"I'm sure we'll be fine." Mary Catherine's smile was cheerful. "If you have more pressing business, Kevin, Dae and I can see Jake and take care of the other things. I don't want to put you out."

"Not a problem." He swallowed some coffee and quickly finished his pancakes. "I'm going to get ready. Pick you up at Chris's house." He kissed me goodbye and left through the back door.

"What a nice man," Mary Catherine said. "I can see why you love him, Dae. And it's easy to see why he loves you. You're a lucky couple."

"Thanks. I'm going to get ready too." I put the dishes and cups in the sink. A car horn honked in the driveway. "It's Howard," I said to Gramps. "Let me help you out there."

But before I could move, Howard was in the house and taking care of the situation. He'd brought a collapsible wheelchair. If I would have suggested it, Gramps would have ignored me. Because it was Howard, it was a great idea.

"See you later Dae, MC," Gramps called out. "Be careful out there."

I put on a deep blue sweater and jeans before I stuck my feet into flowered rubber boots. If we went to the excavation site, I'd need them. I offered a pair of boots to Mary Catherine, but she said she'd be fine.

We struck out for Jamie and Chris Slayton's house which was only a short walk from where I lived. We weren't the only ones visiting him. There were cakes, pies, and casseroles all over the kitchen and dining room. I put the cookies I'd brought on the kitchen table and went into the library where Chris was seated in an armchair. His ankle was in an elastic bandage, but otherwise he seemed unharmed.

"Thanks for coming, Dae." He glanced at Mary Catherine. "I don't think I know your friend."

I introduced her. Chris hadn't moved to Duck yet when she'd lived here. They shook hands, and Jamie brought in a tray with cups of hot chocolate and cookies on it.

"The banner looks great up there, Chris," I told him. "Next time don't try to do everything yourself."

He laughed. "Look who's talking."

"I'm glad to see you're okay," I told him. "I don't like to have important meetings without you."

"Don't worry about that," Jamie said sharply. "He'll be there tonight if I have to put him in a wheelchair and push him over. We need that gambling ship to bring people to

Duck in the off season. I hope you plan to vote for it, Dae."

"You know Gramps, Chief Michaels, and Sheriff Riley are completely against it, right? Chris has a signed request from them not to allow the ship to dock here." I knew how Jamie felt. But I wanted her to know that there were people against the gambling ship too.

Jamie dismissively waved her hand. "That's because they're old and they aren't trying to make a living at retail. You know what I mean. Just think how much busier Missing Pieces would be with an extra few hundred people every day."

I had thought about it, as I was sure every other business owner in Duck had. I could see good and bad points to voting for the ship. Of course it wasn't only my vote—unless it came to a tie that I had to break. I hoped it wouldn't come to that because I wasn't sure which side I'd fall on.

"Either way, Jamie," Chris said. "We'll find a way to make Duck the best town on the Outer Banks. I don't want everyone to get too one-sided over this. The vote is going to be close."

"Any idea on who you plan to appoint to the board to take the place of Mad Dog and LaDonna?" Jamie asked.

"Jamie!" Chris frowned. "Quit trying to influence the mayor."

"What?" She turned to him. "She's my mayor too. I'd just like to know."

Chris changed the subject. "We heard something about Mad Dog planning to ask for his seat again at the meeting tonight."

"And we don't want that to happen," Jamie finished for him. "We need somebody younger, someone who owns a local business—what about Kevin?"

"He's definitely not in the running," I told her. "But Cody Baucum is. We'll see who else shows up."

Before the discussion could get too bogged down in town business, I excused myself and Mary Catherine, telling them that we were on our way to Corolla.

"Going to see Jake today?" Jamie asked with a sly smile. Not surprising since everyone had seen him bring me home on the back of his horse during the election. "Probably not today. We're going to see the wild horses and the excavation site. Maybe I'll be able to see Jake tonight."

Chris shrugged. "The public works guys told me there were a lot of calls again about the horses last night. There was more damage done. What's going on out there, Dae?"

"I'm not really sure yet," I said. "But I hope to find out."

Kevin's timing was perfect again. He'd waited in the truck as Mary Catherine and I had said our goodbyes. We walked through the Slayton's yard, noticing the crushed bushes and demolished outdoor ornaments. There were hoof prints everywhere.

We were discussing it as we got in the pickup. "The horses coming through at night doesn't make any sense," Mary Catherine said. "They're so destructive."

"Wait until you see my rosebushes," Kevin added. "It looks like someone dug them up and crushed them into pieces. There are hoof prints all over the yard and the verandah. I'm going to have to replace some boards that couldn't stand up to the horses."

"Maybe your insurance will cover it." I scooted beside him on the bench seat.

"Not sure how I'd explain the horses being there." He backed the truck out of the drive. "I saw Chief Michaels this morning. He said they had more than seventy calls about it last night. He's thinking about asking Sheriff Riley for extra protection until the horses stop invading Duck."

"What about Corolla?" Mary Catherine asked. "Are the horses just coming to Duck or are they trampling flower beds out that way too?"

"We can stop and talk to Chief Palo," I said. "She's very nice. I'm sure she wouldn't mind sharing information."

We followed Highway Twelve out to Corolla, not taking as much time as I would have liked to appreciate the fall scenery, but we were on the clock.

I got a call from Chris telling me that Jake had been arrested so I shouldn't bother trying to go to Kill Devil Hills to see him. I thanked him for letting me know. "He's in jail in Corolla," Chris said. "Just thought I'd let you know since you were going to be out that way."

"I thought she'd wait to arrest him until the lab results were back on Jake's bloodwork," I told Kevin and Mary Catherine after I'd said goodbye to Chris and ended the call. "Maybe Chief Palo isn't as nice as I thought."

"Or maybe she was just doing her job," he said. "Let's reserve judgment on that, shall we?"

"How far is it from here to the wild horses?" Mary Catherine asked.

"It's where Highway 12 drops into the ocean," Kevin replied. "From there you have to take a Segway or rent a Jeep to get out where they live."

She smiled. "Do you think we could go there first and then check in on Jake? I'd really like to see the horses right away."

I shrugged when Kevin glanced at me. "Sure. I guess Jake isn't going anywhere. Let's see if we can find someone who'll take us out there. A Segway is expensive."

"We may not need one." Her eyes were fixed on the horizon. "The horses know I'm on my way."

I realized that she hadn't lived here for a long time and she may not have even gone to visit the horses when she was here last time, although that seemed unlikely. It wouldn't hurt to drive to the end of the road. Maybe someone would be out trying to make some money by taking people out to see the horses.

Tom Watts had always been out there each day, taking people to see the wild horses and explaining why they were so important to preserve. I hoped Jake, or whoever took Tom's job, would be as good as it as he had been. The lives of the horses depended on it.

We made the last turn before Highway Twelve dead ended. Usually at this time of year, there weren't many tourists. The beach was mostly deserted.

But not that day. There were no tourists or wild horse guides—no people—just hundreds of horses, young and old, waiting there. As soon as Mary Catherine got out of the truck, they began trying to move as close as they could to her. They pressed their noses against her and softly whinnied as though she were a long lost friend.

"Oh, it's good to see you too!"

Chapter Fifteen

"Oh my dear friends." She lifted her arms to hug as many horses as she could, pressing her face close to theirs. "It's been too long."

Kevin and I got out of the truck after her and slowly followed her to the last tip of land at the edge of the Outer Banks.

"You think they remember her?" he asked.

"I don't know. You've seen how animals are with her. The only ones that aren't that way are the ghost horses, and she says they aren't really animals. She can't communicate with them."

We stood back and watched her talk with the horses. They kept trying to get closer to her. She was surrounded by all sizes, colors, and ages of the wild herd.

"They definitely like her," Kevin said. "I've never seen them this way, have you?"

"Not ever. Not even for Jake or Tom. She's kind of amazing, isn't she? I wonder what it's like to hear everything animals have to say."

"I think it might be confusing. Just like if you could hear everything humans said."

"Or knew where everything came from," I murmured.

He put his arm around me. "How are you feeling today?"

"Like always after I pass out at a public place—embarrassed and uncomfortable." I put my head against his chest. The wind whipped at us from the rough sea, blowing the tall grasses.

"I guess that's part of having a gift."

"Kevin! Dae!" Mary Catherine beckoned to us to join her. "My friends have plenty to say about what's been happening. The poor dears are suffering."

"Do they know who killed Tom?" It might not stand up in court, but at least we'd have a direction.

"No, I'm afraid not." She shook her head. "But they do know about the excavation and the horse cult. They're as afraid of those demon horses as the rest of us. They say they've always known to avoid that spot. They can't believe we didn't know better."

Kevin reached out a hand to stroke one of the horses' tan manes. "Tell them I've wondered the same thing."

I carefully touched one of the horse's noses and the large brown eyes stared soulfully into mine. "I'm so sorry. I hope none of the horses have been hurt by all this."

"They're worried about their reputations," Mary Catherine translated. "It already upsets them to have some of their friends and relatives removed from the island every year. They're afraid this might make it worse."

"I'm sure no one is going to blame them." I disregarded

some of the extreme comments that had been tossed around at the town hall meeting. "You said yourself that the demon horses aren't real animals."

"But how many people are going to believe that?" Kevin asked. "I've already heard some talk in Duck about getting rid of the rest of the horses."

"Oh no!" Mary Catherine cried out. "These horses have more right to be here than we do. They've been here for a thousand years. The tribal people brought them here for ceremonies with the horse cult. They didn't appreciate being used in that manner, I can tell you. But they don't deserve to be punished for it."

"I'll do what I can to help protect them," I said. "Maybe we should sponsor a wild horse day during the Christmas celebration. I'll talk to Chris about setting that up."

Mary Catherine kept one arm around a small gray and brown colt. "They understand that it's a problem getting along with humans. They appreciate whatever you can do, Dae."

I saw movement out of the corner of my eye. Thousands of gulls, pelicans, and other sea birds had come to roost on a few large rocks and a solitary tree near us. As I pointed them out to Kevin and Mary Catherine, a group of dolphins jumped out of the water, calling to us and laughing.

Mary Catherine waved to the dolphins and shouted back at them. "Thank you! I'm glad to see you here too."

Kevin raised his eyebrows. "What a show. I feel like I'm in a Disney movie."

I glanced at my watch, hating to put an end to the camaraderie, but if we were going to see Jake, and go to the excavation before I had to leave for the shop, we needed to go now.

Mary Catherine understood. She told each horse goodbye, and commented on each colt saying how lovely he or she was. "You know the mothers like to hear that."

"I suppose so. That's incredible. Your gift is really special."

"It's always been a big part of my life. Not always a good part, as I can hear the poor things suffering and can't always help. But I do what I can, like you do."

We walked back to the truck across the cold sand. A few fishermen were making their way to the water. Mary Catherine frowned and called fishing an abominable sport. Kevin hustled us into the truck, and we left.

The sea birds followed us from the beach to the Corolla police station. They were joined by a few hundred other birds—wrens, starlings, and crows. They perched on a tree near the pickup after we'd parked. Kevin glanced at them, but didn't say a thing.

Chief Palo was looking out the window as we walked up. She opened the glass door for us and nodded at the noisy group of birds. "Looks like you've brought some friends."

She didn't know how right she was. I smiled, and said hello, but didn't enlighten her. "I was wondering if I could see Jake Burleson. I'm not family, but I'm a friend."

She sipped some coffee after offering each of us a cup. "I don't see why not. It's not like he's really even my prisoner. Sheriff Riley is coming later to transport him to the county lockup in Manteo. This is kind of a courtesy that he let him stay here today."

"Thanks. I'd like to hear what he has to say," I said.

"He's more coherent today. We got him a change of clothes, and he took a shower. He even ate some breakfast. Just go down the hall there. The door isn't locked." She shrugged. "Where is he gonna go anyway?"

Kevin and Mary Catherine accompanied me, though I wished I'd insisted on seeing him alone. I wasn't worried about Mary Catherine so much as Kevin after their altercation at the Blue Whale.

But Jake was Jake again. He was sitting in a ladder back chair tossing cards into a bucket as he waited for the sheriff. When he saw me, he got to his feet and offered me his chair. He pulled another up for Mary Catherine.

"Boyfriend." He nodded at Kevin as he always had.

"Fiancé." Kevin corrected and nodded back. "Cowboy. How's it going?"

"I've been better." Jake's gaze came back to me. "Miss Dae. I hope you're well. I'd like to apologize again for what happened."

"You weren't yourself," I replied. "How are you feeling?"

"Not too bad considering they say I killed my best friend." His eyes narrowed. "Know anything about that? I hear you found him—no surprise."

"That's about it. I'm sorry. The sheriff and Chief Michaels think you killed him because he started siding with the archeologists about you leaving your property."

He shook his head. "That's just stupid. I'd never hurt Tom."

"I didn't think you'd hurt Dae either," Kevin gruffly remarked.

"I wouldn't—not knowingly. I was out of my head. I can't describe it."

"Maybe you were out of your head when you killed Tom too."

I knew I had to end that discussion. "No one thinks you meant to do it, Jake. I think you were drugged. They did some blood work at the clinic."

"Why would someone drug me?" he asked. "That doesn't make any sense."

"And according to the blood tests, it didn't happen either." Chief Palo knocked on the doorway, but she was already in the room with us. "Sorry. Sheriff Riley is here."

"Don't I get a lawyer or something?" Jake asked tersely.

"As a matter of fact," Chief Palo said. "The Wild Horse Conservancy is hiring an attorney for you. They said he'd be there when you're arraigned."

"Just don't say anything until you talk to him," I advised.

Sheriff Riley and Dare County District Attorney Luke Helms joined us. After nodding to us, Sheriff Riley instructed one of his deputies to put handcuffs on Jake, and tell him his rights.

"Good morning, Dae." Luke smiled at me and shook hands with Kevin. "This seems like an odd place to find the mayor of Duck."

"Not so odd," I told him. "Jake is a good friend. I can't believe you're arresting him for killing Tom."

"His blood work came back clean. He had motive and opportunity. Everyone knew he and Tom had been arguing over this thing with the horses. We found what we think is the crime scene at Jake's house."

"In short, Mayor, it looks like your friend killed Tom Watts and dumped his body on Duck Road. He tried to convince everyone that he was crazy or drugged. I think we know better than that now." Sheriff Riley hitched up his pants. "I hereby take custody of this man from you, Chief Palo. Have a nice day."

Jake was escorted from the room.

"Don't worry," I told him. "We'll figure out who really killed Tom."

"We will?" Kevin asked.

"Yes. We will."

We waited to leave the police station until Jake was in the sheriff's car, and they were backing out of the parking lot. An older woman with streaked gray and black hair walked into the police station. Her black suit was sharply creased, and her matching shoes and bag looked expensive.

"Hello." She held her hand out to us. "I'm Mayor Lisa Fitz. I don't know if you voted for me, but I thought I should introduce myself to my constituents."

Chief Palo smiled. "This is Mayor Dae O'Donnell from Duck, ma'am. And her friends, Kevin Brickman, and Mary Catherine Roberts."

"All from Duck?" Mayor Fitz asked. "Is there a convention that I didn't know about?"

"No, ma'am. They were here visiting the prisoner Sheriff Riley just picked up," Chief Palo explained.

"Sheriff Riley? Isn't he from another county too?"

"Yes, ma'am. It was his prisoner. The murder was committed in Duck, but the suspect was from Corolla. We were holding him until the sheriff could get him."

Mayor Fitz glanced around the police station. "Well, next time, let's try to have a prisoner of our own, shall we, Chief Palo?" She vaguely glanced our way and then left.

Chief Palo apologized. "She's new. Only lived here the necessary ninety days to file for public office. She'll get used to things."

"Thanks for your help and understanding." I shook hands with her. "We're headed over to the excavation. I don't know exactly what we're looking for, but I want to take a look out there."

"If you don't mind, Dae, I'll ride over there too. I haven't been out there since Tom died. I'd like to see who's taken over and such."

"Sure." I glanced at Mary Catherine and Kevin. "We'll meet you over there."

Two Corolla police officers came into the station. They were talking about the dozens of calls they'd received during the night. "It's crazy out there," one of them told Chief Palo. "Everyone thinks we're being attacked by horses. No one has seen any horses, but they keep saying they hear them."

"I know." Chief Palo put on her hat and jacket. "Mrs. Evans called again to say that horses ruined her statue garden. I don't know what's wrong with everyone."

"Whatever it is must be contagious," I said. "We're having the same problem in Duck. I've seen the hoof prints—some of them burned right into the pavement. There's been some property destruction our way too."

We discussed the situation for a few minutes. The stories sounded the same from both towns. I didn't mention having heard the horses or feeling their presence. Things were strange enough as it was.

"Bobby, go out to the wild horse trailer and ask them if they know what's happening," Chief Palo said to her officer.

"I'll do that, ma'am," he replied. "But I'm telling you no horses—wild or otherwise—are out jumping on porches and smashing statues. That's just plain crazy."

I noticed he glanced my way when he said it. Maybe he knew me. Maybe it was just the weirdness of the situation.

Kevin, Mary Catherine, and I left the police station with Chief Palo following behind us in a squad car. It couldn't hurt to have her with us. Dr. Sheffield had invited me to take a look, but that had been before Tom's murder. He might have had a change of heart.

"I guess that answers the question about the horses in Corolla too," Kevin said. "I had a feeling that would be the case. I'm sure it's the same coming up through Sanderling too. They just rely on the sheriff taking care of their issues."

"I don't like the way this is going," Mary Catherine fretted. "It's no wonder the horses are worried. I'm worried too. You know it doesn't take much for something like this to blow up into an event everyone will regret. We can't let that happen."

Chapter Sixteen

I'd been to Jake's horse ranch several times since I'd met him. It wasn't much—just a few acres with an old barn and house on it surrounding by fencing. Now there was a large red sign at the long drive that proclaimed the spot a historic dig.

There were no horses in the pasture now. Jake had to give up taking care of them while the excavation was going on. Too many people were going in and out to make sure the injured animals weren't in danger. It had been a difficult decision for him because caring for the wild horses was his life—as it had been Tom's.

That was why the two of them were such great friends. Tom had probably endorsed the excavation because he thought it would be a good thing to prove how long the horses had been on the island. He'd probably hoped it would bring in more publicity and donations to take care of them.

Jake had thought that too, at least in the beginning. He'd wanted to know more about the bits and pieces he'd found on his own. But his curiosity had put him in a position that was impossible for him.

I could see covered areas with signs all around the property. The first area that Jake had begun digging had yielded the large stone horse. I was surprised to see it completely out in the open. The horse was exactly like it had been in my vision. The red-brown stone was carved with the same intricate markings I'd seen in the vision. The area around it even appeared like the square dimensions of its underground tomb that I had visited.

We parked by the old barn. The three of us waited for Chief Palo before going any further. There had been no guards or anyone stopping us from going into the site, but as we got out of the truck, Dr. Sheffield appeared.

He was dressed in jeans, a long-sleeved blue shirt, and a Corolla baseball cap. He was a long, lean, no-nonsense kind of person. His assistant, Duran, was at his side, as always. I was beginning to think the two were permanently linked together.

"Mayor O'Donnell." Dr. Sheffield hurried to my side. "Mr. Brickman. What a pleasant surprise. I believe we met at the election party, Mrs. Roberts. Welcome, all."

He was in an effusive mood. I had to wonder how much of his giddiness was directly attributed to losing his longtime critic to a murder investigation.

"Dr. Sheffield." I shook his hand, my most friendly mayor's smile on my face. "It's good to see you, even in these difficult circumstances."

He hung his head. "I know what you mean. I can't believe that Tom is dead or that Jake killed him."

"That's yet to be seen," Kevin said, surprising me.

"Is there some new evidence that shows someone else is responsible for Tom's death?" Duran voice was heavily laced with sarcasm. "We heard that the murder scene is right in his house. Am I mistaken?"

"No." Chief Palo stepped in. "That's the latest on the investigation, sir."

"It's just so sad," Duran added. "The two of them were so close—until Jake lost it. He's been getting scary for a while now. He actually tried to collapse the dig around the big horse. Can you imagine?"

"I don't understand why Tom turned against him," I said. "I know they disagreed as to how much good the dig could do for the wild horses. I didn't realize it had become more than that."

"Jake threatened Tom with a shotgun a few weeks ago," Dr. Sheffield explained. "They'd been arguing again. Jake told him to get off his property. When Tom didn't leave right away, Jake escorted him off."

Duran shivered. "There were a bunch of us there that day. It was *frightening*."

It was the first I'd heard of the incident, but since I'd been busy with my own problems, it wasn't surprising that I hadn't known. It was still hard to believe, even with the audience of archeologists willing to testify to the event. Jake just wasn't the type to pick up a gun to solve his problems. But I acknowledged that Jake had not been himself.

"Was there something in particular that became the last straw?" I asked.

"It had something to do with digging up the big horse," Dr. Sheffield said. "I actually think he wanted to re-bury it after all the work it's taken to dig it up."

"As soon as he saw it out in the open, he freaked out," Duran continued. "He couldn't even look at it. He kept saying it was evil."

Chief Palo nodded as she glanced around the property. Small groups of people were working everywhere with brown tents covering the spots where they were digging. We stood there as I wondered what to ask or look for that could make some difference.

It seemed even more possible that Jake was feeling the emanations from the horses that I'd felt and they had overwhelmed him. He might not be psychic, but he could be sensitive.

"I'd like to take a peek at the rest of the site," Mary Catherine said. "I might not be out this way again, and it's not every day that one visits a place that could predate most of the historical spots in our country."

"I'd like that too," Chief Palo said. "I'm new to the area. I thought the horses came from the Spanish treasure ships."

"Good God!" Dr. Sheffield eyes widened as Baylor stretched around Mary Catherine's shoulders. "What is that?"

She patted her cat's neck. "This is Baylor. He often travels with me. You don't have to worry. He won't get down and bother a thing. Shall we go?"

Immediately on seeing her delicate shoes, Dr. Sheffield had a few of his workers create a walkway with wood slats to the individual worksites. *So that was why she didn't have to worry about wearing boots.* She was very good at getting her own way.

We went to see the big horse first. It was definitely Sheffield's pride and joy. I could feel the terrible evil coming from it long before I was looking up at it. It was even worse in person than it had been in the vision. But at least here I could get away from it.

Osisko was there too, pointing toward Jake's house.

"I'm sorry. I'm not feeling very well. I think I'll go back and sit in the truck for a few minutes. If you have to move on, that's okay." I didn't have to feign illness. Staring at the statue had made me queasy.

"I'll come with you," Kevin offered.

"That's okay." I squeezed his hand. "I'll be fine. Probably just some bug going around. You know how it is at this time of year."

Dr. Sheffield was gracious about me leaving the tour. "I hope you feel better, Dae. You're always welcome here."

"I could make you some mint tea," Duran offered.

"I think I'll just close my eyes for a few minutes." I started walking back toward the truck, hoping none of them would feel so bad that they needed to follow me.

Osisko moved with me toward the house after I'd left the group. He used his bone to point to the front window.

I knew I was going to have to go inside and look around. It was a crime scene, and Gramps would have killed me if he'd known I'd crossed the yellow tape. But I thought someone might have missed something small that could clear Jake's name from the case the police were building against him.

I waited until the side of the barn was between the tour and Kevin's pickup before I made a sharp right to get into Jake's house. There was crime scene tape across the kitchen door, but not the front door that faced the highway. I started thinking that I could say I needed to use the bathroom if anyone found me. It seemed a rational excuse.

There were always gloves in my bag. I needed them when I went to auctions and visited antique dealers. I slipped on a pair as soon as I walked into the house. Kevin had taught me that. I only needed to touch what was necessary—not everything. I didn't want to risk passing out.

There had been a scuffle in Jake's house. He didn't have a lot of clutter, more the type to only have what he needed. But now everything that had been on the sofa, the mantel, and the table, was on the floor. Papers had been ripped to shreds and thrown everywhere. I noticed the outline of what I assumed was Tom's body on the hardwood floor. There was still a blood stain where his head had been. I moved closer, and squatted down beside it.

"I knew I'd find you here," Kevin said.

I jumped and almost fell into the blood stain. "What?"

He laughed. "What are you looking for?"

"Something that proves beyond a shadow of a doubt that

Jake didn't kill Tom. You asked."

"That seems unlikely. The best thing would be a good alibi. You could always say you were with him when Tom died."

"Gramps would kill me if I lied for you, much less Jake. Short of that, there must be something else."

Kevin crouched down on the other side of the outline. "Look at the hoof print."

I noticed the bloody mark that was clearly a hoof print. "Were the horses in here too?"

"Doubtful. And there's just the one print. A horse couldn't come in here, gallop over Tom, and leave no hoof prints but this one before it took Tom to Duck Road."

"So Jake couldn't have done it. He wouldn't have done anything that might be bad for the horses."

"I didn't say that, and the police won't take that as proof that Jake didn't kill Tom," Kevin corrected. "Someone tried to make it look like a horse did it, but that could have been Jake."

"Or Dr. Sheffield killed Tom to pin it on Jake so he could take his land."

He shrugged. "It's possible. It's not the weirdest thing I've ever heard." He bent down close to the wood floor.

"What are you looking at?"

"See if you can find some tweezers," he said. "There's something wedged between the floorboards. I don't think I can get it out with my fingers."

I got the tweezers I'd seen on Jake's desk near the fireplace. Kevin maneuvered them between the cracks in the old wood. He came up with a thin slice of white plastic.

"That could be anything." I wasn't very impressed.

"It could be something important." He studied it as he held it between the tweezers. "It looks like the edge of a name badge."

"Everyone out here has one." I sulked. "How is that going to help anyway, even if it is a name badge?"

"I know someone who can touch things and see who

they belong to," he reminded me. "Want to give it a try?"

"I'm scared to do it after yesterday. What if I pass out again?"

He didn't hesitate. "I'll take you to the pickup, and they'll know you were really sick."

"That's not a great plan."

"Got a better one? It's not old. I don't think it could harbor much evil in a slice this small."

"No. Let me have it." I took off my gloves and grabbed the piece of plastic from him.

Jake was arguing with Tom Watts. It was about the excavation. Tom was convinced they would get more donations for the wild horses with the horse cult tie-in. Jake was equally adamant that nothing good could come from it.

"You're just worried about losing your land," Tom accused.

"Yes, I am. I don't want those freaks digging everywhere until there's no room for the horses. Why can't you see that?"

"It's not that. You don't care about the horses." Tom pushed his pudgy finger into Jake's chest. "It's all about you."

"Get out of here," Jake yelled as he pushed Tom away from him. Tom had been wearing a plastic name tag that broke as he fell. A splinter of it lodged between floorboards and had been ignored by the crime scene team.

The experience was just like being there in the room with the two men arguing, but it wasn't so involved that I couldn't shrug it off.

Kevin was staring closely at me. I jumped when I opened my eyes.

"Are you okay?" he asked.

"I was until I saw you standing there." I sat down in a chair and tried to catch my breath. "It's just as well for Jake that the crime scene people didn't find this. It was just him and Tom arguing. Nothing useful to us at all, but could look bad for him."

"I know you don't want to hear it but—"

"I don't." I put my hands over my face. "I don't believe Jake killed Tom. If it had been during this big argument, maybe. They were both really hot. But I didn't sense anything like that from the plastic."

Kevin shrugged.

"Besides, maybe there's something to what you said about the single hoof print. How *can* there be one hoof print?"

"I don't know, but I agree that it doesn't make sense."

"Why are you helping me try to prove Jake is innocent?" I eyed him suspiciously, putting my hand on his chest as I moved in close. "You hate Jake."

He put his arms around me. "It's true that I don't like Jake Burleson, but I can see that we're not going to be able to talk about anything but him until we figure this out."

"You mean because you want to talk about the wedding?"

"No." He kissed me. "Because I want to talk about Christmas, and new things you find for Missing Pieces, and everything else, except Jake. I'm really fine with not planning the wedding yet. I wasn't kidding."

"Thanks, Kevin. Mary Catherine was right—you are a great catch."

Duran walked in, looking for us. "Why are you in here?"

"Mayor O'Donnell wasn't feeling well. We stopped in here so she could use the restroom."

Duran glanced around. "This is a crime scene. The police don't want anyone here."

"We were just leaving." I wished I'd thought to take pictures of the room. "When did you and Dr. Sheffield leave Duck after the party?"

"What are you insinuating, Mayor O'Donnell?"

"Nothing. I know the police are looking for other people who may have been on the road that night. You had to come right by that spot to come home. Maybe you saw something important and didn't realize it."

"We've already spoken to the police," he said. "And we didn't see anything. I think you should leave now." He held the door open.

His familiarity with Jake's house was irritating. He didn't knock to come in, and something about the way he held the door seemed possessive to me. He and Dr. Sheffield were already counting on Jake losing the house, and what was left of the land being excavated.

Kevin and I walked outside. Mary Catherine and Chief Palo were returning from their tour of the site. I apologized to Dr. Sheffield.

"That's quite all right," he said with an engaging smile. "I'd be happy to take you on a personal tour anytime, Dae. It will have to be soon, though. We're planning on sending the big horse to Raleigh for further study."

Kevin's eyes narrowed when Dr. Sheffield used the word *personal*.

I ignored it. "Thank you. Maybe I'll take you up on that when things settle down. What's next for the site?"

"We've done some satellite imagery. We know there are pieces buried under the barn and the house. It's unfortunate about what happened to Jake and Tom, but our research may be the recipient of their quarrel. I've applied for a grant to purchase this entire tract of land."

"Don't you think you should wait until a jury finds Jake guilty before you take his property?" Kevin asked in an unpleasant voice.

Dr. Sheffield's gaze lighted on him. "Not really. We were headed in that direction anyway. The common good, and all that. This is an important find, Mr. Brickman. I'm sure Jake can buy another piece of land with the money we'll pay him for this one—if he's not in prison."

"How very practical of you," Mary Catherine said.

Dr. Sheffield loved it. "Thank you. Now if you'll excuse me, we have a lot of work to do preserving the big horse and getting it ready for transport. I'll be accompanying it, but I'll be back."

"What do you think the ancient people did out here with all the horse statues?" Chief Palo asked. "How does it relate to the horses on the island?"

"That's exactly what we're trying to find out," Dr. Sheffield answered. "It was nice meeting all of you. Please feel free to visit again."

I noticed that Osisko was close by listening to our conversation. I didn't know if he could understand us the way I could understand him, but there was something to learn from body language. His presence made me question my grandmother's words about not being able to move forward beyond our times. Osisko had a physical presence—he'd touched me. How was he able to come forward to our time?

It seemed unlikely that I would be able to have a conversation with him that would answer those questions. He might not even know. But I was curious.

We started back to the truck and the police car. Chief Palo glanced back at the retreating figures of Dr. Sheffield and his assistant. "You know, there's something about Sheffield that I don't like. I think I'm going to do some digging of my own, and find out what there is to know about him. I'll catch you later."

Chapter Seventeen

I glanced back as Kevin drove the truck out of Jake's drive. There was no sign now of Osisko. I wondered what it was like for him to see the big horse unearthed again after so many years. Did he still feel responsible? It had to be frustrating for him after he'd given up his life to keep the demon horses from returning.

"That place gave me the willies." Mary Catherine shuddered. "I'm glad to be out of there. One way or another, I agree with the horses. We have to find a way to bury the site again, and end this excavation. That man has no idea what he's digging up."

"I'm hoping we can prove he's actually the one who killed Tom," Kevin said. "I like him even less than I like the cowboy."

"And that's saying a lot." I studied the side of his face. "It was the personal tour thing, wasn't it?"

He raised his brow. "What do you think? It took a long time for me to work up the courage to ask you to marry me. I think you saying yes takes any personal tours with that jackal off the bucket list."

Mary Catherine laughed. "Good way to put it. Where are we off to now?"

"I have a Santa, sleigh, and eight reindeer waiting for me to put them on my roof," Kevin said. "I'm hoping to win grand prize for the best decorated business."

"What's that?" I asked. "A free dinner or something?"

"No. A free ad in the Outer Banks online and print editions of their magazine. I'm surprised you didn't know that before me. You're usually up on these things."

"Wow. I don't have a sleigh and reindeer. What's second prize?"

"Dinner at an oyster bar in Manteo." He grinned. "Planning on taking second place?"

"Maybe. I haven't even looked through my Christmas stuff yet. That's what I'm going to do when we get back."

"You want to meet for lunch?" he asked. "I hear the Blue Whale is serving delicious homemade soup and their awesome grilled cheese sandwiches today."

"If that includes some yummy dessert that the famous chef at the Blue Whale Inn has cooked up, I'll be there."

"Me too," Mary Catherine chimed in. "I love soup."

Kevin dropped us off at the Duck Shoppes. I felt a little guilty leaving Treasure at the house since Mary Catherine had Baylor with her, but I hoped it was going to be a busy day. Besides, Treasure wasn't as sedentary as Baylor. Sometimes he tried to run out of Missing Pieces. He could learn a few things from Mary Catherine's cat. I'd apologize to him later.

Everyone along the boardwalk was decorating their shops. August Grandin was adding lights to his Christmas duck menagerie. Trudy was getting help from Tim putting up sparkling, lighted snowflakes on her big windows.

Mary Catherine and I stopped to admire her snowy windows.

"When are you putting up your decorations, Dae?" Trudy asked.

"Right now, I hope. I might have to go to the store to get some things. I know I've taken in some used Christmas decorations during the year. I'm not sure exactly what they are."

"Where were you this morning? I thought you'd be here before me." Trudy gave an extra spritz of fake snow to the large plate glass window.

"We went out to see Jake. Mary Catherine talked to the horses, and we had a short tour of the horse cult excavation out in Corolla," I told her.

"She talked to the horses?" Trudy asked. "How did she do that?"

"It's something I was born with," Mary Catherine explained as hundreds of sea gulls landed around her on the boardwalk rail and the rooftops of the shops. "Horses are very easy to communicate with. They have a kinship with man, much like rats, dogs, and cats. They understand us, as opposed to a whale."

Trudy's perfectly made-up eyes widened. "You talk to whales?"

"I have been known to have a conversation with one from time-to-time. They are very noble creatures with a large world view, not surprising I suppose."

That was almost too much for Trudy.

Tim and I glanced at each other. He knew how she felt about these things too, and changed the subject. "I don't know if you've heard or not, Dae, but Sheriff Riley had to release your friend Jake right after he got him to Manteo."

"What? Are you sure? That's great! What happened?"

Tim took his time relating the tale. "Jake has an alibi for the time the ME puts on Tom's death. He was drinking with some friends at a bar in Southern Shores. His buddies, and the bartender, vouched for him. Sheriff Riley was really mad."

This was great news as far as I was concerned. "Does he have any new suspects in mind?"

"Not that I've heard. He's meeting with Chief Michaels and Chief Palo to see what else they can figure out."

"But the crime scene is at Jake's house, right?"

Tim shrugged. "That's what I heard, Dae. I haven't been out there. Maybe you should ask Sheriff Riley what he thinks."

"What about the hoof marks that were on Tom?" I continued, though I could see it was distasteful to Trudy. "Is that what killed him?"

"The ME said that was odd, now that you mention it," Tim said. "He said all the hoof prints came from one hoof. Crazy, huh?"

That made sense with what Kevin and I had seen at the crime scene too. But the question still remained about how a horse could use only one hoof. "Thanks for telling me. I'm glad Jake is out of the picture." I'd feel better though when the picture was clearer and we knew what happened to Tom.

"I don't know," Trudy said with a deep frown between her brows. "It kind of makes me scared to think that the wild horses are out there trampling people. When did they start that? They've always been gentle and shy when I saw them."

How to tell her that it probably wasn't real horses, but some kind of demon/ghost/hybrid that was intent on destroying things? *Probably not a good idea.*

"Everybody thinks it's a one-time thing, Trudy," Tim said. "Tom's blood alcohol was high. He could've easily passed out or fallen down on the road and the horses just ran over him. They didn't know any better."

Mary Catherine didn't like the sound of that. "We can't allow those wonderful creatures to be blamed for the supernatural evil coming from the excavation site. Perhaps we should speak to the sheriff about what's really going on." I took her arm, and waved to Trudy. "We're going to look for Christmas decorations now. I'll see you later."

Trudy let Mary Catherine's dark words pass right over her. She was good at that. "Good luck with the decoration contest, though I think none of us have a chance against Wild Stallions."

I followed her gaze and saw Cody and Reese Baucum working on the restaurant at the end of the boardwalk. They were putting up lighted dolphins that appeared as though they were jumping from the water to the roof. A lighted Christmas version of Neptune, King of the Seas, was waiting for them with his holly encrusted trident.

"Wow! Where did they find something like that?"

"They probably had it specially made," Tim said. "I don't know if anyone can beat it."

Mary Catherine and I continued down the boardwalk to Missing Pieces. It looked odd on the other side of my shop to see Shayla's place empty and dark. The blinds were drawn, and there was a note on the door that said Mrs. Roberts Psychic Reader was closed.

"Coincidence is a strange thing, isn't it?" Mary Catherine was looking at the shop too. Baylor lazily raised his big head to take a peek. "Shayla leaves Duck as I arrive. I wonder what the significance is in that."

I opened the door to Missing Pieces and went inside despite the dipping, swirling gulls that seemed like they wanted to get face-to-face with Mary Catherine. I wasn't afraid of birds, but I wasn't crazy about one flying in my face either. "I think I put all those old decorations in the closet in case someone wanted them for the holidays."

"How do you decide what to keep and what to throw away?" she asked as she sat on the burgundy brocade sofa.

"I can't explain it. There are some things that I find, or that make their way to me, that I know someone will be looking for. These decorations, and some of the used clothes

I take in, are more for people who might need them, but are low on cash. I give a lot of things away or there wouldn't be any room in the shop."

The box of Christmas decorations had come from a woman who'd moved to Duck over the summer from somewhere in New Jersey. None of them had been made in the last ten years. The lights were large, colored bulbs. There were spinning circles made from gold and silver foil, and a dozen or so old fashioned ornaments.

"I think this is all I'll need for the shop." I sighed as I glanced around. "I wish I had an original idea to go with this stuff. I can't think of anything except hanging it all up and seeing how it looks together."

"Since your friend Trudy decorated her window, maybe you should decorate your door,' Mary Catherine suggested. "Nothing says welcome like a well-decorated door."

"I suppose that's true, and it will maximize my decorations too."

We tacked the big lights around the door frame and then strung the gold and silver foil spinners on the Missing Pieces sign. The ornaments wouldn't stay on the sign or the doorway. I brought them inside and hung them from the ceiling around the shop.

"That looks lovely." Mary Catherine clapped when I turned on the lights.

"I wasn't planning on winning anyway. I just want the shop to look like Christmas. Maybe we should put a decoration next door on Shayla's shop, too, for the same reason."

A woman with long, curly reddish hair and wonderful blue/green eyes came in before we could leave. She was carrying a large box in one hand as though it was very light.

"Hi. I'm April. We had these extra decorations left over at the church, and I thought maybe you'd know someone who could use them."

I peeked in the box. There was a large array of Christmas decorations including some wonderful old carved

Christmas elves and a large, lighted eight-point star. "Great. Thanks. I might use some of them myself, if that's okay."

"Oh, sure. I knitted some of the ornaments in there." April began wandering through the shop with an eagle eye, looking for treasures. I'd seen her in Missing Pieces before but she'd never purchased anything. "I'm looking for something for my grandmother for Christmas. She's got everything, you know? It's always so hard shopping for her, but I don't want to give her a gift card either."

"I know what you mean. Take a look around. We're going to put up a few of these decorations next door. If you see something you like, let me know."

"Thanks. I love looking around in here, but I usually can't afford to buy anything."

Mary Catherine and I put up a few tin stars around the doorway of Shayla's shop. I thought about Mary Catherine's observation regarding Shayla and the shop. It did seem odd that she'd arrived at the same time that Shayla had been called home. It had been a similar circumstance when Mary Catherine had decided to leave and Shayla had arrived. Maybe she was right about coincidences.

"That looks very nice." Mary Catherine watched the tin stars moving gently in the breeze from the Currituck Sound. "A bit whimsical and old fashioned."

"Something wrong with old fashioned?" August Grandin asked as he wandered toward us from the Duck General Store. "I like old fashioned. At least I'm not overwhelming the boardwalk with all that junk Cody and Reece are putting up. I think that helps me make my decision about being on the town council."

"I thought you never wanted to be part of the politics that ran Duck," I reminded him of his words from when he'd turned down a chance to run for the first town council after Duck had incorporated.

"A man can change his mind, I believe. That still one of our inalienable rights, isn't it?"

"Definitely. I guess I'll see you at the meeting tonight," I said. "Good luck."

"Who else is running?" he asked.

"Cody Baucum and a few others. It should be an interesting discussion."

"What discussion?" he asked as he walked away. "I'm the best man for the job. Cody's just a young pup. There's no comparison."

"Okay. Thanks for telling me." I waved to him as I went back into Missing Pieces, not wanting to get into an argument with him.

"Sounds like you're going to have your hands full, Dae," Mary Catherine whispered. "I can't wait to hear everything tonight. I hope it's okay if I go too."

"Sure. It will be good to have someone there who doesn't want to be on the council."

Mary Catherine and I had some tea while April continued perusing the store. I really didn't think she'd buy anything this time either, and that was okay. Not every customer had to be a buyer.

"Who's judging this decorating contest?" Mary Catherine asked.

"I'm not really sure. Probably someone from Outer Banks Magazine. Like I told Kevin, I didn't even know there was a contest last week. Usually either I know about it or Nancy tells me. I don't know what happened this time."

"You know," April said suddenly. "I think I'll take this old cookbook. Grandma is always talking about how good food used to be. Maybe she'd like looking through this."

"A nice choice." I took the heavy, green hardback from her. "You know, this cookbook was put together by a group of women from Duck who were trying to raise money to start the first history museum. It has a lot of great recipes. I always knew someone would like it."

"What year is it from?"

I read the second page in the book. "It was published in 1938. Each of the recipes has the name of the woman who submitted it. I recognized many of their names, including my grandmother, Eleanore O'Donnell."

April lovingly took the book from me and searched through the names and recipes. She gave a loud squeal when she found a name she recognized. "Look! There's my grandmother's recipe for duck soup. My grandfather was a prolific duck hunter. I can't believe she doesn't have a copy of this. I know all her cookbooks, and I've never seen this one."

"She may not have bought a copy of the book for herself," I explained as I put the book on the glass counter near my cash register. "Not all of the women did. I think they thought about it as just a fund raiser and not something for themselves."

"This is so wonderful. Thank you so much for having it here." She touched the book again. "I hope I can afford it. I know it's old."

I looked into her happy face. There was no doubt the book belonged with her and her grandmother. "I'll take a dollar and fifty cents for it."

"What?" April glanced back at Mary Catherine who shrugged. "I know you want more than that. Tell me, please. I have some money saved for it."

I started wrapping the book in Christmas paper. "That's it. It's not very valuable, except in a sentimental way. It belongs with you."

"Thank you so much. My grandmother is going to be so surprised. You said your grandmother has a recipe in here too. Do you have a copy of the book?"

"Yes. My grandfather bought copies for everyone at the sheriff's department. He kept one for himself. That's just the way he thinks."

April was so excited when I'd finished wrapping the book and handed it to her. I really wasn't sure what the book was worth, but I knew what it was worth to her.

"I can't wait until Christmas now," she said. "I don't know how I can ever thank you enough."

"I should thank you. I always have to sell things to make

room for new things. Selling this will make that possible. Merry Christmas, April."

She hugged me. "Merry Christmas, Dae."

Chapter Eighteen

There were a few more potential customers who didn't buy, but mostly the rest of the morning went slowly. At noon, I closed Missing Pieces, and we walked to the Blue Whale for lunch.

I could smell the bread baking before we reached the three-story inn. Kevin had enough time to get his reindeer, sleigh, and Santa up on the roof before he'd started lunch. I didn't plan to tell him about the display at Wild Stallions. Who knew what the contest judges were looking for anyway?

He had also decorated every window with a large holly and fir wreath, and a candle. There was garland swung swag-style on the verandah. Even the mermaid in the fountain out front was decorated. She looked happy with a Santa hat on her stone head.

We passed two of Kevin's guests staying at the inn as we opened the door. Mary Catherine took a deep breath of the warm, bread-fragrant air, and put her hand to Baylor's soft fur. "What a wonderful aroma. I could live here, couldn't you, Baylor?"

The big cat meowed and went back to sleep around her shoulders. I honestly didn't know how she'd ever trained him to ride that way. I'd never seen a cat that kept so still.

"He isn't easily impressed," she said. "If this had been a tuna factory, I'm sure he would have been keener on the visit."

Kevin greeted us at the kitchen door. He had some flour on his shirt and cheek. His face was red from the warm kitchen.

I kissed him lightly. "Mary Catherine wants to live here with your homemade bread."

"She's my kind of woman—easily impressed."

"I know. I might consider living here if you'd been baking cinnamon rolls. Just plain bread?" I shook my head. "Not much incentive."

"I baked cinnamon rolls first since you were coming." He held up a large tray of iced rolls.

"Now that's the kind of man I'm looking to grab for my sixth husband," Mary Catherine laughed. "I'll have to keep that in mind when it's time."

"I have potato soup too." Kevin showed us to the small table set in the kitchen where he and I had eaten many times. His guests ate in the bar at the polished table, or in the sitting room near the fire. He had a huge dining room that the town had rented several times for important events. The Blue Whale Inn was an asset to the community, as I was sure it was meant to be.

We ate lunch, talking about the coming Christmas festivities. Mary Catherine told Kevin about the display at

Wild Stallions.

"I guess I'll have to look for something to beef up my decorations." He ladled soup into bowls. "Those Baucum brothers are showoffs."

"And I'm pretty sure Cody will be on the town council after tonight," I added. "I'd vote for him over August Grandin or Mad Dog anyway. I guess we'll see who else shows up."

"I'm not interested, even if no one else shows up." Kevin cut three large chunks of bread. "I know how much time you put into meetings and so forth, Dae. It's not for me."

"I'd love to do it if I were a Duck resident," Mary Catherine said. "You'd always know what's going on."

"You're right." Kevin grinned. "That's a bad thing too."

"I didn't ask you again," I said. "I was just explaining the circumstances."

"Thanks. What did you think of Santa and the reindeer?" He effectively changed the subject.

Mary Catherine and I both told him that we thought the decorations on the Blue Whale were nice. He told us that the decorations at Mike's Surf Shop were good too. Nothing flashy, like what they had at Wild Stallions, but creative—Christmas surfboards with mannequins dressed as Santa and his elves.

"I suppose you already heard about Jake's release," Kevin said.

"Tim told me. It happened really fast, didn't it?" I asked.

He poured more sweet tea for us. "You must be glad."

"I'm glad they figured it out right away."

"The ME found only one hoof print on Tom too. He found hundreds of different prints on the street and in the yards around the crime scene. I think we're on the mark about the single hoof print at Jake's house."

"But what does it mean?"

"It's too bad one of us don't speak with the dead," Mary Catherine suggested. "I knew a woman once who could do that. It was scary, but she got results."

"I've seen places and people, situations too, by touching clothing or other personal items, but they usually only point me in the right direction. It's probably just as well. I'm not sure I'm ready to have dead people hanging around all the time."

"It's the same thing with me." Mary Catherine shrugged and Baylor changed position on her shoulders. "Of course with animals it's difficult because they see things in ways that we don't. I once had a conversation with an injured turtle that had seen his mistress killed. Naturally I had to fill in a lot of dots on that one."

Kevin told us a few stories about working with his psychic FBI partner. They mostly looked for missing children—some they'd found alive—others hadn't made it through the ordeal.

I was surprised by his openness. He usually didn't like to talk about the past. He'd been changing a lot since he'd first come to Duck. I thought of it as loosening up. I was sure it would take anyone a while to get over the life he'd led.

After cinnamon rolls and coffee, he drove Mary Catherine and me back to Missing Pieces in his golf cart. Two of his guests rode with us too. They came in the shop with us and bought some Duck souvenirs. I keep postcards, towels, mugs, and other inexpensive items on hand for those occasions. They don't make a lot of money, but I think every shop in town should carry some.

Traffic was brisk on the boardwalk. I was hopeful that the ads already in place for OBX Christmas were starting to pay off. It hadn't been cheap to be included in the event. Maybe that was why the magazine had decided to host the Christmas decoration contest. I realized it was more a goodwill gesture opportunity for the local shops than anything else.

I sold a complete set of Duck towels that featured the last few years of our Jazz Festival. They were very colorful and nice collectors' items. We only made a few hundred of them each year. I thanked my customer who was from Raleigh before I noticed Jake standing in the doorway watching me.

When my transaction was over, I excused myself to Mary Catherine and stepped out on the boardwalk to talk to him. We sat on one of the benches facing the Currituck Sound. A group of men were renting kayaks and pushing off from the sandbar next to the boardwalk.

"I just wanted to stop in and thank you before I head back to the ranch." His eyes were fixed on the horizon where the sky met the water. "You probably saved my life."

"I was happy to hear you were released. I knew you didn't hurt Tom."

His smile was lazy in his lean face. "Well I'm glad someone was thinking something positive about me. I don't deserve it—especially from you, Miss Dae. I can't tell you what a selfish idiot I felt like after the other night. I hope you know that wasn't me, not the real me. If I'd been in my right mind, I would never have done something like that to you. I wish Brickman would've hit me a little harder. I hope you can forgive me."

"Nothing to forgive," I told him. "I knew something was wrong with you. Do you know what happened?"

"I don't know." He pushed his hands through this hair. "It was like trying to think through cotton candy. I don't know if I had a breakdown or what. I finally woke up, and was me again."

"Maybe someone did all this to get you off your land." I thought about the nonchalant way Dr. Sheffield had acted about taking the land for the excavation. "Or not. Have you ever thought that you might be susceptible to psychic forces?"

He laughed. "I'm sorry. People have accused me of a lot of things, Dae, but that isn't one of them."

I explained how many of the things he'd said to me sounded like my visions from the past when the demon horses were being called.

"Demon horses?" He put his hand on my forehead. "Are you feeling all right?"

"The demon horses, whatever they are, may have killed Tom, but I don't believe they did it without direction."

"How does someone tell a horse that's not really there what to do? That's kind of outside my realm of experience. But if it happened, my money's on Sheffield. He's been the one pushing the whole time. He wants me out of there in the worst way."

I didn't go into the bad feelings I got from the excavation. He'd known how I felt about the horse statues. There was no way to really describe how much stronger I felt about them since going out to the site again.

"What do you think I should do?" he asked.

"I think we should check into Sheffield, and everyone else working out there. Someone wanted you and Tom out of the way. That could also be the same person summoning the demons. I know it sounds crazy, but I think they really exist."

"Whoa now. I don't think you should get involved any further in this. You've done enough, and I thank you for it. This is a killer we're talking about. I'll do the checking. It might be nice if I could call and talk to you about it from time-to-time, just to clear my mind. But your new fiancé won't thank me for putting your life in danger."

I didn't argue with him. I didn't plan to let him go it alone either. Maybe if we both checked into what we could, we could find some answers. "Do you need a ride back home?"

"No. Officer Tim brought me out here from Manteo and told me he'd get me to Corolla by the end of the day. I was glad to have a chance to talk to you." He put his hand on my shoulder. "Your friendship means a lot to me, Dae. I'm glad that hasn't been ruined by all this."

"Not at all." I pushed my hair out of my face where the strong breeze from the water had blown it. "We'll figure this out, Jake. I think we owe it to Tom."

He nodded, and said goodbye. I watched him leave the

boardwalk before I went back inside.

"I hope everything is all right," Mary Catherine said. "He seems like a very sincere man."

"He is, and he has a good heart. I'm not sure where to start to help him. How do you find murderous demon horses?"

She had been staring out the open door. "Maybe *he* could help." She pointed to Osisko who was perched on the boardwalk rail outside the shop.

"You can see him too?"

"I can right now. Is this the prehistoric man you were describing from your vision?"

"Yes. I've seen him all over the place. He was the man who first brought the demon horses out of the fire." I was relieved she could see him too. It made me feel less ridiculous. "I think he might be a shaman or something. He said he was a horse man. It was his affinity with the horses that helped him call them to kill neighboring tribes."

"A terrible burden to bear. No wonder he wants to make amends."

"Yes. He died to keep them from coming back, but now they're back anyway."

"Poor soul." She left Baylor in the shop, and closed the door so he wouldn't follow her.

We walked toward Osisko, and I searched for something to say. There had to be some way to communicate with him here as we did in his time during the vision.

"You've seen the horses, haven't you?" I asked him.

"Not the living horses."

He cocked his head and stared at me.

"The horses that come out of the fire." I tried again.

That time he nodded.

I sat on the bench near him. "How do we kill the demon horses?"

"Not die." He used the bone he was always holding to trace an image in the soft wood of the bench. It was a stick figure of a man holding a bone beside a large fire.

"They have to be called back." Mary Catherine interpreted. "Someone else had to call them. You were right, Dae."

He pounded the bone on the wood like he was applauding.

"I think he's telling us that someone called the demon horses and is sending them out to kill again."

"I think you're right," I agreed. "We have to find the person calling the horses. Someone knows the ceremony."

"Probably an archaeologist who researched the horse cult," she murmured. "Maybe someone who came here for this reason."

Osisko jumped up on the rail, precariously balanced. He crouched low as though ready to take on any threat. The charred bone was large, too big to be a human bone.

He pointed to my eyes with the bone. "You see."

"I need more than that," I said. "If we start a big fire, can you call them back? Should the big horse be buried again? I don't understand."

His expression was comical, as though he was talking to a small child that didn't understand. "You see." Osisko pounded the bone again and then jumped from the boardwalk rail into the Currituck Sound.

"Oh my goodness!" Mary Catherine exclaimed as we looked over the edge of the boardwalk.

There was no sign of him. No bubbles or splashing. If he was swimming away, I couldn't see him. "I'm glad you saw him, too, this time."

Mary Catherine stared out at the water. "I wish that made me feel better. What are we going to do, Dae?"

Chapter Nineteen

Duck town hall was filled to capacity that evening. Even Gramps was there in the crowd to see me sworn in for a second term as mayor.

I had to wear the official mayor's coat the seamstresses in town had created for special occasions. Lucky for me it was chilly and damp in November. The only other time I'd worn it was at the Fourth of July parade.

The heavy wool coat was too big for me, I assumed because no one had ever considered that a woman would be mayor. It seemed as though they'd made it for a large man like Mad Dog—maybe *for* Mad Dog. I'd wanted to ask them to take it in, but Gramps thought that was presumptuous. Maybe now that I was mayor for another term, I'd ask them for that favor. They could always let it back out when someone else became mayor after me.

The coat was meant to reflect our history with pirates. It was covered with red sashes and gold medallions that resembled pieces of eight. There were two red ribbons and real gold doubloons that went around my neck. The sleeves went past my wrists even though I was wearing a long-sleeved shirt with lace cuffs. We were Bankers—our ancestors had survived the harsh life at the Outer Banks to earn the title. These things were part of our heritage. I didn't want to mess with that.

With one hand on the oldest Bible in town, dated 1610, I took my second oath of office. I smiled at Kevin and Gramps in the audience and posed for pictures that would be posted online and put up in the new town hall building.

When I was officially mayor again, I used my gavel to bring the meeting to order. We all said the Pledge of Allegiance to the U.S. flag and then Nancy read the minutes from the last meeting. That brought us to new business.

The primary objective of new business that night was putting two temporary council members into the empty seats. I noticed right away that Mad Dog was sitting in front near the council dais. He had a big grin on his face as though giving him back in his old seat was all but done. I hoped he was wrong.

"The council will hear from citizens who wish to be considered for our two vacant seats," I explained to everyone. "There will be a deliberation after we've heard from every person who has told us their qualifications for the positions. Council will vote after that, with the mayor breaking any tie between the two seated councilmembers."

I hoped that was a suitable explanation of what would take place.

Our remaining councilmembers nodded their approval of my words. We were off to a good start—no one wanted to debate the proceedings.

Mad Dog was up first, of course. He approached the podium and leaned close to the microphone. "My name is Randal 'Mad Dog' Wilson. I grew up in Duck, as did every other member of my family for the last three hundred years. I helped bring about the town charter, and I've sat on the council since we became a town. I would still be seated but for a rule that required me to give up my place to run for mayor. A rule, I might mention, that I plan to change when I take my seat on the council again. Thank you."

There was a smattering of applause from some of his old buddies who'd no doubt voted for him to be mayor in the election. I brought my gavel down again for quiet.

Next up was Cody Baucum. He explained how he and his brother had come to live in Duck and open Wild Stallions. "I plan to live in Duck the rest of my life and raise my kids here. I want them to appreciate this wonderful place that I've come to know—without massive changes being brought by outsiders. I know Duck was incorporated as a city in the first place because you wanted to keep it the way it was. If I'm on the council, this will be my prime directive. Keep Duck small and prosperous! Thank you."

There was more applause for Cody, with a few boos from Mad Dog's friends.

I noticed that Martin Sheffield was in the audience. I was surprised to see him there since he technically didn't live here. Why would he be at one of our meetings when nothing we did would affect him? I could see if it was a Corolla meeting.

Jake was across the room from him giving Dr. Sheffield looks that could kill an elephant. Sheffield had a tougher hide. Kevin was staring at Jake as though he wanted him to go away as much as Jake wanted Dr. Sheffield to vanish.

I brought my focus back to the woman at the podium. Martha Segall was the town crank. If there was something she could possibly complain about, she complained. If not, she made something up to ridicule. She was telling everyone about being born and raised in Duck and how she'd clean up the messes made by everyone else on the town council.

August Grandin came up with his story and agenda after Martha. His platform was popular since it included doing away with all taxes for local businesses. There was strong applause for him. I saw the two council members beside me whispering after his introduction.

The last person who wanted to be considered for the council was our fire chief, Cailey Fargo. Her tone was confident and deliberate. She knew aspects of problems that would have to be considered by the council for any sustained growth. I recognized some of her ideas from meetings I'd had with Chris Slayton. The two were obviously on the same page. I didn't think that was a bad thing.

"Thank you for volunteering for these positions," I said when the room was quiet. "We'll take a fifteen minute recess and give you our choices for council members when we return."

"Fifteen minutes?" Mad Dog shouted. "It seems to me a choice as important as this one should take more time."

"I'd like to remind everyone that whoever takes these council seats tonight will have to run for election in eighteen months. If you're not happy with our choices, you can vote them out and run for office yourself. Thank you. There's coffee and hot tea in the ante-room, and I think we have some goodies from Duck's Donuts." I hoped everyone had paid attention to what I said. It seemed they did when people started moving out of the council room to grab a hot drink.

I opened the door to my office. It had been a large storage room when I'd first become mayor. It had a good window that overlooked the water. I'd had it painted a nice, watery blue and put in all the nautical related artifacts I could find. I had a ship's bell from a freighter that had gone down in a storm in the early 1800s, and other reminders that Duck had prospered—and been destroyed many times—by our proximity to the water.

Council member Dab Efird immediately made himself

clear about putting Mad Dog back into office. "He might win in the next election, but it won't be with my help. We need some fresh thinking on the council."

I was delighted when Council member Rick Treyburn agreed with him. "I'd prefer someone who is business oriented, like Cody Baucum."

"He's so young," Dab debated. "What about Cailey Fargo? She's earned her keep around here for many years. I think she'd be good for Duck."

Rick wasn't sure about that idea. "I think our fire chief might try to influence our spending. What about August? He's kept the General Store open for years. He'd be good with finances."

"But he's so old," Dab said. "I could go along with Cody, I guess—if you could go along with Cailey. I think we'd find she'd do a good job without involving the fire department."

"I could do that," Rick agreed. "As the mayor reminded us, we'll all be up for election in eighteen months."

"What do you think, Madam Mayor?" Dab asked. "You seem to have the most recent take on what people are looking for since you've just won re-election. What about it?"

"I'm happy to agree with both of you," I said. "I think Cody would give us a younger perspective that would be useful moving into the future, and Cailey has always had a good head on her shoulders. Don't forget that she hasn't always been fire chief. I think the two of them would be good for Duck."

"All right." Rick grinned. "I guess we're agreed." The two men shook hands.

"But we can't go in and announce our decision yet." Dab glanced at his watch. "If Mad Dog is unhappy with the idea of a fifteen minute decision, think how unhappy he'll be with a five minute decision."

So we agreed to sit in my office for the full fifteen minutes. We talked about the Christmas celebration and the next item up, which would be old business. We couldn't discuss it too much outside the council room or that would be a violation of our oaths of office. I had no idea how these two men would vote on the proposal to allow a gambling ship to dock close to the Blue Whale. Cody and Cailey's decision on that was a mystery too.

I still wasn't sure how I felt about it. Part of me felt like Gramps and Sheriff Riley—I wasn't sure a gambling ship was what the town needed. On the other hand, it might make a difference to getting more local businesses to stay open during the winter months when everything usually closed.

At the end of fifteen minutes, we went back to the council room where people were beginning to take their seats. Nancy handed me a note from Dr. Sheffield. He was asking for a few minutes of my time after the meeting. That explained why he was there, but I couldn't imagine what he'd have to say that would make him sit through town business.

I banged my gavel and re-opened the meeting. When the room got still, I announced our decision to have Cailey and Cody on the town council.

Mad Dog was furious. He pushed his bulky six-foot-six, three-hundred pound body up quickly from his chair. "And this is what we can expect for the next eighteen months? A lot of nothing."

He exited the room with a few of his friends. Gramps gave me a thumbs-up on the council members we'd chosen. I didn't see Dr. Sheffield as the second part of the meeting got underway. Maybe he was waiting for me outside. Jake smiled and waved before he left.

"On to old business," I said after the new council members had been sworn-in and taken their seats. "Mr. Bullard is here representing the interests backing the gambling ship that wants to dock in Duck. You have the floor, Mr. Bullard."

Mr. Bullard and Chris started a presentation that included the possible income the town could expect from the gambling ship, and well-documented information from other small towns that had embraced a similar situation.

Bullard was a short, round man who kept mopping his brow with a white handkerchief. He had an excellent voice and presentation manner though, and his PowerPoint ended with an image of what the gambling ship would look like. The image was that of a pirate ship, with modern conveniences, of course. The ship would go out twelve miles each day to allow its patrons to gamble on slot machines, drink, and eat.

What sold his pitch was the ship. It had been modeled to look like the 1720's Spanish treasure ship that haunted our shores, the *Andalusia*. People in the room broke out into excited applause when they saw it.

Chief Michaels stood, and held out his hands for silence. "I know you all are excited about the idea of the gambling ship, especially now that you've seen it. Yes, it has clever marketing, but what's going to be the cost to the soul of Duck if they put it in here?"

Sheriff Riley got to his feet beside him. "They have facts and statistics that say how much Duck will prosper by allowing them to dock here. We have facts and statistics from some of the other coastal towns that have gone along with this idea. It's not a pretty picture like they paint. Crime of all kinds from burglary to assault, even rape, goes up when the gambling ship opens. I don't live here in Duck, but I'd hate to see this happen to you."

Luke Helms was there too. "I've seen the evidence the sheriff and our police chief are discussing. I may be the Dare County DA, but I live here in Duck too. I implore the council to vote against the gambling ship being allowed to dock here. Thank you for your time."

"Gentlemen, your remarks are improper until after our guest has finished his presentation," I said. "Continue, Mr. Bullard."

"I'm finished, Mayor O'Donnell. That concludes my presentation. Thank you for allowing me to show you what we have."

Dab Efird nodded. "I like the sound of this, Mr. Bullard. How long are we talking about between us giving our approval and the ship setting up here?"

"Probably six to nine months." Mr. Bullard was packing up his materials.

Cody Baucum smiled. "I can imagine how great this could be for Duck."

Chris Slayton stood up to address us. "Mayor and town council members, staff recommends that we table the idea until we have a chance to fully examine the statistics that have been given to us by law enforcement this evening."

"Thank you, Chris," I said.

"Madam Mayor," Rick Treyburn began. "With all due respect to Mr. Slayton, our town manager, we've already put off the vote on this project. I think we should take it up right now."

I shrugged at Chris as he sat down. "All right. All those for the project, please say aye."

There was no reason to call for the nays. All four council members voted unanimously to allow the gambling ship to dock in town. My vote on the matter didn't count since I was only allowed to break ties.

The gavel came down on the matter. "The ayes have it. Welcome to Duck, Mr. Bullard."

The man smiled back at me. "Thank you."

"And God have mercy if our worst fears come to unfold," Sheriff Riley said before dramatically storming out of the meeting.

Chapter Twenty

There was no more business, so. I closed the meeting. A large number of people were excited about the gambling ship. They flocked into the ante-room where the donuts were still plentiful and the coffee was flowing.

"I'm not sure how I feel about it," Kevin said when I reached him. He was seated in a chair beside Gramps. "Maybe that's my law enforcement background warring with my innkeeper's persona."

"You only need common sense to see where this is going," Gramps ranted. "What do people think will happen when a few thousand gamblers show up every month?

Obviously crime will skyrocket. I don't think the benefits to the economy will outweigh the other aspects."

"Well, it's done now," I said. "I'm exhausted. Let's go home."

Kevin offered to drive me and Mary Catherine back to our house.

Gramps didn't want to get in the golf cart with his broken leg. His friend, who'd brought him to the meeting, was still there and would take him home. "I might as well eat some donuts." He smiled and hugged me. "I really only came to see Dae sworn in again as mayor. I'm proud of you, honey."

"Thanks, Gramps."

There were dozens of Duck residents standing around on the boardwalk, talking about the meeting. Some called out good wishes as we walked by going to the parking lot. I saw that Sheriff Riley and Chief Michaels had cornered Mr. Bullard before he could leave. The gambling ship might be on its way to Duck, but it was going to be one of the safest ships they ever ran.

I looked for Dr. Sheffield, but didn't see him anywhere inside or on the boardwalk.

It was very cold, with the wind blowing off the icy water. Mary Catherine had left Baylor behind and shivered in the night air. "You get used to having that hot-blooded scoundrel around your shoulders all the time. I wish I had him with me now."

"I'll turn on the heat in the golf cart," Kevin volunteered as we went down the stairs.

All the lights were on inside the bookstore and coffee shop in the parking lot. No doubt there were plenty of people debating the merits of allowing the ship in Duck as well as the choice for new council members.

I heard a sound like thunder in the distance. The fine hairs on my arms and neck stood up as the sound came closer.

"Must be a storm on the way." Kevin took out his keys

for the golf cart.

"Not a storm," I told him. "It's the horses."

The windows in nearby shops rattled with the force of the invisible horses passing in the night. The trees and bushes swayed with the pounding of their movements. Mary Catherine grabbed my arm, her hands trembling, and two car alarms went off in the parking lot.

"I can't see them, but look at the road." Kevin pointed. "Where are those sparks coming from?"

"The horses' hooves. They strike the ground with such force that it causes sparks," I explained, not taking my eyes from the road. "They're flaming when they first emerge from the fire."

People came out of the coffee shop to see what was going on. A few others came down the stairs from the boardwalk. The horses continued by in a steady, freight train cacophony.

"What the hell is that, Dae?" Mad Dog asked as he walked into the parking lot.

"Demon horses from Corolla," I answered him honestly. "They run up and down the roads every night between here and there. I don't know why."

"Demon horses?" Martha Segall said. "That's crazy. Is that what keeps running down my plants and tearing up my yard?"

"Yes."

"*Bah*. Whoever heard of such a thing?" She walked away, but didn't try to leave the parking lot to walk down Duck Road to her house. It wasn't *that* crazy.

Mary Catherine tugged at my sleeve. "What's that in the middle of the street? I don't think that's a demon horse, do you?"

By now the parking lot was full of Duck citizens and visitors. Chief Michaels and Sheriff Riley walked out just as the horses had passed us. The night was so quiet when the horses were gone—not a bird cried from under an eave. No dogs barked.

"What's that in the road, Sheriff?" Mrs. Euly Stanley asked. She was a frail, older woman with a will of iron who ran the board of directors at the Duck History Museum.

Sheriff Riley strode into the street, followed quickly by two of his deputies.

"Now what?" Chief Michaels asked as he descended the stairs a few moments later. "Don't tell me we've got another horse hit and run."

"I don't know," I told him. "I'm sure Sheriff Riley will let us know in a minute."

Chief Michaels jogged out to the street. The two men crouched close to what they'd found and then stood up to discuss it.

One of the sheriff's deputies returned to the parking lot. "Sheriff Riley says everyone here has to stay put for now. Looks like another dead man in the road."

* * *

The coffee shop stayed open for people who were trapped there waiting for the county medical examiner to arrive. Mary Catherine, Kevin, and I waited it out in the golf cart so we could see what was going on. Even with the lights from the parking lot around us, it was hard to tell what everyone was doing on the road. Chief Michaels had called Tim to help him. They lit flares, and kept traffic moving around the crime scene.

Our other Duck police officer, Scott Randall, knocked on the plastic that surrounded the sides of the golf cart keeping out most of the cool night air. "Mayor O'Donnell—the chief wants to know if you and Mr. Brickman will help take statements from everyone who was here when the man on the road was found."

I knew Kevin had been deputized the first year he'd been in Duck. It was helpful to sign people up before emergencies. There were more than a hundred deputized civilians in town. I was one of them, too. I had been since I was eighteen. People expected it from the sheriff's granddaughter.

"Sure, Scott," I said. "Who's that on the road?"

"Sorry, ma'am. The chief told me to keep my mouth shut about that." Scott was a quiet young man with gentle brown eyes. He seemed less likely to be a police officer than anyone I knew.

"Okay. I don't want to get you into trouble. We'll start taking names and getting contact information."

"Thank you, Mayor." He nodded to Kevin. "Mr. Brickman."

"You should've held out," Mary Catherine said. "If you'd said no until he told you what you wanted to know, he would've told you."

"I'm not curious enough to risk losing Scott on the police force," I explained. "His feelings get hurt really easy."

Her smile made her look a lot like her cat. "And such a handsome young man."

I ignored that remark and took two yellow legal pads from my bag that I always brought to town meetings. I handed one to Kevin.

"I'll start in the coffee shop," he said. "Maybe that will keep us from getting duplicates. Meet you out here."

"Sounds good." I kissed him lightly. "You don't think I should have been mean to Scott, do you?"

"It would be interesting to know who it is." He shook his head. "But I like Scott too, and you're right about him."

Mary Catherine stayed in the golf cart. Gramps called to find out why I wasn't home yet. I was glad he'd made it out of the parking lot before the horses, and the dead person. I guessed that automatically laid out a short window of opportunity for whatever had happened on the road. Gramps had only been gone about ten minutes before we'd reached the parking lot.

I went back up to the boardwalk and started telling everyone what had happened. Chris Slayton was also deputized. He took a sheet of paper and started writing down the names of people who were left in the ante-room finishing the donuts. The meeting room was empty, except for Nancy who was cleaning up after the crowd.

"Another dead man on the road?" Her dark brows shot up. "Are we having some kind of crime wave before the gambling ship even gets here?"

"I don't know yet. This is all the information I have."

"I'll just start transcribing my notes from the meeting," she said with a sigh. "Maybe it will all be over by the time I'm done."

"I hope so. Thanks, Nancy."

"Just be careful out there, Dae. Trouble likes to follow you sometimes."

I told her I'd be fine, and started out on the boardwalk to write more names. I noticed the lights were on at Wild Stallions—probably Cody and his family celebrating. I walked down there to share what had happened and take down their names. It almost seemed redundant since we all knew where they lived and worked.

Cody was nervous after I'd told him about the second dead person on Duck Road. "I hope this isn't a bad sign," he said. "We just said it was okay for the gambling ship to come in. I don't want people to think I'm soft on crime."

His brother, Reese, who was a few years older, chided him. "Don't get all paranoid. I'm sure there's a good explanation for it. And if there's not, that's on the police, not you. The gambling ship is gonna be good for all of us, right Dae?"

I really didn't want to talk about my mixed feelings on the subject, but I thought I had to say something. "I live with the former sheriff, and I'm engaged to an ex-FBI agent. I'm not sure what to say about the gambling ship yet. I'm hoping we can come up with some good plans to keep those bad things from happening in Duck."

Reece laughed and hugged me. "And that's why she just won re-election as mayor, folks. It's not about what goes wrong, Cody. It's about how you handle it. Just don't freak out and say something you'll regret about whatever has happened."

Cody's wife was standing beside him. She held his hand,

and smiled up at him.

"I'll try not to say anything" Cody said. "You have what you need, right Dae?"

"Sure. Thanks."

Cody and Sally's little girl started crying. The after-the-meeting party was breaking up. I left Wild Stallions to see who else was on the boardwalk.

Mad Dog was still there, of course, seated on a bench spouting his usual rhetoric about the town being run badly. Cole Black and his wife, Molly, were there listening. So was Mark Samson from the Rib Shack and August Grandin.

"And there's our new mayor," Mad Dog said as I quickly wrote their names and tried to walk by unnoticed. "I keep wondering if anyone else is ever gonna notice how our murder rate has gone up since she became mayor."

"Leave the girl alone," Molly said. "Dae's done a good job for us. It's nothing on her that we've started having so many new people come in. It's not like she can close Duck off to the rest of the world."

I thanked her. "I guess I might as well be the one to tell you that there's another dead man on Duck Road. I don't know who it is yet or how he got there. That's why I'm taking names."

Mad Dog slapped his thigh. "That's what I'm talking about. Horses trampling the yards, and killing people in the street. What's your plan to prevent this from happening again, Madam Mayor?"

"I don't have one right now. I don't think anyone does. But if you come up with one, Mr. Wilson, I'm sure everyone will be happy to listen. Goodnight."

I walked away from the group, but Mark Samson hooted. "I guess she told you, Mad Dog. That girl has some spunk."

Chris met me at the end of the boardwalk with his list. "We had a good crowd tonight. I counted fifty people. I wish the council would've voted to hold off on the gambling ship. Jamie and Phil are excited about the idea—I'm just not sure. I've done a lot of research, but I only got those crime statistics tonight. There was no time to check into them."

I put my hand on his shoulder. "You gave the best recommendation you could with the information you had. You advised caution until we knew more about the project. That was all you could do."

"Thanks, Dae." He smiled as he handed me his list of names. "I'm glad you're going to be mayor again for another term. I'm honored to work with you."

"Wow. I appreciate it. Let's not get too mushy. I got my Christmas decorations up today. Nothing like Cody and Reece, or even Kevin, but I'm excited about the OBX Christmas plans."

"Me too. We're putting the decorations up on the coffee house and bookstore this weekend, if the weather holds. We're going to put everyone else to shame anyway," he bragged. "Jamie says we're gonna win the contest, and that's that."

I laughed as I left him there and walked down the boardwalk stairs to meet Kevin in the parking lot. I stopped abruptly when I saw his golf cart with Mary Catherine inside. There were at least fifty cats on the front, sides, and back. I was pretty sure she hadn't even noticed. She was on her cell phone, and looking out at Duck Road.

"Yeah." Kevin grinned as we met. "How do animals find her anyway? You think it's a pheromone thing?"

"I don't know. I think they sense she can understand them. Maybe they have something to say."

"Maybe so. I guess we should give these names to Chief Michaels."

"Good idea." I linked one arm through his. "We can find out what happened at the same time. He won't mind. After all, we're deputized, right?"

"If you say so."

We walked together to the road where the smell of burning flares made my nose twitch. More deputies had been called, and I saw Chief Palo's car parked at the edge of the pavement. What was she doing here?

"Brickman," Chief Michaels acknowledged him. "You got those names for me?"

Kevin took my list and added it to his. "What's going on?"

"Is Jake Burleson on one of those lists?"

"I didn't see him." Kevin turned to me. "Did you, Dae?"

"No. I saw him in town hall during the meeting, but not after. He walked out right after Dr. Sheffield."

"I saw him there too," Chief Michaels said in a gruff voice. "Looks like they let him out too soon. His business with the archeologist wasn't over yet. That's Dr. Sheffield under that tarp over there. He's dead just like the other man Burleson didn't like anymore—Tom Watts."

Chapter Twenty-one

"That's why Chief Palo is here," I muttered as I turned away from the scene.

"Jake's going to have a hard time getting out of this," Kevin whispered. "Why was he at one of our meetings anyway?"

"I think he just wanted to wish me well." I dug the note Nancy had given me out of my pocket. "Dr. Sheffield wanted to talk to me after the meeting."

Kevin glanced around the parking lot. "So where's Jake?"

"Maybe he left early like Gramps." I shrugged. "Just

because Dr. Sheffield is dead doesn't mean Jake did it."

"I can't imagine a single lawman who would agree with that supposition right now. I know Horace and Ronnie won't. Jake was here. He had access and motive."

"What's his motive?"

"The same as it was for Tom—getting them off his property."

"Things aren't always the way they appear, as with Tom. If Jake were going to kill Dr. Sheffield, why announce to the world that he was here by waving to me from the audience?"

"I don't know, Dae," he admitted. "But I'm not buying that Dr. Sheffield was killed by marauding demon horses."

"I think someone sent them to kill Dr. Sheffield."

"Even though we know they didn't kill Tom?"

"Mary Catherine and I saw Osisko today. We sort of talked to him."

"What did he say?"

"The same thing he said when I saw him in the vision. I can stop the demons, but I don't understand how. I think he said someone is controlling them. I guess it's not Dr. Sheffield."

We got in the golf cart with Mary Catherine. "I was wondering what you two were doing out there," she said.

"I could ask you the same thing." I smiled and opened the side of the golf cart so she could see what I meant. "You have your own cattery."

"Oh my stars!" Her eyes and face were full of delight to see the large number of cats perched on and around the golf cart. "I didn't even notice them. For the most part, a cat's thoughts are as quiet as their movements, except for Baylor, of course. He's noisy inside and out. I never have to wonder what he's thinking."

"What are they thinking?" Kevin stared at the cats.

"They're scared," Mary Catherine told him. "The horses frighten them. They'd like to leave Duck as so many of the dogs have, but they're attached to certain people they can't abandon."

"Did they see what happened to Dr. Sheffield?" I asked.

"Is that who's on the road? Is he dead?"

Kevin nodded. "It looks like Jake Burleson again. But as Dae reminded me, it looked like Jake did it last time too."

Mary Catherine was silent for a moment with her eyes closed. "All the cats are scared. They didn't see the man die, but they felt the presence of the horses. They think there will be other deaths."

"Great," Kevin muttered. "What are we supposed to do against demon horses we can't see?"

I was staring off into the brush that surrounded the parking lot. The overhead lights picked out a familiar figure. "There's Osisko. He has a way of popping up at bad times."

Kevin couldn't see him. "Are you sure? I don't see anything."

"I see him. Don't you think you should get a net or something?" Mary Catherine asked. "He was jumping around like a gazelle on the boardwalk earlier."

"We can't capture him. He has something else to say. I need to talk to him."

Kevin was skeptical. "How do you know it's not Osisko that's responsible for everything, Dae? Maybe he's just leading you on."

"He's not. He died to keep this from happening, Kevin. He wants to stop it again. He's here to help us."

"All right. Take Mary Catherine with you since she can see him too. Don't take unnecessary chances—and don't let him touch you. We know how that ended last time."

I told him I'd be careful. I wasn't sure how Mary Catherine felt about approaching Osisko again, but she climbed out of the golf cart with me.

We approached him cautiously. "Hello again."

He nodded, hopping from one foot to another with the charred bone in his hand.

"I was wondering if you saw what happened with the horses."

"Death."

"You're right. But did you see the demons? Can you see them?"

"What's he saying, Dae?" Mary Catherine whispered. "How can you understand him?"

"I'm not sure. I guess we're on the same wavelength."

He started toward me with his hand outstretched.

I took a step back. "No. Not again. Tell me what I need to know."

He pounded his chest and shrieked.

I understood his frustration. "I'm sorry I can't understand everything you're saying."

He closed his eyes, and covered them with his hands. "You. Me. The same."

That made me want to run back to the golf cart and forget the whole idea. At the same time, I understood what he was saying. He'd purposely touched me at the hospital because he and I shared a similar gift. He could be one of my ancestors, maybe the first with the gift.

"No. I can't do it again. Just tell me. I'll get it."

He shook his head. "No. You see."

"Dae, I think we should go back to the parking lot," Mary Catherine said. "He seems to be getting worked up."

I thought about it for a moment, debating what my next move should be. What if the only way to understand what he was saying was for me to touch him? I had to know what was going on.

It would've been a lie to say that I wasn't afraid. There was always the fear of being trapped in that other place where my visions took me. But I knew I might be the only person who could end the problem we were having. I had to take the chance.

"Okay. Hurry. Let's get this over with."

"Are you going to touch him?" Mary Catherine asked, horrified. "Didn't Kevin say that was a bad thing?"

I braced myself for the contact, but was surprised when he smiled kindly, and took my hands in his. The world tilted and spun away from me. No words were necessary to tell me that I was back in the past again.

There were hundreds of torches and a huge fire in the middle of the pit. It was the same scene as before. People danced in the light, and caressed the big horse. Shadows of flames moved across the runes marked in the stone. Overhead, a full moon watched the proceedings on earth.

The ocean was much closer than it was in present day. The land was swampy, sucking at the dancers' feet as they twirled and dipped around the fire. A constant drumming sound came from wood stick being beaten against a hollow log.

I looked for my companion. He was still there beside me, clutching one of my hands. We didn't speak. I understood what was going on without him telling me.

There was an apex to the dancers' frenzied movements. They dropped to the sandy ground around the fire and the drumming ceased. Out from the shadows came Osisko. He was much younger, barely more than a child. He was also completely naked, his thin body glistening in the moonlight. He raised his arms and threw back his head to shout the ancient summoning at the moon.

It was only a moment before the demons answered his call. From the depths of the fire, they came from the earth below. Their heads and necks twisted as they pushed at one another. Their hooves and legs competed for space as they tried to be the first ones out.

I couldn't understand the words Osisko was screaming, but I could see it excited and pulled at the demons. He didn't stop until the first horses were formed in the sizzling red and black skins. Their hooves struck the ground creating sparks and fire where they met the earth. Their yellow eyes stared balefully around them at the night.

The young Osisko stopped the summoning. He stared into those evil yellow eyes, and called out the name of another tribe, pointing in the direction he wanted them to go. The demons ran off, but young Osisko stopped the new demons who tried to struggle out of the fire.

"That's how we stop them?" The words were hoarse from my throat.

The shaman and the dancers stared at me. They'd heard what I'd said. As they advanced toward me, the version of Osisko who'd died for his sins, pulled at my hand.

"Go. Go now!" he yelled.

"Dae? Dae? Are you all right?" It was Kevin. "Where's the man? Where's Osisko?"

It was difficult to catch my breath. It felt like I'd run for miles. Tears were streaming down my face. My mind was so full of the evil horse demons that I could barely think.

"Sorry. He's gone. He held my hands. Osisko controlled the demons then. Someone controls them now. We have to find out who it is."

"We will," Kevin promised as he put his arms around me. "You weren't supposed to touch him."

"I couldn't help it," I whispered against his shoulder. "It was the only way. He can't explain and I can't see it without him. I know—I think I know—how to stop it. He was showing me the scene for a reason. The horses can be sent back."

We walked back to the golf cart. Duck Road was clear enough that people were leaving the parking lot.

Mary Catherine was anxiously awaiting us. "I'm sorry, Dae. I thought it was better to get Kevin. Are you all right?"

"I'm fine," I assured her. "Thanks."

"I think they came for the body. The police are directing traffic out of here. Now might be a good time to leave."

I told her what had happened as we got back in the golf cart. "All that power and anger. They could take out entire tribes in a night. That was why they finally realized that they had to bury the horse statue and not summon the demons again."

"But why Mr. Watts and Dr. Sheffield?" she asked. "Whoever is doing this must want the excavation to continue. Why kill them, and not Jake?"

"I still don't believe that the horses killed them," Kevin

said. "Maybe the person summoning the horses today isn't to that level yet where he can use them to kill people. We know from the evidence that there was only one hoof print on Tom that struck the fatal blow. I doubt if even a demon horse can be that agile."

"Even so," she argued. "Why not kill Jake since he's the instigator?"

"It's gotta be the opposite," Kevin said. "The shaman summoning the demons doesn't want the dig to continue."

"But why?" I asked as we were finally rolling down Duck Road toward my house.

"I think that's something you'll have to ask him when we find him," Kevin said.

"Are there any plans to do that?" Mary Catherine wondered.

"Not yet," I replied. "But I think we'd better come up with one fast."

Chapter Twenty-two

Gramps was still up when we got back. He wanted to hear everything about what had happened. I gave him a little more information than he was ready for when I told him about Osisko.

"Kevin, I thought you were going to keep her from doing that kind of thing," he remarked. "It could've been much worse."

"We talked about it, Horace," Kevin said. "You know her. She does what she thinks she should."

Horace frowned. "What are you going to do now?"

"I've thought about it since we left the parking lot," I

told him. "I think we have to catch the present day shaman in the act of summoning the demon horses."

Mary Catherine laughed. "You've thought all of fifteen or twenty minutes and come up with a plan that may get you killed?"

"It makes sense. There are a lot of people working out there. It could be any of them—we know nothing about the workers. One of them might have come just to control the demons," I explained. "We could question them, but I doubt they would admit to it. This is the last night of the full moon. In both visions, they summoned the demons during the full moon."

"Can you hear yourself describing a plan to catch someone who uses demon horses to kill people?" Gramps asked. "It's crazy."

"That's why I'm talking to you about it," I argued. "Chief Michaels couldn't handle this and neither could Sheriff Riley. But you understand these things because of Grandma Eleanore. You know they're real. Kevin too. You have law enforcement smarts, but you can also see the other side."

Gramps shook his head. "Better put on some coffee. I think best with a cup in my hand."

As we started planning, I could see that he hated that he couldn't be at the site with us, but he was willing to help us get it together. So was Kevin.

"You have to assume there might be more than just the shaman who's summoning the demons." Gramps held a cup of strong hot coffee. "All of those diggers out there could be his accomplices."

Kevin agreed. "It will be harder now that Dr. Sheffield is gone, but we should try to get a list of the men and women working there. If we consider that they could be involved, numbers can make a difference."

"We don't have time for that. It will be another month until the next full moon. We're not going to be able to come up with anything near the number of people working out there," I reminded him. "Right now there's me and you."

"And me," Mary Catherine said. "I know I don't look like I could bring much to a fight, but I can call the wild horses and every other animal on the island to help us. I can be quite formidable if I put my mind to it."

Gramps smiled and squeezed her hand. "I'll say. You knocked me down when I wasn't looking."

Mary Catherine kissed his cheek, and I went to get a package of chocolate chip cookies. It was so wonderful to see them look at each other that way.

There was a knock on the front door, and I veered from the kitchen to answer it.

Jake was standing on the porch. "Can I come in?"

I opened the door wider and peered outside. "Everyone is looking for you. They think you killed Dr. Sheffield."

He snorted. "What else is new? I guess from now on if anyone dies around here, it's gonna be my fault."

"Especially when it looks like you're the one with the most motive," Kevin said.

Jake stopped. "I'll come back later, Dae. I don't want to interrupt anything."

"You might as well come in." I closed the door. "We're talking about something that concerns you—getting rid of the demon horses."

I wasn't sure how he'd take it. For a moment he was uncertain, but then he relaxed. "Well why didn't you say so? Do you folks know more about them than I do? All I know is that they want to destroy everything. I could feel it as they dug up the big horse statue. I just can't figure out why."

"Get a cup of coffee," Gramps invited. "Dae will enlighten you."

Jake went to the coffeemaker. "Got anything stronger?"

"I think we'd best keep it straight," Mary Catherine said. "We need our heads about us to get through it."

While the cookies were being passed around, Jake took a seat with a cup of coffee. I ran through all my visions, and the information about Osisko. "I know now what I'm seeing, what he's trying to tell me. We're coming up with a plan to catch the present day shaman who summoned the horses—maybe to kill Tom and Dr. Sheffield—maybe to create a distraction so he could kill them. We could use another person to help out."

"You know there's nothing I wouldn't do for you, darlin'," Jake drawled. "But how do we fight something we can't see?"

Kevin's eyes narrowed at Jake's endearment, but he ignored it. "We can see the people doing the magic. That's who we need to stop."

"Makes sense," Jake agreed. "Who do we like for this shaman fella?"

"We don't know," I admitted. "All I've seen is the one from the past. Maybe Osisko can help us. He knows exactly what's going on. He's just not great on explaining it."

"But he's real, right?" Jake asked. "He's not like a ghost or something, is he?"

"Not exactly," I said. "Mary Catherine saw him too."

"But she talks to animals." Jake smiled at her. "No offense, ma'am."

"I'm not a bit offended by what I do." She smiled back at him. "Speaking with animals doesn't make me crazy, if that's what you're worried about."

There was another knock on the front door and I went to answer it—it was Chief Palo.

"Dae." She nodded and looked past me into the crowded living room. "Jake. I've been looking for you."

"You have to hear what they have to say before you take me in again, Chief. It may sound a little crazy, but it's what I've been trying to tell everyone for the past few weeks."

Chief Palo took off her hat and jacket. "All right. You've got five minutes."

Five minutes later, she was overwhelmed and skeptical about my information. "And you believe this?" she asked Gramps and Kevin. "Sheriff Riley explained about Dae's 'gifts', but he never mentioned anything like this."

"I was sheriff for many years. I was a deputy for even longer. I've seen and heard some crazy things that many people didn't believe," Gramps said. "My granddaughter has been right more times than she's been wrong about some things. I don't pretend to understand it, but I know it happens."

"Sheriff Riley and Chief Michaels are never going to believe it," Palo flatly stated.

"They will when it's real," I told her. "They always do. They don't like it, but they believe it."

Chief Palo shook her head. "What can I do to help?"

"We don't have a lot of time, or many people to get this done," I said. "If you help—and you ignore Jake for a while—maybe by tomorrow it will be over."

She stared at Jake. "All right. I'll help. But Jake, you'd better be standing right next to me the whole time. If you're playing me for a fool, I'll make sure you don't get out of jail again."

He nodded. "I'm not going anywhere, ma'am. I want to stop these weird people from trying to wreck Duck and Corolla, and I want my home back."

"Then let me grab a cup of coffee, and you can fill me in on what we're planning to do."

I did most of the talking, but Gramps and Kevin jumped in to help plan the strategy.

"You'll have to catch them summoning the horses, doing something tangible," Chief Palo added. "No one is going to believe it if we don't."

"Agreed." Kevin drew a rough map of Jake's property.

"I could've done that, boyfriend," Jake said.

"Maybe," Kevin agreed. "But I thought of it first, cowboy."

Jake added information to Kevin's map, pointing out the possible areas where the summoning could take place. "The only thing I don't get is why they'd summon the demon horses again tonight after already accomplishing Sheffield's death."

"I think that's where you come in." Kevin slapped him on the back. "You have to make them want to summon the horses again to kill you."

"Me?" Jake asked. "It seems like they would've already done that if they'd wanted me dead."

"We have to figure out why they summoned the horses to kill Tom and Dr. Sheffield and not you," I said. "Anything come to mind that might help?"

"What about the note from Dr. Sheffield?" Mary Catherine reminded me. "What did he say?"

I'd almost forgotten the note Nancy had given me at the meeting. I found it in my pocket and read it again. "He said he wanted to talk about the big horse being sent to Raleigh."

"Why would he want to talk to you about it?" Gramps asked.

Kevin took a look at the note. "That's it? Why was that so urgent?"

Jake thought about it. "I don't think some of the workers out there are happy about it. I heard him arguing with Duran. I didn't pay much attention then but now, I wonder if that's why Sheffield was killed. If they plan to use the big horse to raise these demons, taking it away would be a bad thing."

"That makes sense," Chief Palo said.

"What if Tom died because of his close association with the wild horses?" Mary Catherine suggested. "I can tell you that the horses are devastated by his death. They really considered him a dear friend and loyal to their cause. What if the man summoning the demon horses doesn't want the real horses around for whatever he has planned?"

Gramps nodded. "That could be true, as much as any of this. Jake is close to the horses, but Tom lived and breathed for them. If they don't want the wild horses here, getting rid of him would be a good idea."

Jake sipped his coffee. "Tom was the one who got the grants to keep working with the horses. He fed them, and found medicine for them. I could see where his death could cause the area to lose the wild horse population. It's already a struggle to keep them here."

"But why wouldn't the shaman of the demon horses—I can't believe I just said that—want the other horses here?" Chief Palo bit her lip to repress a smile.

"We don't know their complete history," Mary Catherine said. "But I do know that the horses I spoke with resent having the demons here. Maybe they were partially responsible for the cult disappearing."

"I can't believe you said that with a straight face." Jake laughed. "If I didn't know better, I'd think we were all out of our minds."

"Saying we're not insane," Kevin continued, "what could they have in mind? What can you do with demon horses? It's not like it was a thousand years ago. They run up and down the road and wreck furniture. I don't think they'd stand up well to an AK47."

"There must be something more to it than that," I said. "Maybe they aren't at full power yet."

"Or this shaman fella doesn't get it," Chief Palo added. "If he's trying to pull demon horses out of a fire, he's not exactly living in our times, is he?"

"That's true," Mary Catherine considered.

"So you go in as they're doing this ritual, guns blazing?" Gramps met my gaze. "I don't think much of that plan."

"It could make them move faster. They don't have much time left tonight." I glanced at the full moon hanging above us in a misty white gauze.

"Say I go in and rile these people up," Jake said. "What happens next?"

"Horace is right," Kevin said. "It's not much of a plan—but it's all we have. Let's say we stop this shaman from summoning the horses tonight, and somehow, the authorities believe us and put some of them in jail. It would be a misdemeanor charge at best. The legal system won't be able to hold them for practicing magic. We have to do something to prevent it from happening again."

"We'll have to destroy the big horse," I told them.

"Nothing started happening until they'd dug it up. I don't know how to get a legal conviction against the person summoning them or those helping him. But at least we can stop the demons. That's probably the best we can do."

"I think I missed the part about how to actually stop the demons." Jake scratched his chin. "Do we know how to do that?"

I took a deep breath. "I think Osisko will help me."

"So you're getting rid of the demons?" Kevin asked.

"I don't think so," Gramps chimed in.

"Let's take it one step at a time, huh?" I didn't want everyone falling apart before we even got to Corolla. I was convinced this was the right thing to do, but I had to keep my team together.

Everyone studied the crudely drawn map on the kitchen table. Kevin began to assign roles to the participants. He had Jake going in by himself. I pointed out that two people should go in together.

"Who did you have in mind to go in with him?" Kevin asked.

"I think you should go in with him," I responded.

Both men had a dozen reasons why that wouldn't work. They didn't sound valid to me. "Jake needs someone with him in case the reaction is bad from the shaman," I told them. "You'd be good for that, Kevin."

"I could go with Jake," Chief Palo volunteered.

She'd barely spoken when she got a call. "There's a bad wreck on Highway Twelve in Corolla. It shouldn't take long to clear it up. Can you wait for me?"

I didn't know what to say. After she left to answer the call, the idea of waiting started making me nervous. If this wasn't resolved tonight, who knew what could happen during the month between? Jake could go to jail. Whoever was taking over the excavation from Dr. Sheffield could move matters up to a point where it would be even more difficult to destroy the cult.

"I know what you're thinking, Dae," Gramps said.

"There aren't enough of you to go around. You have to wait for Chief Palo."

"We have the element of surprise," I told him. "At least we do right now. After tonight, who knows?"

"I agree with Dae," Mary Catherine said. "We've only lost one person."

"One person with a gun," Jake reminded her.

"I don't need a gun," she replied. "I have hundreds of wild horses waiting to help us. I've been talking to them while we've been discussing this."

"I hate to say it, but I'm with Jake on this," Kevin said. "I know it won't be easy, but we should take this opportunity to get a few more people involved. I'm not knocking the horses, Mary Catherine, but I'd take two people with guns over a dozen horses."

Even with Kevin, Jake, and Gramps against the idea, I Knew we had to go. "We can't wait. We can leave a message for Heidi. She can meet us out there. We have to do something tonight."

Mary Catherine agreed with me. "I believe this is true. Something big is coming. I can feel it. We don't have a few hours to wait. We have to take control of the situation, gentlemen."

Jake held up his hands. "All right. You convinced me. I'm in."

"Kevin?" I asked.

"I'm not letting you go alone, Dae." He glared at Jake. "You better be ready to do your part of this."

"If I'm not, you can always shoot me, boyfriend."

"Not a problem," Kevin retorted.

"Let's go," I insisted.

Chapter Twenty-three

I helped Gramps into bed. I could tell he was still in a lot of pain with his broken leg. "You know we might be able to get some stronger pain meds from the doctor so you don't have to make that face every time you move."

He grunted as he pulled the blanket over him. "And lay around sleeping all the time? I don't think so. This is gonna take weeks to heal, Dae. I'm not giving up my whole life for a broken leg."

"Okay. Just offering." I kissed his forehead. "This wouldn't have anything to do with a certain pet psychic staying with us, would it?"

He smiled. "I'm not saying she could take the place of your grandmother, but I wouldn't mind giving her a chance to try. You like her too, don't you?"

"What's not to like? We're kind of on the same wavelength. She's fantastic. I hope she decides to stay in Duck."

"Me too." He settled back on his pillow. "I wish I could be out there with you, honey. I'm keeping my cell phone next to me. Call when you know something. And don't take any unnecessary chances. Let Kevin and Jake do the heavy lifting."

"I will," I promised, switching off the light. "I love you."

"I love you too, Dae."

I closed his bedroom door, and went downstairs.

Mary Catherine was waiting in the kitchen. "Jake and Kevin went to get some weapons."

"Good. We'll probably need them." I took Gramps's shotgun from behind the door, and looked for the shells. "Are you sure you want to do this?"

She took a pearl-handled revolver out of her handbag. "I'm ready, even without the horses."

Her face was set in grim lines. "I'm glad you're here, Mary Catherine. You've been a big help."

"Thank you, Dae. That's why I came."

"And I'm glad you'll be there tonight. I don't know what's going to happen out there, but I know I'll feel better with you there too."

"Thank you, dear." She hugged me. "I'd best go change now. It's become quite cold out there."

Mary Catherine went to her room to change into something more appropriate for assaulting a group of people performing a ritual on a cold night. I went to mine to do the same.

Treasure was sitting on the bed. He was concerned about what we were going to do. "It's going to be fine," I told him. "I'll be back by morning. I don't think Baylor is going with Mary Catherine either. This won't be a good place for cats to be."

I stepped into the bathroom to change clothes. It was cold outside, with a biting wind. I pulled on wool pants, heavy socks, and a sweater to wear under my jacket. I covered my hair with a red knit cap, and put my feet into boots.

Picking up my gloves and the shotgun, it felt like I was in some small town movie about alien invaders where everyone goes out to fight them. I hoped it was one of the movies where the small town people won the fight. I already had most of my Christmas shopping done, and I didn't plan to miss the holidays.

Mary Catherine was waiting downstairs. She was completely dressed in black including a black wool cap covering her bright hair. Baylor was protesting by meowing loudly and snagging her pants with his claws.

"You're not going," she told him. "It's going to be dangerous enough for us. I can't protect you out there." He meowed again. "Oh, I know. You're big and brave. You can take care of both of us. But you still aren't going. That's that. Go take a nice nap until we get back."

"Treasure wanted to go too," I told her. "He was afraid Baylor was going, and he didn't want to be left behind."

Mary Catherine wasn't surprised. "It's in their nature to be protective of the ones they love, not to mention that they're predators. Of course they'd want to go to war."

I took gloves out of my bag. "I just hope Osisko shows up. I don't have a clue how to stop the demon horses. I have a feeling that AK47 Kevin was talking about won't work."

"I know what you mean." She sighed. "I'm ready to go when you are."

"Are you sure?" I asked. "Last chance to get off the train."

"I never get off until the end of the journey." She laughed. "Let's go."

Kevin stopped for us at the end of the drive. "Jake is already on his way out there. I hope he waits, and doesn't jump in by himself."

"At least he's back to being himself." I was firmly wedged between Kevin and Mary Catherine. I wasn't going to complain though. I was happy not to ride in the back again.

"That doesn't make me feel a lot better," Kevin said.

"I know you don't like him, but we can trust him," I reminded him. "There's something to be said for that."

"I'm sorry." He started down Duck Road. "I'll try to forget that he wants to be with you too."

I kissed his cheek. "He'll get over it. Did you bring some guns?"

"The back is full of them."

"Not that I think they'll help with the demon horses," I added. "But they may keep the horse cult followers out of our way."

"Is there some magic potion or spell to get rid of the demons?" Kevin asked.

"Not as far as I know. I think Osisko will guide me when we get there."

"Ghost man from the past," he muttered. "Great."

Driving down Duck Road to Sanderling, and then Corolla, was unsettling. It was probably just in my own mind. The road was brightly lit from the full moon hanging over us. There were several points where I could see the water in the distance.

There was no sign of the Andalusia—our local ghost ship that was sometimes spotted on moonlit nights. Maybe its ghostly crew didn't want to be around with the demon horses.

I'd only seen the Andalusia once in my life, though like every other resident of the Outer Banks, I was always looking. Some had even tried to take photos of it, but none existed. There were drawings of it in the history museum dating back to the 1700s.

"What do you think it is about this area that seems to make everything so strange and dramatic?" Mary Catherine asked as we passed large dunes that gleamed in the silver light.

"Maybe it's knowing that it could all be taken away at any moment," I said. "The early residents that we call the Bankers knew that. They stayed through storms and floods. They did whatever they had to do to survive. But the one thing we have in common is not knowing what the tides will bring tomorrow. I think it goes with the whole Graveyard of the Atlantic theme, don't you?"

"Yes. I think that may have been what drove me off last time I was here. A person can only handle so much truth. You and I have more than our share, Dae. Living in the city with a million other people sometimes makes you feel safer."

"I've never lived anywhere that big, but the more people around me, the more I worry about touching something that will make me see things I don't want to see."

We kept driving toward Corolla until we reached Jake's long drive. From the road, everything was dark. There were no lights at the house or the barn. The place looked deserted.

"Looks like they have a fire going behind the barn where the big horse is," Mary Catherine pointed to an eerie orange glow at the back of the property.

"Great. Not something I wanted to see." It would probably mean the horse cult was trying to summon the horse demons again. I was really hoping I was wrong. "This is why Osisko wanted us to come out here. They're after someone else."

"Or something else," she whispered. "They must have something more in mind than just killing off a few random people. It would be nice if we knew their game plan."

"What could it be?" My tone matched hers. "World domination through invisible horses? How much damage could they really do?"

Even though my words were brave, my hands were shaking as Kevin turned out the lights before we drove on Jake's property. There was a cold knot in the pit of my stomach. He pulled the pickup into a field beside the horse pasture. *Now what?*

Where was Jake?

"Obviously, we have to stop them from summoning the demon horses again," Mary Catherine spoke as though she were trying to get her thoughts together. "Maybe we could hose down the fire. Once it's out, they can't summon the horses out of it, right? Then I can call in the wild horses."

"Even though these people are doing an ancient ceremony," I reminded her. "They probably still have modern weaponry. They could shoot the horses."

She tapped her finger on her chin. "I suppose that's true. I can't have them come in here and die."

"Exactly. I'm not sure what plan B is."

"Plan A is to get in there without them noticing," Kevin reminded us as he got two rifles out of the back of the pickup. "If we can sneak in there so Dae can do her thing without firing a shot, it would be great. We aren't the police."

"Good plan." Mary Catherine took her revolver out anyway.

I grabbed the old shotgun. I might not have to shoot anyone, but it made me feel better.

"Ladies." Kevin nodded. "I'll take point."

"What does that mean?" Mary Catherine asked.

"It means I go in front. You stay behind me," he explained.

"What about me?" Jake asked from the darkness.

Mary Catherine and I jumped.

"You scared the crap out of me," I whispered the complaint.

"Sorry," he replied. "Looks like your friends have been busy tonight. They're dancing up there in some kind of animal skins, screaming at the big horse, and howling at the moon. This is like a bad movie."

"Did you call Chief Palo?" I asked him.

He nodded. "She didn't pick up, but I left a long message. Are we gonna wait for her?"

We all looked at Kevin.

"Your call, Dae," he said.

I cleared my throat, and tried to sound tougher than I felt. "Let's go."

"Do you see Osisko?" Mary Catherine whispered as we started toward the barn, our breaths frosty in the night air.

"No. Not yet." *Please be here. I don't know what to do without you.*

"Who are you looking for?" Jake asked.

"Our guide," I explained. "He was part of the horse cult at one time."

"The ghost man," Kevin told him.

Jake let out a sigh. "You gotta be kidding me. I thought it was someone real."

"He's real enough," I said.

Mary Catherine made a faint sound as her foot caught on one of the boards that had been used to cover the holes in the ground. I put out my hands to make sure she didn't fall. As I did, one of the spotlights from the house came on.

We'd been caught trying to sneak up on the horse cult.

"Welcome ladies and gentleman," a familiar voice said. "We were hoping you could join us tonight."

Chapter Twenty-Four

It was Duran.

He was wearing a dark robe like you'd expect to find on a monk. Behind him were his followers. They were all people working here, about a dozen or so, dressed in monk's robes too.

"Robes? *Really?*" I muttered.

"I suppose they didn't have the option of seeing into the past as you did, Dae," Mary Catherine whispered. "They didn't know what the original horse cult members wore."

"What do we do?" I asked Kevin. "Is this part of Plan A?"

"Not exactly," he said. "But we can work with it. Don't panic."

Jake's gaze was intent on the horse cult members. "I don't see any weapons."

"That's what I was thinking too," Kevin said.

"How about a change of plan?" Jake suggested. "Kevin and I go in shooting. Whatever we don't hit, the pet psychic sends her horses after. Maybe you can throw rocks at them, Dae. There's not that many of them."

"We'll all go to jail permanently," Kevin reminded him. "We have no proof of any wrongdoing at this point."

"Jail is better than dead, my friend," Jake said. "Dae, is your spirit guide saying anything right now?"

"No." I didn't see Osisko at all. I'd been stupid for leading us into a trap. What was I thinking?

"So we need proof that they're bad men?" Jake shook his head. "Any idea how we get that?"

"We have to make them act," I said. "This is still your land, Jake. You have a right to be here. They don't. If we make them believe we're here to stop them, they may act without thinking of the consequences. It's not much, but it might slow them down. And we can't get in trouble because we're not doing anything illegal—if we don't shoot them."

Kevin took a deep breath. "Dae—"

"This has to stop." I stepped in front so Duran would see me. "You have to stop these cult rites. People are dying."

Duran brought the staff he held down hard on the sand. "Leave us alone. We weren't bothering you."

"You've been bothering me, and my town," I told him. "The statue has to be destroyed. Our ancestors buried it. The statue wasn't supposed to be found. The demon horses have to be sent back where they came from, and never summoned again."

It was a strong statement. I was actually hoping one or two of them might come over to our side after considering the consequences of their actions. But Duran had chosen well. Not a single one of his followers showed any remorse or sided with us.

"That's never going to happen," Duran said. "From here it just gets bigger. There were horse cults all over the world at one time. Descendants of those people are patiently watching, waiting to join us. We can overthrow governments, and make the world what we want it to be."

"And exactly what is that, buddy?" Jake demanded. "What's your philosophy about?"

"It's about destroying modern civilization," Duran raged. "Once we're done, there won't be governments, internet, or any of the things that make life the way it is today. Once our horses have ravaged the earth, people will sit by fires in the darkness again. They will worship the old Gods, and follow the ancient ways."

"Listen to yourself," Kevin said. "The old ways are gone, and a bunch of demon horses aren't going to change that. Give it up. You can't win this, Duran."

"The wild horses will stand against you," Mary Catherine said forcefully. "They will call on horses around the world to fight you. You can't hope to win against them."

"You are a silly old woman," Duran said. "The horses will join us when they understand what we're doing. You can't keep them from following the demons that are so much like them."

"I think now might be the time to start shooting," I said to Jake.

"I think you're right."

He took out his gun, but we weren't prepared for the dozens of horse cult followers who came up behind us—and those people were armed.

"Did you think we were backwards because we follow the horse cult?" Duran asked. "Just because we believe in the horse demons as the center of the world doesn't mean we won't defend ourselves against invaders. Get their weapons."

Jake laid his gun on the ground, and put up his hands. "Sorry, ladies. A man should know when he's outgunned so he can live to fight another day."

"If there is another day," Mary Catherine muttered.

"Sorry, Dae." Kevin relinquished his rifle and sidearm. "Everyone stay calm and watch for opportunities. We can still get out of this."

"It's okay," I whispered back. "This might be what we needed."

I saw Osisko walking slowly toward the fire behind the barn. We were on the right track. My heart was pounding. I thought I might be sick. But we were doing what had to be done.

The four of us were quickly rounded up by the cult followers. They took us to the area where the huge fire was blazing beside the big horse. There were more followers tending the fire, probably fifty or so all together. We'd sadly underestimated their numbers. It shocked me that people had come tonight who weren't part of the excavation team. Why would anyone want to do this?

"I think we should have waited," Mary Catherine said as she was tied to a tree.

"Hindsight," I answered. "What should we do now?"

"Well, the gun idea didn't work," Jake said. "Maybe the animal psychic could call in some help."

"I've been trying to do that for the past ten minutes," she said. "I don't think they can hear me, or they're scared."

Jake fought the cult members when they tried to tie him to a tree. One of them picked up a rock, and hit him in the head with it. He slumped forward as they held him, and wrapped the rope around him.

"This would've been a lot easier if all the cult people were from the past and didn't understand cell phones." Kevin stared at his phone that had been smashed on the ground at his feet.

It made me angry. "Why do you want us here, Duran?" I yelled. "Do you need an audience?"

"It will be nice to have someone that's not part of our group to witness what we do here tonight with their own eyes," he said. "But more than anything, I want you to understand the power of our demon horses, and what they can do. Maybe you'll decide to join us when you understand."

"That's not going to happen." Kevin pulled at the ropes on his hands and feet. "Save the show for someone who cares."

"What do you have in mind?" I asked.

Osisko was staring into the fire, sparks flying all around him as the huge logs shifted and burned into coals. The fire was as high as the horse statue.

"My horses are going to make things the way they should be, the way they were when my ancestors first brought horses to the island. We're going to destroy the bridges."

"You can't." I wondered if the demon horses could actually do that much damage. Remembering the feeling of their raw power, I shivered in the cold night air. "You'll cut us off from everything—food, power—everything we depend on to live."

"That's my dream. Once things are quiet out here, we can take over the towns close by on the mainland and consolidate our power with other sites like this. Imagine the thousands of people on the island feeding life to the demon horses as they realize that new gods are being reborn. It's going to be wonderful."

"Don't try to reason with him, Dae," Jake said when he came around again. "He's insane. He can't understand what's going on."

But I couldn't keep still. There had to be some way to reach him. "What do you think will happen when the demon horses need more energy to feed? When they can't get enough, they'll turn on you. That's what happened the last time they were summoned. They began killing the people—our ancestors—that had called them."

I suddenly knew why Osisko had died to stop the horses. I could see it clearly in my mind. That's what the demons had wanted. The bonfires they came from were just the beginning. They wanted to dominate humans.

He laughed at me. "You don't understand, Madam Mayor. They are grateful for my help in bringing them back. I knew the words, and the ceremony. My ancestor was the one who originally summoned them to earth. I have the horse totem. They won't turn on me. It won't be long before they're able to take over the world."

It was stunning to think that Duran and I were related, however far back in the past. That probably meant he had a gift too. It might be the only reason he could call the demons.

"Yeah," Jake mocked him. "A bunch of horses are gonna take over the world. You've got some weird ideas, little man."

There was a sudden burst of flame from the huge fire. We were close—the heat was almost unbearable. In the orange light, I saw Osisko watching, and listening to his descendent. Surely this was the time to act if he was ever going to. He knew what Duran was doing. He knew the consequences. We couldn't help him, but there had to be something he could do.

Duran's disciples took their places around the fire and began chanting. Osisko crept closer to me, and began to untie my hands.

He pointed to the big horse that looked alive in the glow of the fire.

"I don't know what to do or how to stop it," I whispered to him. He hadn't spoken but I knew what he wanted. The cult members were too busy looking for the demon horses to notice what we were doing. It was possible Duran could see Osisko too. "What should I do?"

He put out his hands flat on the tree as though he were setting them on something to understand it as I would.

"I think he wants you to touch the horse," Mary Catherine said. "I think that may be the answer, Dae."

"No. Don't do it," Jake said. "I saw what happened to you after you touched one of the small horses. You may not survive if you touch the big horse."

"We'll figure out something else," Kevin reasoned with me. "There's another way besides you touching that thing." I was scared, no doubt about it. I also didn't understand how touching the big horse would help. All I would be able to see was how it was made, and the terrible things it had been called on to do in the past. How would that make any difference?

Yet I knew that Osisko understood how my gift worked. He knew how to stop the horses. I had to trust him, and myself. "I can't stop this by touching the horse."

He jumped up and down like a monkey, slapping the charred bone on the sand.

"Don't do it," Mary Catherine urged. "Help me get free. We can get away from here, and I can call the wild horses."

"Let's get the sheriff, huh?" Jake said. "It's not like I don't believe the horses would help. I don't want to see any of them get shot either. We need backup with guns."

"Let's just get out of here," Kevin said. "You can't do this alone."

I'd finally freed myself from the tree and the ropes, and started toward Mary Catherine to get the rope off her too. Osisko had other ideas. He grabbed my arm in a surprisingly strong hold, and began pulling me toward the big horse on the other side of the fire.

"No!" I fought him off. "I have to free my friends first. You don't understand."

He wouldn't listen. We skirted the edge of the clearing, and were finally within arm's length of the horse. He grabbed me and dragged me to the feet of the statue. The cult members were too entranced by the fire and the chanting to see what I was doing.

"Dae!" Kevin called out, the fire gleaming on his angry, frightened face as he fought to free himself.

I kept pulling back as Osisko tried to propel me forward. We were standing close to one of the horse's legs. He outstretched one of my arms and I fought him, suddenly terrified that touching the statue could be the end of me. I'd thought that he understood my gift, but it seemed I was wrong.

I finally screamed out of fear and frustration. The flames from the center of the fire changed color from red/orange to black.

The demons were coming.

Chapter Twenty-five

As the legs, torsos, and heads began to emerge from the inferno, a cold certainty that the horses could do everything Duran had predicted grabbed me. The terrified faces of the cult members surrounded me. Maybe it was one thing to practice summoning the demons—which was what I believed had happened—and another to have them destroy the bridges that connected us to the mainland. Anyone who lived here knew what that would mean.

As the first horse clawed its way out of the fire, three cult members shrieked and ran away. The remaining members continued to chant.

It was a now-or-never situation. The demons had to be stopped. I didn't know what I could do by touching the horse, but I had to try. There wasn't time to go for help. This was happening now.

I reached for the large horse's stone leg, the smoke from the fire blowing into my face, choking me. Duran noticed what we were doing.

As my hand went flat against the cold stone, Duran rushed at me, screaming the chant he'd been repeating. *Too late.* The impressions and power of the horse began to surge through me.

Unlike the smaller stone horse that Jake had compelled me to touch, this one was clear and easy to understand. I saw the stone workers carving it, and a priest of some kind blessing it. It was thrown in the fire as soon as it was completed. The red stone glowed until the horse's body was completely orange. It was as though the stone had absorbed the fire.

It had been created for only one thing—destruction. That was why the early cult members had finally entombed it where it could never come near fire again. The blood shed by the demon horses flooded through it, and through me. I could feel the demons rising from a dark place to answer the summons of the stone horse, and the cult members, again.

Words that I didn't understand spewed from my lips. I was above all of it, coldly dispassionate, like the horse I was touching. My rational mind still clung to my thoughts, and who I was, while the demons tried to rip away everything good and human in me.

Duran stepped quickly back from me. His face contorted, filled with fear. He stared at me, shaking his head until he finally ran out of the circle of light created by the fire.

Chief Palo had arrived, bringing Sheriff Riley with her. They were rounding up the remaining cult members and putting them into a van. Kevin was walking into the firelight, staring at me. Mary Catherine was untying Jake.

"Get her away from that horse," Jake yelled at Kevin.

"Somebody tell me what's going on," Sheriff Riley interrupted.

"No!" Mary Catherine stopped Kevin from coming toward me. "Not yet. Osisko believes she can stop the demon horses. You can't take her away yet. They'll destroy everything."

"What demon horses are you talking about?" Sheriff Riley demanded. "I should have all of you arrested for being crazy."

"I can see them," Chief Palo yelled. "Look! Right there beside the fire. They're huge. Someone has to stop them."

All weapons were directed toward the horrible creatures coming from the fire. Bullets meant nothing to them. They weren't made of flesh like real horses. They kept fighting to be free, to destroy everything they encountered.

"Dae can do it," Mary Catherine said. "She's holding them back right now. Just give her some time."

I understood her words, but I wasn't sure she was right. I was frozen to the stone leg, unable to move. There was friction between me and the stone that was holding my hand in place. It felt like my hand would tear away from my wrist if I tried to move it.

"We have to get her out of there," Kevin growled. "This could kill her."

"Not yet." Mary Catherine put her hand on his shoulder.

Then I could see the red and black horse demons. They were staring at me with their yellow eyes. Mary Catherine was right. They were waiting to be released on their targets. Duran and his followers didn't control them anymore—I did.

I fought to hold them and then realized that they had to return to the black fire. I had to send them away, even though it was the hardest thing I'd ever done. Their power and ferocity made my insides quiver. I could imagine how Duran had felt, drunk on the ability to control them. It was like holding back a hurricane. Their thoughts whispered obscene promises of wealth and power.

"Dae?" Kevin yelled. "Can you hear me?"

I could hear him, but I couldn't answer. It was all I could do to hold the demons in place and begin the process of turning them to go back into the fire. I was disconnected from the normal functions of my body. All my energy, everything I was, went into keeping the horses from achieving the goal Duran had set for them.

They were slowly returning to the flames. Their mighty hooves struck against the earth leaving fire where they fought to stay. Sparks flew out with their angry breaths. They didn't want to go back. They didn't want to listen to me. They recalled the past when they'd been called to rain fire and death on humans.

But I kept pushing them until they had all jumped back into the fire.

Osisko was still beside me. He was smiling and crying. His hand was on my face, and I knew I'd done the right thing. This was how he'd managed to stop the horses the last time they'd been called a thousand years ago at this spot. He'd been the one who had decided to bury the stone horses so they could never be brought back. He'd convinced several tribes to get the job done, although it took years and many men were lost. He was the one who'd ordered them to bury him alive with it. He never dreamed that one of his descendants would bring them back.

As the horses began to fade into the fire, the flames turned red again, and died down. There was no one to feed the fire. I could feel the energy draining away. As it did, my hand slid down the length of the horse's leg. I blinked, and realized it was over.

Mary Catherine ran to my side, followed quickly by Jake and Kevin.

"Are you all right, Dae?" she asked. "Do you need to go to the hospital?"

"I'm fine." I smiled and stared back at them. It wasn't the truth, but I couldn't discuss what I'd experienced yet. It was all I could do to get up from the ground. My muscles didn't want to cooperate, and my brain was mush.

Osisko was gone, probably for good this time. Mary Catherine shrugged when I looked at the place beside me. I understood—she couldn't see him either.

"Let's get back to your place." Kevin put his arm around me.

"Maybe she should chill for a while on my sofa," Jake said.

"She needs to go home," Kevin said more forcefully. "I think you've gotten her in enough trouble already tonight. Get out of my way."

Jake put his hand on Kevin's arm. The two men glared at each other.

"Boys, I think Dae needs to go home. If you can't manage it without your egos getting in the way, I'll take her home." Mary Catherine ended their debate.

Kevin and Jake were silent. Sheriff Riley walked over. "Exactly what am I supposed to do with these people?"

"Arrest them for the murder of Dr. Sheffield and Tom Watts," Kevin said. "They called back the demon horses and used them to kill both of them."

"I can't arrest someone for calling up demon horses," Sheriff Riley said. "I knew I shouldn't have come. Palo!"

She put her hand on his arm. "There's more to it than that. Just hear them out, Tuck."

I'd never seen Sheriff Riley back down that way before. Chief Palo was letting everyone know about their relationship in a big way. How was he going to handle it?

"Heidi, you know we can't arrest people for doing things with demons. That's crazy—I won't get re-elected."

"Let's figure this out," she said calmly. "There are old witchcraft laws on the books, right?"

"Yeah, sure, but I don't want to be the one to use them." He stared at what was left of the enormous fire as the night settled around us. "Besides, I never saw a thing, not really. I shot where you said to shoot."

"We'll just hold them for now," she suggested.

He agreed with that. "Okay. You keep 'em in your jail until we figure it out. Maybe we can prosecute the ringleader, if nothing else. Anyone know who that is?"

"It's Duran, Dr. Sheffield's assistant." Jake gave him a brief description. "He's the one you should look for."

"You mean he got away?" Kevin glared at Jake. "Nice going, cowboy."

Jake took a step toward him, one hand raised in a fist.

"Settle down, gentlemen," Chief Palo said. "Don't make me lock all of you up for trespassing while we try to make sense of this."

"This is my property," Jake reminded her.

The conversation swirled without me taking part in it at all. I just couldn't get the images of the demon horses out of my mind. My brain felt stuck on them like a song repeating over and over again. The chant Duran has used to raise them still burned through me. It was all I could do not to go back and try to bring the demons out again.

When they'd finished deciding what each of their first steps was, Sheriff Riley glanced at me. "Someone take her home. She looks like a zombie or something. I don't want Horace blaming me for this."

Chief Palo handled any debate from Jake and Kevin by saying she would drive me and Mary Catherine home in her police car. There was a touch of the general ordering her troops in her voice. Kevin and Jake went to their vehicles without saying another word.

We got in the car, and Mary Catherine put her hand on my forehead, staring into my eyes. The dash light was dim and slightly green. "I believe I understand how you feel, Dae. The first time I spoke with a blue whale, I had the same expression on my face. You're overwhelmed, but you'll feel better once you're home and you get a good night's rest. Just sit back, and try not to worry about a thing. Everyone else will take care of what needs to be done."

It seemed like a short trip to the house. Mary Catherine and Heidi helped me out of the car. Jake and Kevin had managed to beat us there. They helped me upstairs, and I collapsed on the bed. I vaguely remember Mary Catherine helping me out of my clothes and boots before I fell asleep.

The night was fraught with nightmares and the horrors I'd seen by touching the big horse. To think that could have happened to people in Duck and Corolla made me violently ill. I crept back to bed after my visit to the bathroom, wishing there was something to take this away from me.

My grandmother's watch was in the drawer of my bedside table. I never wore it because I was afraid something might happen to it. I clutched it then out of misery and fear. What if I could never get past what I'd seen? How would I live with this in my mind for the rest of my life?

There was a way to go back in the past. Grandma Eleanore had told me at our impromptu tea party. I closed my eyes, and allowed it to happen. When I opened them again, I was seated at the kitchen table downstairs, bright sunlight coming in through the windows, but at a time when she was still alive.

"My goodness, Dae!" She jumped visibly. "I didn't expect you."

I noticed that she was winding the same watch I'd held to get here. "Is this before or after we met when I touched the first horse?"

"I'm not sure what you're talking about so I'd say before. I assume we had some conversation about it?"

I watched her delicate hand as she set the time on the worn gold watch. She seemed younger, not as frail. "When I came back last time, you were looking for something on the island where Rafe Masterson used to bury his treasure."

"Don't tell me anymore." She held up her hand. "It's not good to know too much about one's future. I'm so happy to see you, honey. What brings you back to me?"

I told her everything that had happened as she made pancakes and bacon for breakfast. She listened patiently, and didn't interrupt until it was all out. Just telling it made me feel better. Still, the monsters lurked at the edge of my awareness.

"You had quite an adventure," she said. "I'm sorry I can't offer you pancakes."

"That's okay. I just wanted to see you again. I knew you'd understand." I glanced around the kitchen. Some things were different, but many things hadn't changed. "When am I? I mean, have I been born yet?"

"Not yet. Your mother is pregnant. You'll be here soon." I watched her finish making breakfast, thinking about her warning not to get too far ahead in her timeline. She'd died before I was born. I'd thought she was sick, but she looked healthy. Maybe it had been something that had come on quickly. I suddenly realized that we'd never talked about how Grandma Eleanore had died.

I also thought about Osisko coming forward from his time to help me with the horses. I wanted to ask her about it, but Now wasn't the time.

"Hush now. Your mother and your grandfather don't have our gift. They won't be able to see or hear you."

My heart started beating fast and I started crying. I was going to see my mother again. My heart was filled with joy, pushing away the evil and darkness I had experienced.

"Morning, Mom."

Chapter Twenty-six

My mother, Jean O'Donnell, with her flyaway hair like mine and the smile I'd never forget. She was so young—and so pregnant.

I wanted to touch her, call out to her. I sobbed with her loss as though she'd just died. My heart was breaking. I wanted to feel her arms around me so badly.

"Good morning, sunshine," Grandma Eleanore said to her. "Eat your breakfast before you run out the door. It's not good to go without eating when you're pregnant."

"So you keep telling me." My mother smoothed her hand over her baby bump. "But if I keep feeding her, she's going to burst right out of me."

"That won't happen." Grandma Eleanore laughed. "She'll just be healthy and beautiful like her mother."

"Who are we talking about now?" Gramps asked as he poured himself a cup of coffee.

"We're talking about your granddaughter." Grandma Eleanore smoothed his tie down against his brown sheriff's uniform. "Sit down and eat. The bad guys will wait until you get there."

Gramps looked so young and handsome. He was still a deputy with Dare County. He wouldn't run for sheriff until the next election.

This was an important time in my family's history. I was on the way. Gramps would be sheriff soon. Grandma Eleanore would die. Everything would change. It was hard knowing, and not saying anything, but I was new to this and had to assume my grandmother knew what she was talking about.

Gramps and my mother left for work. It was beyond wonderful being there with them, even if I couldn't interact. Being with my mother brought back all my memories of her. The way she laughed. The way she cut her pancakes into tiny pieces before she ate them. All those details we miss about the ones we love when they're gone.

My family's love and warmth soothed the pain in my heart. The demon horses couldn't touch me here. I wished I could stay forever, but Grandma Eleanore reminded me that I should go.

"I loved having you here." She smiled. "I hope our timelines cross again. But you can't stay. What do you think is happening to you while you're gone? Tell me about it when you get back. I hope your grandfather is all right. He understands the rudimentary aspects of our gift. Your mother has always been a little skeptical. I hope she got over that as you grew up."

I didn't tell her that I'd evidently found a secret she hadn't discovered. I could see her whenever I wanted to. I wasn't sure if this little jaunt back into the past was possible because we were both holding her watch at the same time, but I planned to find out. I'd always wanted to know her and learn about our shared gift. Now I could.

"You're right," I told her. "I love you. I'm so glad we had this chance to talk."

"So am I. Remember not to let those things that you see when you touch something get inside you. Don't make them part of you, Dae."

"I'll work on that." I waited a moment, but nothing happened. "I'm not sure how to get back."

"What did you do to get here in the first place?"

"I held your watch and thought about you."

"Then you'll have to think about home. And Dae, much as I love you, don't keep visiting. You can't live in the past."

I closed my eyes and thought about sitting in my bedroom, holding her watch, with Treasure asleep on the bed beside me. When I opened them again, I was back in my time. It was morning, and the sun was streaming in through the windows in my room.

"Thank goodness!" Mary Catherine took a deep breath and hugged me. "I was beginning to wonder if you'd ever wake up."

I stretched, stiff and sore, but feeling better. "How long was I asleep?"

"Three days." She got off the bed. "I thought I might have to kill Kevin and Jake. They've both been here every minute asking after you. I wish one of them would shoot the other, and put an end to the rivalry."

"That seems a little harsh." I slowly got out of bed. "I'm starving."

"That's always a good sign. How are you feeling mentally?"

"I think I'm okay. I saw my family, Mary Catherine. She couldn't see me, but I saw my mother again." Just saying it made me break down in tears.

She put her arms around me. "There, there. I'd be crying

too if I could see my mother again. How are you managing to go back that way? Is it safe?"

"Perfectly safe," I lied. She didn't have to know about Grandma Eleanore's warning. "It's just part of my family's gift that I didn't know about until recently."

"Well, that's good. I guess since you're up and moving, I'll go down and tell everyone. Horace has been beside himself. Take a shower, Dae. Dress warmly. The weather has gotten colder the last few days. I'll see you downstairs."

I did as she suggested with renewed energy and hope inside me. I planned to go back again to see my grandmother and my mother too, if possible. I'd limit the trips and try to go back before the time I was at today. Maybe I could see my mother as a child. The idea was exciting, and the danger seemed trivial.

The shower felt great. I ran a brush through my damp hair and then pulled on jeans and a green sweater. My boots were still covered in mud and sand from Corolla. Still feeling a twinge of that terrible darkness that had been inside me, I let them stay where they were and put on my tennis shoes.

I couldn't wait to get to Missing Pieces and find out how the Christmas decorating was going around Duck.

Kevin, Gramps, and Jake were impatiently waiting downstairs. I hugged all three of them, despite daggered looks from Kevin. Jake was still my friend. I wouldn't let my engagement to Kevin change that.

It was between breakfast and lunch, but I ate some chicken soup that Mary Catherine had found frozen in the freezer. Gramps had made too much the last time. It was a good thing that everyone else had already eaten.

"Coffee?" she asked me.

"That sounds great, thanks. But you don't have to wait on me. You're our guest."

As I finished eating, the three men joined me at the table.

Gramps was getting around much better. It seemed he'd make a full recovery quickly. "Are you sure you're okay?" he asked.

"I'm fine. I guess I was just exhausted after everything that happened."

"Do you want to talk about it?" Kevin asked.

"No. Not yet." I smiled to reassure him. "I'm all right. Has anything else happened since that night?"

Gramps, Kevin, and my two friends glanced at each other as if they were uncertain if they should tell me something.

"It's okay. You can tell me," I assured them.

"The police haven't been able to find Duran," Kevin said. "They have everyone out looking for him. They had to let his followers go, but I figure without him, they don't know how to summon the demon horses anyway."

That put a dent in my happy mood. "But they have the big horse secured, right? They can't get to it, can they?"

"They have sheriff's deputies on duty twenty-four/seven," Gramps said. "You don't have to worry about that, Dae."

"There's nothing the police can do about what happened to Tom or Dr. Sheffield, is there?" That sense of mourning and darkness filtered into me again. I couldn't change what had happened.

"I don't think so," Gramps answered. "But I don't want you to dwell on it, honey. You get better. Tend to your shop. Leave the rest of this to the police."

I wished it were that easy.

"We have another problem," Jake said in his ironic voice. "The state wants to send in other archeologists to resume the excavation of the property. I told them no. They said my land could be forfeit to them if I don't agree to let them do what they want."

I stared into his eyes. "We can't let them do that."

He nodded. "I know."

"Horace is right, Dae," Kevin said. "You shouldn't worry about this. You did your part. You won't believe all the Christmas decorations that have gone up. It's like Santa dumped Christmas all over Duck. Why don't we take a look?"

He was trying to distract me. I let him. There wasn't anything I could do about finding Duran or about the state wanting to dig around on Jake's property again. Kevin had his golf cart there, but I insisted on walking to the Duck Shoppes.

There was an icy breeze coming from the Atlantic. It had lightly frozen anything that had been outside from plants to outdoor furniture and cars. The crystal glaze covered everything and added a festive look to the town decorations.

All the metal horse statues that commemorated our heritage were dressed for the holidays with red Santa caps and warm plaid blankets over their backs. Some were even wearing holly behind their ears.

All the shops were decked out for the contest. Some had followed the lead of Wild Stallions and gone crazy with decorations and lights. Game World had a huge lighted display of Santa and his reindeer. Most had stuck with more traditional decorations—beautiful wreaths, holly, and mistletoe.

There were pine trees, real and artificial, stuck in the most unlikely places around town. The surf shop had both a lighted tree, and a Santa on a surfboard. Santa was wearing a Duck T-shirt and shorts. The coffee shop and bookstore was festooned with red bunting that covered the whole building. The rental company that owned the Duck Shoppes had also hung ribbons and garland along the boardwalk.

"At night, the whole place glows," Kevin said as we walked hand-in-hand into the Duck Shoppes parking lot. "Wait until you see it."

"What did you decide to do about the Blue Whale?"

"I'm saving that for a surprise when you come to dinner tonight." He kissed me lightly, and put his arms around me. "It's good to have you back. I was terrified you wouldn't wake up."

"I could've been back sooner," I admitted. "I visited my grandmother again. My mother was there too. I stayed longer than I should have. It was hard to leave. My mother was pregnant with me, Kevin."

He took a deep breath of the salty cold air. "I don't know anything about actually travelling back in history, but I'm sure there are some limitations and guidelines. I know you've missed your mother. Just be careful."

"My grandmother said the same thing. I won't randomly go back, I guess. But it made me feel better being there with them. I can't describe everything I saw when I touched the big horse. But I never want to see or feel anything like that again."

We walked to the boardwalk. There was ice covering the Currituck Sound. "I'm sorry. I shouldn't have let you do it," he said

"You couldn't have stopped me," I told him. "It was what I needed to do to push the demon horses back into the fire. There was no other way."

"Let's work on alternatives for the next time there seems to be no other way, huh? A good plan can keep you from going through anything like that again."

He hugged me again, and I stared out at the sound. There were no boats out today. The wind was blowing hard and steady, pushing at the frozen boardwalk where we stood.

"It's good to see you, Mayor O'Donnell," August Grandin said as he walked by. "That boating accident that killed those three young men right out here on the sound could have been prevented. I hope you'll bring in some safety experts for the future. We don't want to get that kind of reputation."

He nodded, and went on his way. I was stunned by the boating accident. We had never had that kind of tragedy since I'd been mayor. I wondered what had caused it.

"Sorry. You were supposed to be looking at the decorations," Kevin reminded me.

"That's okay. But I think I'd like to stop at town hall."

"Dae, let it go for now. It's the holiday season. Get in the spirit."

I knew I wouldn't forget what August had said even though Kevin bought me a white mocha at the coffee shop, and we had a chance to see Phil playing Santa for some school kids from Duck Elementary. I walked back to my house with him when he got a call from his assistant at the Blue Whale. I didn't go with him since he was a surprise for that night. It gave me an opportunity to catch up on what was happening in Duck.

Mary Catherine went with me. Gramps was at his weekly pinochle game. I didn't feel as though she were trying to keep an eye on me—more saving herself from a boring afternoon.

Jake had driven to Raleigh to discuss closing the excavation instead of re-opening it. He called when he was on the road. "I don't know if I have a chance of persuading them that it's a mistake. But I have to try."

"Thanks. I hope you can convince them to leave it alone."

"There's only one other alternative if they don't agree," he drawled. "We both know what that is, right?"

"Try your best to convince them," I said. "If you can't, we'll do what we have to."

"I'll be back as soon as I can."

"Good luck."

Mary Catherine and I had reached the boardwalk as I pushed 'end' on the call.

"Trouble?" she asked.

"I hope not." I filled her in on Jake's trip to the capital. "It was what he tried to do to begin with. He couldn't do it then. I don't know if anything has changed now."

We walked into town hall to have Nancy bring me up to speed on everything that had happened while I'd been asleep. Instead we walked right into another crisis.

"What's wrong?" I asked her and Chris Slayton as they manned the phones.

"There's been an accident," Chris said. "An electrician wiring Christmas lights was injured. We're trying to find a helicopter to transport him."

I faced Mary Catherine, and though I could see the answer in her clear blue eyes, I asked the question anyway. "It's not over yet, is it?

"No," she answered. "I'm afraid not, Dae."

Chapter Twenty-seven

Cailey Fargo came in, grim faced, wearing what I thought of as her battle gear. It was plain black pants and a shirt with the Duck Volunteer Fire Department emblem on it. Her face was smudged, and her hair was wild. "Any luck yet with that helicopter?" she demanded.

"I think I've got one," Nancy said. "He can be here in ten minutes."

"Good enough." She nodded. "The emergency services people say he needs the hospital in less time than they can get him there driving. He stopped breathing after the electrocution, but he's breathing again and his heart rate is finally steady."

Nancy finished her conversation with the helicopter pilot. "I told him to set down in Duck Park. I think that's the closest place we can find."

"I'll make sure he's there." Cailey nodded at me before she left. "Mayor."

"Are you feeling better, Dae?" Nancy asked as Chris sank down in an office chair and put his head in his hands.

"Yes. Thanks. Sorry it had to happen at such a bad time."

"It's like we're cursed," Chris said. "I keep thinking what else can go wrong. It's been ever since those horses started coming through at night. I know it doesn't have anything to do with it, but it's like I can feel something left behind of them."

It seemed he was arguing with himself, and he finally got up again. "I'm going to see Jamie and eat lunch. You want something?"

"I'll take a roast beef sandwich if you're going near Duck Deli," Nancy said. "Dae? Mary Catherine?"

"We're fine, thanks Chris." He knew about my gift but only on the most basic level. I'd found his car keys once in a trash can by holding his hands.

I wished I could tell him the truth about the demon horses, but I wasn't even sure what that was now. If the cult members couldn't get to the big horse, why did I still feel that something was wrong?

"See you later, Dae."

We watched him leave, and I sat in the chair he'd left, talking to Nancy. "What happened to the men who drowned?"

Her pretty face was sad when she explained. "It was just one of those dumb accidents, like today with the electrician. Except that it seems to be happening every day. I think it's the curse. You know, the one Rafe Masterson put on Duck when he was hanged for piracy."

"Is that something that happened recently?" Mary

Catherine asked.

"No. About four hundred years ago," I said. "He cursed Duck. I can't believe you lived here for any length of time and didn't hear about the curse."

"Maybe it was during one of the good times," Nancy said. "I'm not from Duck, but I've seen enough to believe it. This town is definitely cursed."

"Can't you get a priest or something?" Mary Catherine asked.

"I think they've tried that. Everyone knows about the curse. Maybe that's part of the problem," I said.

"Well, I don't know about that." Nancy got up and paced the floor. "All I know is that this town is falling apart. We have to do something."

"What did you have in mind?" I asked her.

"I don't know. Maybe we could get a bunch of sage and smudge the whole town," Nancy suggested. "It can't hurt. My cousin is a witch, and she swears by sage."

"I'm in," Mary Catherine agreed. "Where do we get the sage?"

"Shayla probably left some in her shop," I told her. "You have the key, right?"

"I do—somewhere. I'm sure I can find it. What a marvelous idea."

We left Nancy at town hall, and went to Shayla's shop next to mine on the boardwalk. Mary Catherine had the key in her pocket. We went inside—it was dark and very quiet. I missed Shayla. We didn't always see eye-to-eye, but it was lonely without her.

"You were right," Mary Catherine picked up several bunches of dried sage held together by green ribbons. "How much do you think is enough?"

"Let's just take it all, and I'll buy more for Shayla later."

We took it down to Nancy, who was on the phone with her cousin the witch, trying to convince her to come to Duck and help us.

Nancy would get in touch with me when she had an

answer from her cousin. Mary Catherine and I went to Missing Pieces, and opened the shop. There wouldn't be much traffic in this weather, but while I was there, I might as well try to sell a few things.

"I've been in colder places," Mary Catherine said with a shiver. "But this is unnatural cold. I feel like I can't get warm. All the animals are feeling it too. I hope sage is the answer."

As she spoke, several mice were sitting on the ledge outside under the front window. A few gulls had joined them, pecking at the glass to be let in.

"I'm sure you could sit still somewhere and animals would cover you to keep you warm." I laughed. "I wonder why the horses didn't come when you called them at the ritual. You don't even have to call the other animals."

"I don't know. It was as though there was a block between me and them, maybe it was the magic summoning the demon horses. It was disturbing, but as soon as you'd called back the demons, I could feel I was back in touch with them. It was too late then."

"It was some powerful magic." I wrapped my arms across my chest. "No wonder some of it is still left."

"Jake wants to destroy the big horse, doesn't he? We talked about it while you were asleep."

"I don't think he really wants to," I replied. "I think he feels like he has to if the state won't leave him alone. I guess I agree."

"Dae! And you such a history buff."

"You know the police won't always be able to guard the big horse, even if Jake is able to convince the state to stop digging here. Duran said he had other friends who wanted to try their hand at controlling that much power."

"Can't it just be reburied?" she asked as the door to the shop chimed and a customer walked in.

"Good morning," I greeted my customer and ended the conversation about the demon horses. "It's freezing out there, isn't it? Would you like some hot tea?"

"No, thank you." The tall, straight man was white-haired, probably sixty. He wore an old fashioned black suit. He walked quickly through the shop as though he knew exactly what he was looking for.

"Can I help you?" I asked.

"I'm looking for something in particular, something I heard that you possessed." He turned sharply to face me. "You are the owner, Dae O'Donnell, is that correct?"

"Yes." I was getting a bad feeling about this conversation.

"I'm looking for the St. Augustine bells. I heard that you had them here."

His tone, and the way he regarded me, made me feel that he was daring me to tell him that I didn't have them.

"I have the bells, two of them anyway. They aren't for sale."

"I have the third bell. I want to purchase the other two."

It had only been a few years since I'd run across the first exquisite silver bell made by the St. Augustine monks hundreds of years ago. The legend of the monks, and their desperate attempt to save the bells from the marauding Spanish army, was something anyone knew who'd read about lost treasures.

I'd been able to get the second bell last year from Dillon Guthrie. Our pact was that I would let him know when I came across the third bell. He believed it would come to me, and wanted to buy them all when it did. He wouldn't let them to go to this man, no matter what the price.

I was still on the fence about selling them to Dillon. They were very valuable, but my finder's soul wanted me to keep them.

"I'd have to verify that the bell is authentic," I said. "You're welcome to bring it here, if you like."

He smiled. "I don't think so. Perhaps we could meet in some neutral place. You bring the bells you have, and a figure on what you're willing to sell them for. We'll see if we can work it out."

I nodded. "I won't sell the other two bells, but I might have a buyer for yours."

His eyes narrowed. "I'm not selling either. I want the other two. I've searched for them for years."

"Leave me your information. We can talk again after the first of the year."

We exchanged cards, and the man left Missing Pieces.

Mary Catherine let out a long breath. "That was intense! I take it these bells are worth a lot of money?"

"Yes. More money than most people see in a lifetime." I thought about contacting Dillon to let him know that I might have found the third bell. It seemed the wrong thing to do after just writing him off. That decision would also have to wait until after Christmas.

The weather got worse. Thick ice and fog settled in around Duck. Mary Catherine and I huddled in the shop until I thought there was no point in staying. No one was coming out in that weather. We bundled up, and headed home. The streets were almost deserted, and what light traffic there was skidded and screeched across Duck Road.

"It's a bad day to be out." Mary Catherine skidded and screeched herself as she almost fell on the ice.

"I guess we should have left sooner." I grabbed her arm. "Let's just make it home in one piece. I'm stocked for the bad weather."

"What about dinner at Kevin's place?"

"I'm sure he'll understand. The weather changes quickly. The ice should be gone tomorrow."

But I wasn't sure if the thick gray pall that had settled with the ice would leave us. I felt it in my bones, and in my soul. If there was a curse on Duck, this was it. I wasn't convinced that any amount of sage could change it. I wished I could grab Grandma Eleanore's watch again and disappear into the past until it was over.

The ice crunched under our feet as we talked and slipped going into the driveway.

"I have a wonderful recipe for tomato soup that might be

just what we need tonight." Mary Catherine's spirit wasn't diminished by the pall as I opened the door to the house.

"Sounds great. I hope I have all the ingredients. I'm sure the local grocery store closed hours ago, and I don't think we want to drive anywhere else." I closed the door behind us, and called for Gramps. There was no reply. "I'm surprised he hasn't called if he can't get home from Howard's place."

Mary Catherine was taking off her jacket when she glanced into the living room. "I think I may know why, Dae."

I followed her line of vision. Gramps was tied and gagged in his recliner. Duran was standing over him.

"Welcome home." Duran bowed mockingly to us. "I'm glad the bad weather didn't stop you ladies from getting here."

I put my bag and jacket on the kitchen table. There was no weapon close at hand, unless I counted a steak knife or two. Gramps's service revolver was in the drawer beside him. I wouldn't be able to reach it in time.

"What are you doing here?" Duran might have the upper hand, but I didn't have to sound like he did. "You picked the wrong house to come at us. Sheriff Riley and Chief Michaels are here every evening for dinner. We were just talking about what we planned to cook. Please—stay for supper. They should be here any minute."

I noticed Baylor taking up a protective stance in front of Mary Catherine, but he wouldn't be much help. Duran could strike him down with his staff.

There was a hideous, preserved horse hoof on the top of the solid stick. I hadn't noticed it at the ritual with everything else going on.

At that moment, it finally came to me. "You didn't use the demon horses to kill Dr. Sheffield or Tom Watts, did you? You did it yourself."

He frowned. "Let's see you prove that. The police haven't been able to keep any of my followers. We are outside your paltry justice."

"True. But they don't have a staff that will show blood

and skin tissue from striking your victims. You killed Tom at
Jake's house to try to shut Jake up. Then you killed Dr.
Sheffield because he wanted to box up the big horse and send
it away. What happened? Why couldn't you get the demons
to do your dirty work?"

If he was upset at all at my revelation, he didn't show it.
"It takes time to get control of them. It was all I could do to
keep them from running away without my direction. But you
know that, right? You pushed them back into the fire, didn't
you?"

"I did," I acknowledged with pride. "And I'm going to
make sure they don't come out again."

"I don't think so. I don't need their help to kill you and
your friends. Once I'm done, I'll call my followers back, and
we'll do everything I promised, and more."

Mary Catherine stepped forward. She'd lifted Baylor and
put him around her shoulders. "That's not going to happen,
Duran. Your time is over. There are creatures you have to
reckon with. I don't know how that will end for you, but we
each make our fate."

As she spoke, I heard the sound of hundreds of horses'
hooves again, in the yard and on the street. I glanced out the
kitchen window. These weren't invisible demon horses. They
were the living, breathing kind. They clustered around the
house, neighing and prancing. Some were jumping up in the
air, their front hooves pawing wildly.

"Stupid old woman!" Duran moved from standing beside
Gramps toward Mary Catherine. Baylor let out a noisy howl
to warn him away, showing his teeth and claws.

But he didn't have to worry about it. Before Duran could
reach Mary Catherine, a hundred bats flew down from the
chimney and straight out at him. They clung to his clothes,
and grabbed his hair. He panicked as he tried to push them
away with his hands and staff. The bats wouldn't move. They
covered his head and chest as he stumbled blindly toward the
back door to get away from them.

I ran to get Gramps's emergency weapon, and held it

toward Duran in case he decided to come back toward me. I grabbed one end of the duct tape that had sealed Gramps's mouth and yanked—probably too hard as he yelped and covered his lips with his hand.

"Sorry. Are you okay?"

"Yes. Give me the gun before you hurt yourself."

Duran had managed to open the back door and tripped down the stairs, falling into the back yard at the feet of the horses he'd wronged. The bats flew away, and he was left with the herd. A large brown stallion with a black tail faced him down, making him back up into another horse.

"Mary Catherine—"

"It's out of my hands, Dae," she said. "I don't know what they plan to do with him, but he's theirs now."

As I watched, the mighty herd of wild horses—more horses than I even knew lived here— nudged and bumped him, threatening with teeth and hooves, until they'd tossed him on the stallion's back. They ran out of the yard and into the street, crossing through the woods toward the ocean until I couldn't see them anymore.

"Call Ronnie," Gramps blustered and raged. "Call Tuck. Get me out of this rope. What's going on, Dae?"

I walked outside and found Duran's staff on the ground. I used a kitchen towel to pick it up and bring it inside. Mary Catherine was untying Gramps. I could hear a siren coming in our direction.

Was it over? What would the horses do with Duran? I wasn't quite sure I believed Mary Catherine when she said she didn't know what would happen to him.

But at least I could give the staff to Sheriff Riley. They might actually have something tangible to use against Duran and his followers. That would be a great Christmas gift for all of us.

Chapter Twenty-eight

Three days later the shore patrol found Duran on the beach. He was barely understandable, talking to himself, and muttering about the horses. There would be a trial for him and his followers, but Duran was sent to a psychiatric hospital on the mainland.

Mary Catherine never said that she'd understood what the horses had planned. I was pretty sure she was lying, but I didn't call her on it. We all have our secrets.

Jake had come home from Raleigh with bad news—the state planned to send another team of excavators and archeologists to work on the horse cult project. I didn't have to ask what he planned to do. I offered to help with whatever he needed.

The next night, Gramps heard a call on his scanner that the Corolla police and volunteer fire department had been called. There had been a powerful explosion that had demolished Jake's house and barn. The explosion also pulverized the stone horse. There wasn't enough left of it to piece together.

Kevin and I went out to help Jake salvage what he could. Heidi Palo was there too. None of us talked about what had happened. The official word was that chemicals, left behind by the excavation team, had accidentally blown up. The state was upset, but that was mitigated by several smaller horse statues that Jake had donated to them.

With the destruction of the big horse, the mood lightened in Duck and Corolla. Christmas was coming, and all the activities that had been planned for OBX Christmas were drawing crowds from the mainland and bringing joy to local residents.

Kevin hosted an open house at the Blue Whale Inn. Everything was lit by candles, and smelled of fresh oranges, apples, and blue spruce. He'd decided to go with a theme— one hundred Christmas trees. They were all sizes and types from spruce and fir to pine, and even cedar. Some were decorated by the Duck Historical Society with memories of people and places that were gone. Some had been decorated by the Ladies Sewing Circle and others by various groups from the area.

He put up his award for winning the Christmas decoration contest with great pride. Cody and Reece hated to admit defeat, but they shook hands with Kevin and munched down his snacks at the open house.

I saw a picture of Grandma Eleanore on one of the history trees. Rafe Masterson was there too, as a photo someone had taken of his painting that was housed at the museum. I enjoyed seeing both of them. I'd managed to stay away from going back into the past to see my mother again.

It was difficult, knowing I could do it. I thought about it a lot. What harm could it do?

Shayla called the day before Christmas to let me know that she was staying in New Orleans. "My Gram isn't doing well, Dae. And I met someone who is seriously interesting. I hate to leave you there by yourself, but I need to find a life for me too. I hope you understand."

"I do. I'll miss you."

"You know you can come down here and we can do your yearly séance for your mother's spirit, right? Maybe the next time will be it."

"I'm not going to do that anymore," I told her. "I found a better way to talk to her, I think."

"Good for you. It's best to leave the dead alone anyway. We'll talk again later. Merry Christmas, Dae."

"Merry Christmas, Shayla."

I hung up the phone. Mary Catherine had been trying to appear as though she wasn't listening, but I knew she'd heard.

"Well?" I asked.

"I'm relieved. And I'm going to stay in Duck and re-open my shop. I may change the name. That's just not me anymore. Maybe I'll sell pet supplies, and give advice to pet owners. What do you think?"

"Gramps will be thrilled," I told her as we bundled up to go to the town singing at Duck Park.

"What about you, Dae?" she asked. "How do you feel about me staying? You've just met your grandmother. I don't want you to feel as though I'm trying to take her place."

I laughed and hugged her. "You don't have to worry about that. I hope you and Gramps will find something wonderful together. I'm glad you're staying."

Gramps's broken leg was well enough that he could drive the golf cart again. He came back for us when the park was set up, and people were coming to sing. Everyone held candles in their hands that Cailey Fargo and Luke Helms lit from one larger candle. We stood close together in the park and sang old Christmas songs as loud as we could.

There weren't many tourists there. It was mainly people from Duck. I looked up at Kevin as we stood with our arms around each other. I was looking forward to Christmas, and the New Year.

But when we got home that night and Mary Catherine had gone to her room, I sat on the sofa beside Gramps and asked him a question that had bothered me since I'd talked to Grandma Eleanore in the past.

"How did grandma die?"

Gramps sighed, and sat back in his chair. "That's not something we should talk about, Dae, especially here at the holidays and all."

"I want to know. I have a feeling she didn't get sick and die." I stared at his worn face as he looked away from me.

"You're right. It was something to do with her gift, honey. She'd learned she could visit the past, you see, by using her gift to touch things and see where they'd come from."

"What happened?"

His hands shook when he answered. "One morning she left—and never came back again."

About the Authors

Joyce and Jim Lavene write bestselling mystery together. They have written and published more than 60 novels for Harlequin, Berkley and Gallery Books along with hundreds of non-fiction articles for national and regional publications.

Pseudonyms include J.J. Cook, Ellie Grant, **Joye Ames** and Elyssa Henry

They live in rural North Carolina with their family, their cats, Quincy, Stan Lee, and their rescue dog, Rudi. They enjoy photography, watercolor, gardening, long drives.

Visit them at:

www.joyceandjimlavene.com

www.Facebook.com/JoyceandJimLavene

Twitter: **https://twitter.com/AuthorJLavene**

Author Central Page: **http://amazon.com/author/jlavene**

11//5

25298156R00146

Made in the USA
Middletown, DE
26 October 2015